A PIRATE'S

TALES

By

S.P. Cammick

Published by Hemingway Publishers

Cover design by Hemingway Publishers

ISBN: Printed in the United States

Table of Contents

About The Author

He grew up on the shore of the Gulf of Mexico. A lifelong resident of southwest Florida, spending thousands of days and tens of thousands of miles cruising the waters of Florida and the Bahamas and weathering countless storms at sea or battened down in a protected anchorage, visiting every cove, back bay, or island within range of his watercraft. He has experienced the eye of three Category 4 hurricanes, one as a child and two as an adult, facing the task of rebuilding after the carnage passed.

As a PADI Certified Dive Master, he dove extensively throughout Florida, the Bahamas, and the Caribbean, from the Blue Holes of Belize to the 5000-foot drop-off of the Tongue of The Ocean and has gone shark diving at Walker's Cay and hundreds of reefs and wrecks in between.

This is a work of Fiction

This is a book of fiction, but many of the tales are woven around a kernel of real-life experiences and events. The characters are fictitious, and the locations and events are depicted in a fictitious manner, but one is real – Gold Fever! The incurable infection was contracted that fateful day in July, "The Day," while sitting on a dock in Key West, baring witness as Mel Fisher brought in the Atocha's Mother Lode.

Weigh Anchor! And join in this voyage of adventure!

Chapter 1

In the summer of 1622 the Santa Margarita lay quietly at anchor in Havana Harbor among the more than five dozen ships readying for the 3,000 kilometer voyage to Spain, 11 of which were Spain's most impressive warships, the Galleons. With Dutch raiders prowling the Caribbean, no trading ships or treasure would attempt the crossing without the protection of the Galleon's massive cannons.

While the Santa Margarita had made the crossing from Spain just five months earlier, the return trip was always the most dangerous. In addition to the Dutch raiders, the specter of hurricanes also weighed heavily on the captain's mind. It was August 22nd and the fleet was already over a month late in departing.

While the sea held many dangers, the Santa Margarita was as capable as any ship in the fleet. Thirty meters long with a beam of ten, the ship weighed nearly 500 tons empty. In addition to her 30 cannons, each weighing 3 tons and 3 meters in length, the Santa Margarita had a standing army of over 100 men. This in addition to the 200 crew and passengers.

But it was not the ship the Dutch coveted. It was the treasure in the hold, 755 bars of silver, each weighing 30 kilograms, over 7,000 coins and gold bars and golden disks that weighed in at 100 kilograms a piece. This was just the recorded and taxed cargo. No doubt, there were several tons of untaxed contraband also stashed throughout the ship. With over 400 million dollars worth of treasure in the Santa Margarita, it represented one of the most valued ships on all the oceans.

The treasure on the Santa Margarita and the other Galleons of the fleet represented a year's worth of the New World's treasure. Much of the silver came from the mines of Potosi. From there, it was carried over the mountains of Péru to the Pacific Ocean, where it was loaded on ships for the 1,000 mile voyage to Panama. Back on land, the bounty was carted across the Isthmus of Panama to the Caribbean. Again, it was loaded onto ships bound for Havana in preparation for the voyage to Spain. Along with the silver were the ghosts of a thousand Mayan and Incan slaves who died in the silver mines of Potosi and even more who perished in the hellish mercury mine of Huancavelica (at the time, mercury was used to extract the silver from the ore).

With the peak of hurricane season approaching and communications indicating that the Dutch fleet was far to the south, the flotilla set sail toward Florida on September fourth. The plan was to reach the gulf stream south of the Florida keys and ride it north, past Florida, to Cape Hatteras. Here, the fleet would head east past Bermuda to Europe. This track should keep the ships far north of both the Dutch and any hurricanes.

As luck would have it, the very next day, the winds began building out of the northeast, making sailing north nearly impossible while signaling the approach of a devastating storm.

The smaller and faster members of the flotilla headed northwest across the barrier reefs of the southernmost keys into the relative safety of the Gulf and Florida Bay. The three Galleons tasked with protecting the flotilla's flank approached the reefs too late. The gathering storm made crossing the shallow reefs too dangerous. The Atocha, the Rosario and the Santa Margarita would ride out the storm south of the shallow waters of the Marquesas.

The captain of the Atocha anchored in only 20 feet of water above the patch reef, while the Santa Margarita set it's three 2,000 pound anchors in 60 feet of water just inside the outer reef line. The Rosario's captain, not satisfied with the limited protection afforded by the shallows, headed west toward the Dry Tortugas. His goal, to out-run the storm and enter the relative safety of the Gulf.

Once the massive anchors were set, the captain instructed his crew to strip the sails and as much rigging as possible. What could not be moved below was lashed as tightly as possible to the deck. As the storm clouds gathered, the captain and navigator took one final look to establish their position. To the northwest was the Atocha, similarly prepared for nature's onslaught. To the northeast lay the Marquesas Keys, an insignificant amount of protection in an otherwise open ocean. After his final check, the captain descended below deck and ordered all hatches and gun ports secured.

As the winds built, so did the waves. Soon, the massive ship was porpoising into the 20 foot seas. The anchor chains straining and ripping at the tree-sized timbers of the hull. The winds continued to increase. The rain and waves felt and sounded like a thunderous waterfall, only the water was horizontal in the wind instead of vertical.

All of a sudden, the thunder ceased, or more accurately, suddenly came the realization that the wind had dropped and the seas subsided. A great cry of relief came from the soldiers and passengers. The crew, however, knew that they were still closer to the beginning of their ordeal, than the end.

The captain ordered his crew on deck to survey the damage and throw overboard the splintered remains of the masts and rigging. While the crew worked feverishly, the captain once again took stock of his position. The massive anchors had held, no doubt, boring further into the reef with every wave. The Marquesas Keys were still to the northeast, but now they were just a collection of sandbars as the vegetation had been ripped from them.

The captain's spirits fell as he turned his glass toward the Atocha. The ship had vanished. Perhaps the shallower water increased the working load on the anchors. A stress even the newest ship of the fleet could not survive. He surveyed the horizon until he spied the Mizzenmast of his sister ship. Rather than northwest, the remains of the Atocha lay nearly four kilometers to the east of its previous position. He could see survivors clinging to the mast and clutching any available timbers to stay afloat. There was nothing he could do to rescue them. Even if the sails were intact, there wasn't time before the fiercer side of the hurricane would be upon them.

The eye of a hurricane is a marvelous thing. While hundred knot winds swirled around them, it was eerily calm and the sun shone brightly. Frigate birds circled high above. They were safe from the storm, but there was no escape. They would go wherever the storm would take them.

As the crew finished once again clearing the decks, the captain marveled at the foreboding sights around him. The sun was bright and warm, the air as fresh as any he'd experienced, scrubbed clean by the terrifying storm and waves that rocked the ship. With no winds to guide them, the confused seas pitched the Santa Margarita in every direction, but it was more of a rocking than the pounding of just moments before. No longer straining against the wind, the anchors fell straight down from the bow, the weight of the chains holding the bow steady as the waves slapped against the hull.

The captain, knowing his fate and that of his ship could still be that of the Atocha, non-the-less marveled at the clouds surrounding him. They towered higher than any he had ever seen. Even the Frigate birds seemed low compared to their towering height. The massive cloud tops were at once, brilliantly white and painted with pinks, purples, and gold. As these towering harbingers of doom approached, they lost their color, and soon, a dark wall of destruction was all that could be seen. As this wall enveloped the ship, the winds increased suddenly to over 100 knots. This time, there were no patch reefs, no low-lying keys, not even the shallow waters of the Gulf to break the waves. They came as locomotives, driven by the winds.

The ship spun around to face the onslaught, but to no avail. The anchor chains, hand-crafted by the finest blacksmiths in Spain, held firm. They did not give a millimeter. The sudden shock of tension was more than the ship could stand. The chains ripped the forecastle from the hull, their weight instantly plunging the crew's quarters and most of the crew to the bottom.

Unencumbered by the anchors, the bow rose out of the water. The stern castle, over 12 meters high, acted as a great sail. The wind and waves pushed the ship north at nearly 20 knots. Four times faster than she ever made under sail. The gaping hole in the bow swallowed the rain and waves in tremendous gulps, pushing the hull deeper into the water.

The remaining passengers and soldiers were frozen with fear. Venturing onto the deck was suicide, staying below certain death.

The four minutes it took to reach the reef line was both an instant and an eternity for the doomed.

As the ship sank deeper into the relentless waves, more water surged in. The keel hit the reef with a horrendous groan, the superstructure separated from the hull.

Five hundred tons of ship, 50 tons of treasure, 260 souls and a thousand ghosts were scattered across the sands.

Chapter 2

Jode and Tripper had a powerful secret. If anyone else found out or even suspected, their good fortune and dreams would be stolen or worse. Whether by the other derelicts along the waterfront, the cops, or state revenuers, the results would be the same, they would lose their new found fortune, if not their lives.

They couldn't let on anything had changed, not now, not here. They had to continue to be the down-and-out harbor bums they had always been, at least for a few more days.

It had been just over 48 hours since Jode made the discovery. He and Tripper had taken Old Moe, their battered old Chris Craft, out to the Marquesas to catch "summer crabs." With lobster season closed, there was a thriving black market for the tasty crustaceans. They could catch many more now and sell them for a much higher price than when the season opened. Of course, this was illegal, but Jode and Tripper never bothered about such minor details.

Jode was scouring the reef for bugs when he saw the monster. It was walking over the coral reef unintimidated by Jode or anything else. It stood nearly 3 feet tall on its spindly legs. The huge lobster had little to fear. Other than a large nurse shark or 200-pound Jewfish, there were few predators to challenge it.

Jode aimed his Hawaiian sling and sent the spear clean through the unsuspecting beast. With one powerful kick, he was on his prey. Holding the spear at each end, the lobster could not escape. It snapped violently, its tail hitting Jode in the face, knocking off his mask. He grabbed his foe by the carapace and held on, pinning it to the bottom. The struggle sent up a cloud of debris. Jode closed his eyes tightly to keep out the salt and sand. Soon, the struggle was over. The effects of the spear and the effort to escape soon drained the monster lobster of its prior strength. With his eyes still closed, Jode felt around for his goody bag, opened it, and stuffed in his prize.

He sat quietly on the bottom, catching his breath and waiting for the dust to settle. Opening his eyes, he located his mask, put it on, and cleared it with one big exhale through his nose. That's when he saw it, a glint of light off of something in the sand. The fight had washed away the powdery sand, exposing a single piece of gold that had laid hidden for nearly four hundred years.

His hand shook as he fanned away the remaining sand and picked up the coin, placing it carefully into the pocket of his B.C. The heavy breathing from the fight had left his tank nearly empty, so he had no choice but to return to the boat.

Tripper was waiting as the bubbles approached. The goody bag of bugs landed with unusual heft when tossed on the dive platform. He opened it and dumped the contents on the deck. Seeing the huge dead lobster, he shouted with delight. He had never seen such a prize.

Jode pulled himself up out of the water to see Tripper holding his catch by the horns, swinging it about, dancing with it, it seemed, but the 12-pound lobster was now just a distant memory. Jode's mind was fixated on the gold coin.

"Quite a catch, Bro! Never seen one this big. We gonna eat it or sell it?" But Jode wasn't paying attention to his question. He dropped his tank and slowly withdrew the coin from his B.C. pocket. Without a word, he held it in his open palm for Tripper to see.

The silence was broken only by the sound of the huge lobster hitting the deck. It slipped from Tripper's hands as if it were as valuable as an old piece of driftwood. They both stood silently, staring at the gold glistening in the bright summer sun.

With the last two full tanks, Tripper and Jode returned to the bottom to search for more treasure. When the last breath of air was sucked from their tanks, they surfaced. It was the greatest day of their lives. They sat drying in the sun, drinking their last warm beers, staring at their fortune: a small gold bar, a gold chain, 3 gold coins, an emerald the size of a nickel, and a small stack of silver coins.

Their tanks empty and beer gone they headed back to Key West. Dreamin' and schemin' of what to do next.

Jode had been dreaming of this day for nearly 20 years. He could never forget the day he got gold fever. Like today, it was an oppressively hot summer day in Key West. He was sitting on the seawall at Mallory Square. It was not the cobble-stoned, Disneyfied, government run Mallory Square of today. There were no city licensed vendors selling t-shirts and beads to ice cream sucking tourists that flooded off the cruise ships like dirty bilge water. No, back then, Mallory Square was real. The entertainers were real, and the sunsets weren't blotted out by twenty stories of "cruisers" ruining the town.

In fact, Mallory Square was where Jode and Tripper hatched their first scheme to separate main-landers from their money. Every day at sunset, the Square would fill with entertainers, pickpockets, and shysters, all doing their best to gain the attention of the well-heeled vacationers. Offering to pose for pictures like the tattooed guy and chick playing guitar, the Snake Man, and the juggler, everyone with either a hat out or hand out, looking for tips.

Soon, Jode and Tripper became the main attraction, "The Sunset Harbor Houdini's." Yup, they put on a hell of a show.

Jode was quite a free diver. Catching lobster, spear fishing, checking props, he could do it all without a tank. If he really focused and relaxed, he could hold his breath for nearly 3 minutes. That was the key that made the trick work.

Jode and Tripper would drag an old canvas bag full of chains and padlocks out to the square. With much fanfare, they would slowly and carefully take out each piece of chain and lay them out by the seawall. It was very important to draw out each step to let the crowd build.

As the spectators became curious, Jode would stand by the seawall in his bathing suit and old T-shirt. Tripper would pick up a piece of chain and wrap it around Jode, pinning his arms to his side. He then would ask some pretty young thing to step forward and "test the chains" to make sure they were tight. Of course, no squeaky clean toots in hot pants and tank top would really want to touch a scruffy-looking fisherman or the rusty old chain, so the "test" was more of a dainty little tug on a loose end of the chain.

Tripper would then start the process over again with the next chain. The next cute tourist was chosen for the "test," and so it went for nearly an hour.

Now, seeing a man wrapped in heavy chains on the edge of a seawall was indeed the greatest draw on the Square. Some people just couldn't bear to watch … they stayed near the back of the crowd, but they stayed.

Finally, when the sun was low, and the crowd had grown to include most everyone on the Square, Tripper would start his spiel...

"Ladies and gentlemen, today you will witness one of the greatest feats of escape since Houdini. My victim, I mean friend here, has been bound with over 50 feet of chain, 5 padlocks, each secured and tested by volunteers from the crowd," motioning toward the least dressed and most attractive young "assistant". "But it is not enough to just escape from these chains. I am going to place a blindfold over his eyes and add one more lock to secure all the chains together."

Tripper would then blindfold Jode and place the final lock with much fanfare. Then, while stepping off the seawall, he would "accidentally" bump Jode, who would stagger and struggle, then fall into the ocean. The crowd invariably would groan and heave in shock. At this, Tripper would pace wildly back and forth, peering into the cloudy green water, searching for his friend. A minute would go by, and believe me, it was a long minute. Tripper would begin to panic. Members of the crowd would push to the seawall, looking for Jode, watching for bubbles, but they would see nothing. Finally at two minutes, an eternity for those watching, Tripper would begin stripping off his clothes. He'd tear off his shirt, fling his belt to the ground, and take off his shoes and then just before he dove in to save his friend, Jode would explode to the surface, gasping for breath.

The crowd would explode in applause, and coins and bills would fall like rain into the old canvas bag.

Yup, Jode had many memories of Old Mallory Square. Most of them are good, but none as powerful as THE day.

He arrived early, wanting to be one of the first to see it. There had been similar rumors before. Twelve years ago, the town was in a similar frenzy. When all was said and done, Mel had recovered five bronze cannons and a few bars of silver. Not much, but enough to keep his investors and the local drinking establishments interested.

This time felt different. All of Key West was buzzing with excitement. Everywhere you went, people were asking, "Do you think it's true? Ya think Mel found the mother lode?"

Private jets descended on Key West airport like seagulls to a picnic on the beach, ferrying Mel's financial backers from all over the globe. The newsies were here too. Not the dorks from the Miami stations that drive down to film every Cuban who washes ashore. No, this time it was the real deal, the national reporters with their fancy equipment and make-up artists. It seems everyone in town had been interviewed at least once. They hung out at Sloppy Joe's and The Bull 'cuz that's where Mel held court for years, telling tales more to draw in unsuspecting investors then to inform. They were everywhere like fiddler crabs at low tide, picking at any crumb of information they could dig up.

Jode sat and thought of all of this as he stared out towards the West, toward the Marquesas where Mel had been searching since 1969. The hot July sun burned down on him, the sweat dripping onto the old concrete. Soon Jode was sitting in an ever-growing circle of moisture.

Then he saw it on the horizon. He recognized it immediately. It was not tall and white, crashing through the waves like some butt-draggin' sport's fish. It was dark and very low to the water. He saw the cloud of black smoke from the struggling over worked diesels first. Then, the dark gray and black hull came into view. The bow was barely 2 feet above the waves as it rounded the Pier House at the end of Duval Street and turned east up the channel towards the Bight. He could see the prop dredgers hanging off the back. They looked like huge pieces of macaroni, nearly 3 feet in diameter and ten feet long.

Mel designed them to swing down over the props to direct the wash down onto the reef. With the props spinning, this sent a fierce current to the bottom, washing away any loose sand and debris, leaving anything heavy, like rock, coral, or GOLD, behind.

The weight of these giant tubes lowered the stern of the boat, but today, the boat was so low to the water it seemed even the smallest wave would swamp it. The small craft had to be loaded to the gills to sit so low.

As the boat passed Mallory Square and the Galleon Marina, Jode stood and followed it on foot, which was quite easy as the burdened vessel was barely making way. It rounded the point into the Key West Bight. Jode followed down the docks of the Galleon Marina, past the A and B Lobster House and over to the city docks on Elisabeth Street.

Mel had done it up right. The crowd was huge. Mel and some of what appeared to be his biggest financiers in front, the news media and cameramen elbowing each other for position, then everyone else in the town.

As soon as the boat was secured, they started unloading. The silver bars came off first, each weighing over 70 pounds and two feet long. They were stacked on shore for show before being loaded into armored cars to be delivered to Mel's well-guarded building on Duval Street.

When the stack of silver grew to 3 feet tall and over ten feet long, the real treasure, the gold, was carried from the boat's cabin. After over 400 years at the bottom of the sea, it was still shiny. Mel took one of the cleanest and longest chains and draped it over his shoulders.

The cameramen went wild. This is what they came for. This is what Mel had searched for over the past 16 years … the mother lode.

Jode was dumbstruck. Such wealth millions, no hundreds of millions of dollars worth. Enough to live like a king for a hundred life times. And there it was, wrestled from the sea and now the property of Mel Fisher and Treasure Salver's Inc.

Jode had spent a lifetime on the water, fishing, working, hunting for lobsters. He vowed that from now on, every time he was on or in the water, he would be searching for treasure.

As the treasure was hauled away, the crowd dispersed to every bar in town. Everywhere you went, there were celebrations. Mel's good fortune would soon become the good fortune for every bar, restaurant and business in town. Not only did all the excitement bring in a throng of well-healed mainlanders ready to throw around their money, but hundreds of bar tabs and store credits, long thought worthless, would be paid.

Mel never paid his divers or workers much. Like his investors, you got paid when the treasure was found. Over the years, every place in town ended up holding accounts for Mel's people. It wasn't a burden. It was just how things worked out. Part of being in Key West, part of the cost of doing business in the Conch Republic.

But this day, THE day, all that changed. Jode strode over to Capitan Tony's Bar on Greene Street to join in the festivities. He had no money, but that didn't matter. He knew several of the divers and, of course the bartender and bar maid. This day he needed no money. Beer flowed like water. Before one beer was gone, someone would shout to buy another round for the bar. It was pandemonium and Jode loved it.

Mel had a grey t-shirt printed up with a black outline of the Atocha on the back, THE date and "The Mother Lode" printed on the sleeve. He handed them out to all his crew. A diver friend of

Jode got one that didn't fit. Without a second thought, he tossed it across the bar to Jode. He put it on, and for that night, he was a treasure hunter and owned a share of the gold.

Chapter 3

As old Moe lumbered East towards the Keys, Jode and Tripper formulated their plan to escape their poverty and the drudgery of day-to-day life at the bottom of Key West's social structure. It was a simple plan, but then again, Jode and Tripper were simple men.

The focus was on stealth and secrecy. If one of the other wharf rats that populate the dark underbelly of the Keys caught wind of their good fortune, the likely outcome would be a fillet knife in the back. Nearly as dangerous, one of Treasure Salver's Inc.'s attorneys with a subpoena could just as quickly steal their newfound fortune.

The first step was to sell their "summer crabs" as they normally would. The cash used to begin the process of returning to the Marquesas. They would tell anyone familiar with their illegal activities that "fishing" had been great, best ever, thus explaining a small increase in their usually meager cash flow. After all, everyone knew if Jode or Tripper got their hands on any cash, it was soon transformed into beer and food anyway.

The key to their plan was to fence the treasure they had on board. Jode had worked in Marathon many years ago, cleaning boat bottoms in the cesspool known as Boat Key Harbor. While plying the waters of the bay, he kept a look out for abandoned or at least unlocked boats. He occasionally helped himself to anything of value and sold it through a local businessman, Carlos, who asked no questions. He was confident he could still find the whereabouts of Carlos at Fanny's, Marathon's best known strip club.

Normally, they would just take the bus to Marathon. It only cost a couple of bucks. They shared the ride with all the maids, kitchen help and day workers that kept Key West running. Most lived in the cheaper upper keys, some came all the way from Miami. On this trip, carrying thousands of dollars worth of treasure up and thousands in cash back down to Key West, the bus didn't seem to be such a good idea.

Starting up Old Moe, they turned south past Mallory Square, around the southernmost point in the US then headed northeast towards Marathon and Boot Key harbor. It was an easy ride and they were tied up at the seawall near The Dockside bar by early afternoon. A short walk up to US-1 and they were soon enjoying a beer at Fanny's. When the barmaid came back to see if they wanted another round, Jode asked if Carlos was around.

"You mean Big Carlos?"

"Ya, I guess. Been a long time since I saw him."

"Haven't seen him yet today, but he is probably at his place out back."

After getting directions to the cottage a few rows back off the canal, they paid the tab and headed out the back door to find Big Carlos. The first thing Jode noticed was the big black Mercedes parked in the shade under the small stilt house. Carlos or Big Carlos had come a long way since fencing fishing gear and boat electronics. As they walked up the steps, the door opened before they even knocked. A tall, dark haired man in a light jacket stood blocking the entrance. There was only one reason anyone ever wore a jacket in the Keys and it wasn't to keep warm.

Jode introduced himself and asked if Carlos was around.

"You mean Big Carlos?"

"Ya, we go way back."

"I'll check."

A couple of minutes later, he returned and ushered them into Big Carlos' office. It was really just the back bedroom with a window overlooking the canal. By the sparse amount of furniture and the business like layout it was obvious this was not where Big Carlos lived. The big man, and I mean BIG, sat behind a wooden desk with the canal view behind him. Not the Carlos Jode remembered, this guy was the same height, about six foot but weighed 250 if he weighed an ounce. He reached over the desk and motioned them to sit in the crappy folding chairs across from him.

"Well, it has been a long time. I see you are doing as well as ever," he said with a smirk. "To what do I owe the pleasure of your visit today?"

Jode cleared his throat and started his pre-rehearsed story. "We have a friend back in Key West who was a diver for Mel back in the day. He's fallen on some tough luck and needs some cash. He asked us to fenc . . uh, find a buyer for his trinkets from the Atocha. For a small fee to us, of course." He had Big Carlos' attention now. Reaching down, he picked up the small canvas tool bag he had brought with him. The tall guy behind him quickly stepped up but just as quickly, was waved off by Carlos. Slowly, carefully, he emptied the bag. First, the gold bar and coins, then the chain, and after dumping the small pile of silver coins on the desk, he reached into his pocket and took out the emerald.

Big Carlos was transfixed by the sight. He carefully lifted the gold bar and held it in his palm, judging its weight and quality.

He did the same with the gold coins. Next, he held up the chain. No dought, appraising its length to see if it would fit around his ample neck. After doing the same with the emerald, he scattered the silver coins to see how many were there, dismissing them as a trivial part of the transaction. "Well, it's a nice little collection. I could offer your friend four large for it all."

"Come on, man, you know it is worth at least ten!" Jode responded too quickly.

"You think so? Maybe your friend should just go back to Mel's museum and see what they will give him." Big Carlos knew Jode's story was bullshit, and Jode knew he knew.

"How about five? We need our cut, and there are expenses to cover."

"Ya, like beers at Fanny's and maybe a lap dance! Tell ya what, I'll give you $4,500 on one condition. Your "friend" comes across any more of this and you call me first. Don't worry about "expenses." I'll come find you and pick it up."

Jode knew he had pushed as hard as he could get away with, so he agreed to the deal. After looking at the gleam in Big's eyes as he fondled the treasure and the hesitance as he counted out the C-notes, Jode knew this was the last time he would see Big Carlos . . . if he was lucky.

Sweating, even though the air conditioner was working overtime to keep the big man cool, Jode and Tripper quickly exited and double-timed it back to the Dockside Bar. After how this encounter went, there was one more transaction to complete before heading back to Key West.

Entering the Dockside, they took a seat at the end of the bar. It wasn't busy yet, just a few boat bums. The tourists and workers would show up later. When Milli came by, they ordered beers. On the walk over, Jode had squirreled away the cash after taking out two hundreds and adding it to the two twenties and a few ones he had before heading over to see Big Carlos.

When Milli returned with the brewskies, Jode made a point of taking out the twenty to pay, making sure she saw the hundreds he had with it.

"Jake in the back? I have a favor to ask."

She glanced at the money, nodded her head, and walked into the kitchen. Now, most of the time, Jake sold a little weed to supplement his income, but Jode had another request to make. After meeting with Carlos, Jode figured he might need a little more protection than just his winning smile and swift feet. When Jake came out, Jode was ready with a story.

"We're heading out to do some shark fishing and figured it'd be a lot easier if we could put those bad boys to sleep before haulin' them aboard. Thought you might be able to hook us up with a little firepower, nothin' fancy, just something that shoots. Maybe a 38 or 357? A rifle would work but could be a little cumbersome in close quarters in the cockpit."

Jake nodded and asked them when they were going shark fishing. Jode told him tonight. He asked if he had the cash and Jode slipped the two hundreds between his fingers so Jake knew they were serious. "Sit tight and nurse those beers, might take me a while. Be back in an hour or so."

Now there was no way Tripper and Jode were going to nurse a beer for an hour, but true to his word, Jake was back just as they were polishing off their fourth. He came out of the kitchen with a to-go bag. Inside was a styrofoam container but it was a lot heavier than a burger and fries. He put it on the counter and Jode looked inside and opened the lid. There sat an old style revolver and a hand full of shells, wasn't sure if they were 38's or 357, but it didn't matter, either one would do. Jode slid the two C-notes over to Jake, left the twenty and change from the last one to cover their tab and the duo headed out the door and back to Old Moe. There was no way they were staying in Marathon with Big Carlos sniffing around.

On the ride back to Key West, they looked over their new purchase and even shot off a couple of arounds into the wake. They were both familiar with guns, just had no reason for one in the Keys. They weren't worried about anyone stealing from them because, until now, they had nothin to steal and if they were the ones doing the stealing, having a gun would make things a whole lot worse if they got caught.

Now that the duo had turned the treasure into cash, they slowly bought up the stores they would need for at least a month at sea, recovering more treasure. One thing they would need that might raise some eyebrows was a Huka rig, a gas powered compressor attached to hoses and regulators that would allow them to stay on the bottom as long as there was gas in the tank. In the shallow water, decompression wasn't a worry. Keeping tanks full 20 miles from nowhere was.

To avoid drawing attention to their plans, they said they were going back into the business of cleaning boat bottoms. Anyone who knew them would scoff at the idea of them working that hard, but it was their story none the less.

They spent some of the loot on beers and shots at the local bars but were careful to keep their new found wealth on the down low. That wasn't easy for Tripper. He loved to tell stories and most everyone loved to listen. Everyone was his friend. Jode tried to keep him quiet, but that was impossible. As the night got later and the beers added up, his stories got a little too close to the truth for Jode's liking, but with a healthy dose of "If I evers," "One day maybes," and "That's what I'd done," Tripper avoided giving them away. The fact that no one ever believed anything he said or any story he ever told helped.

They passed much of their time on the back deck of Old Moe. Day dreaming of living the high life while they sucked down cold PBRs.

With Old Moe loaded down with treasure, they would set a course north to Fort Myers Beach. Slipping behind the Island into Estero Bay, Old Moe would disappear among the other dilapidated old boats and Jode and Tripper would be just another couple of derelicts in the outcast community of misfits.

Finding an old car for sale on San Carlos Island should be no problem. With wheels, the next steps would be a clothes store and barbershop. Soon, Jode and Tripper would be transformed into upstanding members of the middle class.

With their treasure and any other items of value loaded in the car, they would abandon Old Moe and their former lives. The hatches left unlocked and keys in the ignition, they hoped someone would steal Old Moe, both covering their tracks and giving the old girl another chance at life. If not, the overworked bilge pump would drain the batteries until they died, Old Moe dying soon thereafter.

Transforming their treasure to cash, especially any gem stones they found, would be more difficult. Their value would bring out the greed in any potential buyer, always a dangerous situation. Maybe even more dangerous than Big Carlos. Jode had heard of a pawnbroker about 50 miles north of the Beach. He was known to keep several hundred thousand dollars in a safety deposit box to finance his illicit dealings. Even more important, he billed his pawnshop as a jewelry store and fancied himself a gold smith, the perfect combination to suit Jode's needs, but a very dangerous one. This pawnbroker had many contacts with dangerous and undesirable individuals. He had even faked his own kidnapping and burglary to cover up a drug deal gone wrong. They would have to be extremely careful. Once they had cash in hand, the illustrious treasure hunters would drive to Tampa, ever mindful of any tails, buy a nice car, ditch the other in the part of town where it was sure to disappear, and head to Texas, selling coins and slowly converting their treasure at pawn shops and jewelry stores along the way. That was their plan anyway.

As relaxing as it was sitting on the back deck drinking beer, and telling stories, the pull of the local bars, especially now that they had money in their pockets was too hard to resist. Even with the cash burning a hole in their pocket, they still shied away from the expensive tourist traps and stuck with their old haunts. They were almost ready to leave, the boat loaded with equipment and fuel. A couple more days and they would head out for the last time.

Savoring the cold draft, they sat at the end of the bar both lost in their own thoughts and dreams. Suddenly, Tripper reached over and tapped Jode's wrist. "Don't turn around but I think I see that guy we saw at Big Carlos' place. No, I'm sure it's him."

"Did he see us?"

"Can't tell, but if he's here in Key West and in this bar, he's got to be looking for us. Maybe he wants the money back or information on where we got the treasure. Either way, it's bad news for us." Keeping their heads down and whispering softly, they made a plan. Jode would get up like he was going to hit the head, then sneak out the backdoor. Tripper, a little shorter and better dressed would more easily fit in with the crowd and make his way to the other entrance and leave with the first group of guys heading out. Jode would head north, Tripper south, staying with the crowd until he could get to the back streets and make sure he wasn't being followed. They would meet up at the mini-mart near the dinghy dock. After grabbing what they could carry, they would return to Old Moe and leave while it was still dark.

For once, things went as planned and they met a few minutes later at the mini-mart. They each grabbed a case of beer . . . first things first, then loaded up on bread, peanut butter, jelly and as many cans of food as they could carry from the limited selection available and carried them over to the checkout counter. As the clerk rang up the sale Jode grabbed a hand full of cigarette lighters out of the tub on the counter and added them to the pile. They didn't have much weed on the boat but having weed and no lighter would be a crime. When everything was tallied up, Jode took out two crisp new C-notes and laid them on the counter to cover the purchase. The guy looked at the bills, then up at Jode and Tripper, suspicion was written across his face in big letters, but he took the money and handed him back the change. That was precisely why they were careful to hide their wealth. Anyone seeing the two of them with money would know something was up and it wasn't good. Didn't matter now. They were leaving and didn't plan on coming back, ever.

They nearly jogged to the dinghy dock. Tripper jumped in. After loading the beer and groceries, Jode cast off while Tripper pulled hard on the oars as they made their way west towards the anchorage on the far side of Wisteria Island.

Once they were beyond the lights of Key West, Tripper relaxed into an easy rhythm as they rounded the southern end of the island and headed to Old Moe. With the bright lights on shore and the dark waters to the west, there was no way they could be seen making their getaway, whether Big's man was watching or not. They tied the dinghy off to Old Moe and unloaded what little stores they had for their voyage. Not as well stocked as they had hoped, there were no worries of starving. The duo had lived off fresh fish and lobster for weeks at a time. This trip would be no different. At least they had enough beer for a couple a day each, until they made it to Fort Myers Beach.

Having no desire to risk returning to town and knowing Mr. Big was on their tail, Tripper quietly hauled in the anchor as Jode started the engines and idled west through the anchorage. Turning south, they slowly made their way behind Sunset Key and out into the deep waters of the Florida Straits. Once they were far from Key West, Jode pushed the throttles forward to an easy cruising speed of 8 knots, turned on the running lights and relaxed. Both too wound up to sleep, they grabbed one of the still cold beers and went over their plan one more time. Slowly heading west towards their dreams.

Chapter 4

It had been more than two weeks since they made their escape from Key West. The hunting was good and they had found several dozen gold bars, lengths of gold chain and a wide assortment of jewelry and coins. It was not the mother lode but more than they had ever dreamed possible. The days had been long. Each took turns underwater as the other kept watch and pretended to fish. Not an unusual sight out there on the reef. As night fell, they made their way to the lee side of the Marquesas sharing the dwindling selection of rations and resting before starting the whole routine over the next day.

The sweat rolled off Jode's face, stinging his eyes as it journeyed over his bare chest and arms to finally pool beneath the old worn deck chair. The tattered canvas overhead provided no protection from the blistering sun. As it hung low in the sky, its rays intensified by the glass-calm sea. The heat didn't bother Jode.

He had lived a lifetime on the sea. The subtropics of the gulf were where he belonged. The heat on this voyage was more bearable than on most. Jode's first ice-cold beer of the day chilled his throat as it made its way to his empty stomach. Once again, he thanked the gods for refrigeration. The trip to the reef each day had kept the batteries for the fridge charged, and only used a couple gallons of diesel as they idled slowly back and forth. No sooner had the cold beverage arrived, it came pouring out as sweat. At least that's how it seemed to Jode. But he didn't care. There was more beer in the cooler. That was just one reason this trip was different.

It was as different here as it was in the Keys. Key West was exactly the same as it had always been but totally different. Nothing was the same for Jode and Tripper. No, not on the last visit. They arrived with their usual cargo of illegally caught lobsters. Just in time, as the season opened. They smuggled 'em into the fish house as they always had done. They got paid a fair price, then out on the town for some excitement. The excitement they sought could not compare to the excitement they felt within. You see, Jode and Tripper carried with them a secret. A secret they could not share.

They split up their ill-gotten gains. Being careful to set aside enough for fuel and stores for their final trip to Marathon then on to the Marquesas. With money in their pockets, they headed for the usual watering holes. Not Sloppy Joe's or the Bull.

No, those tourist traps would be crowded with mainlanders. They come down to the Keys each summer. They say they're here to catch lobster, but that ain't even half of it.

Like Jode and Tripper, they come to drink, score a little hooch, and maybe get laid. But those mainlanders are different. They swagger into the local bars like they own them. They think they are better 'n all the locals. Their fancy clothes, the jewelry, sporty cars and cockboats. They smell sweeter than their fancy perfume. They strut around like a bunch of dogs at a country fair. Each smellin' the others butt. Kickin' up dirt. Puttin' on a show.

This one has the fanciest car. That one has the fastest boat. This one's got the most jewelry. While another is showin' off his worthless gym bought muscles.

Jode has seen those carpetbaggers too many times before. They strut around like banty roosters. Each tryin' their best to impress every her in the place. All the trappin's of wealth. All the stories of past accomplishments. As the night grows old and the drinks pile up one on top of the other, the stories get harder and harder to believe.

Worst part of this time of year was trying to get laid yourself. With all the money the mainlanders throw around, the workin' girls are busy. Jode couldn't compete with the gold chains, C-notes and fine cocaine. Even the girls that weren't in the business, spent most of their time with the high rollers and big spenders. After all, they're fishin' too and most were out to catch a lunker.

No, early August ain't no time for romance if you're nothin' but a poor local fisherman. That's why Jode and Tripper pretty much avoided the hangouts on Duval Street. At least in the back street local bars, they know the clientele. Sure, the furniture isn't quite clean. The musty smell of stale beer, mixed with salt air hangs like a fog throughout the dark, damp interior. Most of all, you don't have to watch the sickening mainlander's mating dance. That makes the old dump preferable to any bar on Duval. Besides, that's where friends are. If Jode had any real friends. Even Renee, the barmaid, and his sometimes sex partner could hardly be called a friend. Jode didn't make close friends. Most of the time, he preferred to be an observer, rather than a participant. Letting others tell their stories like Tripper did most times they were out and about. Not taking the lead and not following either. Maybe Renee was special, but in an odd sort of way. When they were together, they were close. When they were apart, they were all the way apart. No strings, seldom even a thought. Odd, very odd indeed.

The old Briggs & Stratton engine began to cough and spit and belch. The clamor brought Jode back to the present. Damn, he drifted off and forgot to refuel the damn thing. When it breathed its last, so did the compressor. His first reaction was to jump up and restart the old relic. Looking out over the water to the setting sun, he decided the day was about over anyway. He just had to deal with a very pissed-off diver. Tripper should be breaking the surface any minute. Jode picked up a fresh can of PBR and headed for the dive platform. A helping hand and a cold beer would go a long way in calming down his out of breath partner.

On queue, Tripper broke through the glass smooth surface. After a huge inhale, he let loose with a string of profanity. Jode let the words flow by like the warm humid breeze. There was no reason to respond. As the breeze dies down on its own accord, so would Tripper's anger. It wasn't the first time the compressor stopped in mid-dive. It certainly wouldn't be the last.

Back on board, Tripper took a long pull on the beer, while Jode hosed the salt off him. His anger was likewise washed away, replaced by the excitement of his latest find. Without bothering to dry off, he triumphantly emptied his goodie bag on the deck … six more gold coins, a couple dozen of silver and a cross.

He let the sunlight refract through the green stones. The gold, buried for nearly four hundred years, still shone brightly. "I bet this here will fetch enough to buy one of those fancy cars all by itself." Jode nodded his agreement. After more than two weeks anchored on this very spot, they indeed had enough treasure to buy several cars. Turning their secret stash into C-notes would be more challenging than the long days spent searching the sea floor.

Like Jode, Tripper could put down some beer. With the first can of the day empty, he climbed up on the deck for another. The number of beers left was few, but the days left until they reached the Beach and a new supply were much fewer. They sat without speaking, looking over the latest additions to their haul and draining another can of beer. In fact, neither man was much for words when they were alone. Other than planning their new lives, they preferred to sit in silence. These last two weeks were full of a whole lot of plans and schemes. Not a word of their discovery was uttered while they were out and about in the Keys. The thoughts and dreams just grew larger and more grandiose with no one to share them with.

In a few days, a storm would be moving through. By then, most of the treasure would be on board. The time for dreaming was drawing to a close. Soon it would be time for action. Nonetheless, the evening was spent dreaming out loud. Jode was the thinker of the pair. Though he had scant practice at it. The plan was mostly his.

They would hoist anchor for the last time the day after next. The voyage to Fort Myers Beach would take at least twelve hours to cover the one hundred and ten miles. Anchored among the derelict boats behind the Island, they would blend in with the other displaced watermen. Pawning a few trinkets would get them a car. Jode had the story all laid out in his mind. It wasn't much different as the one he had told Big Carlos.

I worked for Mel Fisher during the early eighties. Before we hit the mother lode, we got paid next to nothin'! But Mel promised us a piece of the action when we found it. That was years ago. Now, I'm down on my luck. All I have left is this last coin, or chain, or jewel. I hate to sell it, but I don't have a choice. Yup, that was going to be the story.

Once they had wheels, they'd head to Corpus Christi, Texas. Stopping at every pawnshop along the way, telling the same story. They would be rich men by the time they got there. The only thing they hadn't decided was whether to buy a shrimp boat and go back into business or just keep driving to Mexico and live it up as rich expatriated Americans.

With all the money, living a life of leisure sounded mighty good, after a hard life spent at the bottom of the food chain.

After another night of cold beer, lousy food, dreaming and scheming, they went below to sleep. The old boat reeked of mold and mildew. Forty years on the water had not been kind to Old Moe. It was more of a surprise when something worked, than when it didn't. Just one more voyage and it wouldn't matter. They could sell her for a few bucks to a down and out fisherman. Maybe just leave her anchored in the Back Bay until she sank, was stolen or blown away by a storm. It didn't much matter, they would be a thousand miles away and thousands of dollars richer when Old Moe met her fate.

The next morning, they awoke to the pitching and rolling brought on by the rough chop. At least the breeze would sweep away the oppressive heat. By late afternoon the chop had grown. Two to three foot seas were now making their way north from the Gulf Stream. Jode and Tripper had been out in far worse. If this were all they faced on the journey to Fort Myers Beach, tomorrow's trip would be a cinch.

For a more comfortable night and to get a small jump on the voyage, they moved the boat to the north side of the Marquesas Keys. Once in the lee of the Island, the waves disappeared. The ten-knot winds would make for good sleeping.

After dropping anchor, Jode went below to cook dinner. He half cleared last night's dinner from the old skillet before putting it on the stove. Neither Jode nor Tripper was much for fancy food. Cut up a few potatoes, maybe an onion. Open a can of corned beef ... cook till done. The hunger from a full day of diving made even this meager offering taste just fine. They washed it down with another beer. Then tossed the dirty dishes into the sink where they would lay undisturbed until needed again.

With the beginning of their adventure imminent, neither felt like talking. After the brief dinner, each went to their cabin to sleep. Just as doing dishes was not something Jode enjoyed, neither was picking up after himself. The bed resembled a nest. Dirty sheets, musty blankets and stained pillows tangled and filled the small bed. Old half read magazines and never read books were strewn about. If rough seas knocked something to the floor, that's where it stayed.

The following morning brought far stronger winds. From the southwest they would pose no problem. The waves would push them toward their destination. It would make steering more difficult, but the following seas would add two knots to their cruising speed. They should be resting comfortably in Matanzas Pass by nightfall. Tripper fought with the anchor as Jode held the boat steady with the controls. Once free, he turned the tiny ship northward and opened the throttles. The old diesels spit and belched as thick black smoke filled the back of the boat. It was several minutes before the wind swept the acrid smoke, first over the boat, then off into the distance.

The seas built as they left the islands behind. The old engines strained and shuddered as they pushed the heavy old boat up the back of each wave, then revved up as the boat slid down the other side. Jode would flail the tiller about, trying to maintain a true course each time Old Moe came falling down the crest of a wave. It was a tiring and nerve-wracking job. He barely even noticed. Years of experience, coupled with his destination of dreams, left his mind to wander as his arms went about their task.

The day was overcast and windy. No blazing sun to deal with. The hundred-mile journey would be rough, but not unpleasant. As was their custom, Jode stayed at the helm. Tripper only relieved him when he had to relieve himself. It wasn't that Tripper couldn't handle the job. He had nearly as much experience as Jode. It was just the way things were, a silent understanding between the two men.

By noon, the seas had built to five feet. Now most mainlanders think five-foot seas are five feet tall. They aren't exactly wrong. The thing is a five-foot wave is followed by a five-foot trough. So from top to bottom, five-foot seas are really ten feet tall. Old Moe struggled more and more to climb the back of each succeeding wave. Once on top, she would shudder and shake as the bow dropped and she plunged the ten feet into the next.

It might have been the wind. Maybe the waves were just too steep, or maybe the old diesels were too tired to continue the fight. Something was wrong, but Jode couldn't figure it out. With each wave, Moe's stern dug deeper into the water. At each succeeding crest, she came down harder and faster.

Yes, something wasn't right, but what? Jode stared intently at the many gauges. Perhaps they would tell him what his instincts could not. Suddenly the amp meter flickered. Once again it bounced to zero and back again. What did it mean? Was it part of the puzzle, or just one of Old Moe's many idiosyncrasies. Jode stood, transfixed as his mind used all its reasoning power to solve the puzzle. His face went white as the blood fell to the pit of his stomach. Water … it had to be water!

It took only a split second for him to connect the dots. The water in the bilge would flow to the stern, making it dig in as the tired old engines pushed the heavy load up the wave. Once at the crest, the bow drops, sending a cascade of seawater crashing to the bow. The alternator, that was the key. Was the saltwater splashing on the alternator itself or onto any exposed connection, shorting out the current? Maybe the water was just hitting the belt, causing it to slip and the alternator to stop spinning? It didn't matter.

Before his mind even reached a conclusion his mouth was barking orders to Tripper. The intensity of his voice made Tripper spring into action. He bounded into the cabin with one leap, throwing back the filthy old carpet; he lifted the heavy wooden hatch to the engine compartment.

Jode was peering over Tripper's shoulder as he lifted the hatch. Neither was prepared for what they saw. He expected to see water, but Jode was shocked by the volume of seawater sloshing through the bilge. The oily greenish-brown liquid had risen nearly up to the engines. Old oil jugs, antifreeze containers and wooden floorboards floated throughout the bilge. Each time a wave rocked the boat, a similar wave cascaded over the interior of the bilge.

Without being told, Tripper jumped down into the knee-deep water. He quickly found the culprit. The seal on one of the raw water pumps had failed. Seawater was spraying into the boat. He yelled for Jode to shut down the offending engine as he closed the sea cock stopping the flow.

Suddenly a wave bigger than most, tossed the diminutive craft. Jode held tight to the tiller. A sharp crack, followed by a thunderous impact shook the boat to its very timbers. Regaining his balance, Jode looked into the salon to check on his partner. The hatch was closed! Without thinking, he dove for the handle and lifted the hatch cover. He first noticed the bracing bar swinging free, a large chunk of splintered teak still bolted to its end. What he saw next made the bile well up in his throat. His knees went weak, too weak to hold up the heavy hatch. He ran to the back of the boat and wretched over the side. What now? His mind was in no better shape than his stomach.

Without a steady hand at the helm, the boat had swung sideways to the heavy seas. Each succeeding wave brought Old Moe closer to capsizing. Jode could not deal with the catastrophe and steer the boat. He had to drop the anchor to point the boat into the wind and seas.

Like a crab, he moved slowly, carefully towards the bow. One moment up on top looking over the cabin into the sea, the next holding on tightly as his feet were immersed in the water of the following wave. The few seconds it took him to traverse the boat's length felt like an eternity. Finally reaching the bow, he sat down with his legs spread for maximum leverage. His hands clinging tightly to the anchor cleat. Afraid to let go, he managed to uncleat the anchor chain with one hand. Once free, it plunged into the sea. First the chain, then the rope came spilling from the rope locker. It moved so fast, Jode was terrified that it might tear off a finger or worse, pull him over with it.

After many moments, the line went slack. The anchor had reached the bottom nearly a hundred feet below. Jode let more line out before cleating off the anchor line. As the line went taught, the bow swung violently into the onrushing waves. Within seconds, the boat began the much more tolerable fore to aft pitching. The anchor would not hold the boat in position, but it would keep it safely pointed into the wind and seas.

With the boat secure, Jode grabbed a pair of old dock lines and entered the cabin to face the grizzly task. He lifted the remaining intact hatch and tied it securely. Stealing himself, he looked into the water below. The greenish tint of seawater was gone replaced by a dirty rust red color. Tripper was floating face down between the engines. Each wave made his arms and legs move as if swimming. One look at his head and there was no doubt that he was not. The hatch had crashed down with such force it split his skull much like a coconut. The seawater had washed away all the blood. The sickening gray of his exposed brain was clear to see.

Still in shock, Jode climbed down and tied a rope around Tripper's chest. Once back out of the bilge, he used the rope to lift his fallen comrade up on deck. There was no time for ceremony. He grabbed a flashlight and a small toolbox and climbed back down between the two dangerously hot engines, one still idling in neutral. He fumbled beneath the gross liquid until he located the water intake of the running engine. Loosening the hose clamps, he pulled off the two-inch hose, while simultaneously shutting the sea cock. Now the engine would be pumping water from the bilge for coolant rather than from the open sea.

Jode braced himself against the still pitching boat as he held the hose down to the bottom of the bilge.

Crouched in the dark, there was nothing he could do to speed up the slow process of emptying hundreds of gallons of bloody water from the boat. His thoughts flashed from Tripper's fate to his own. Being killed suddenly by the broken hatch would be preferable to a slow drowning, trapped in the bilge of a sinking boat. He pushed the macabre thoughts from his mind and concentrated on the task at hand. The water level did not seem to be dropping. With the boat so low in the water, more water could be leaking in than he was pumping out.

He reached over the hot engine and pulled the throttle half open. The sound was deafening, but he could feel the added suction as the water was pulled from the boat. What seemed an eternity was in fact only twenty minutes. Most of the water was gone, at least as much as his improvised pump could remove. He slowed the engine to an idle, reattached the hose and opened the sea cock before climbing out of the bilge. There was more to be done before he could resume his voyage.

Stumbling down to the V-berth, Tripper's room, he found a mass of wet blankets and sheets. The water that had come up through the floor was gone, leaving behind the stench of diesel fuel and blood colored stains. Jode threw the bedding aside and opened the small hatch to get at the bilge pump. It had to be broken; the leak at the engine seal was not that severe. The pump should have handled the problem easily. Upon further inspection, he found the float switch had failed. Reconfiguring the wires, the pump began draining the last remaining water from Old Moe.

Without the automatic switch, Jode would have to remember to turn the pump on and off every so often. Long enough to pump out any water, but not so long as to burn up the aging device.

The boat now secure, he faced his most depressing task, getting rid of Tripper's body.

Bringing Tripper to shore for burial was not an option. It was an accident, no one would deny that. Still, forms would be filled out, questions would be asked and inspections made! No, Tripper would be buried at sea. Jode tried not to think of the crabs and fish picking out his eyes, then devouring his exposed brain as he fastened a weight belt firmly around his friend. He rationalized that Tripper would want to be buried at sea. After all, it was a fitting end to a life on the water. Besides, crabs and fishes are preferable to worms and beetles any day.

Before hoisting the body over the side, Jode quickly went through his pockets finding his wallet; he removed the few remaining bills and through the rest overboard. If by chance the body was discovered, he didn't want to make their job of identification easy. His shake down complete, Jode bid his friend a final farewell and dropped the body into the angry sea.

Unable to steer the boat safely into the swells and lift the anchor at the same time, Jode decided to cut the anchor line and be on his way. There was a spare anchor on board and besides, his remaining days on Old Moe would be few.

Once free of the anchor, Jode's robot-like arms spun the wheel back and forth as the boat climbed each succeeding wave, only to tumble into the next. The loss of one engine made his task all the more difficult. But again, Jode's years of experience allowed his mind to wander as his body worked.

Tripper was gone. What a freak accident. What were the odds? How could so many minor problems build into such a catastrophe? So what, a seal broke. It had happened before. Every two or three years they needed replacing. A thousand to one odds it would happen today. That float switch, again, things like that happen, but today? Another thousand to one. Then there was the auxiliary pump. They checked it before they left. It ran, but how can you check if it pumps water without filling the bilge first? How could it run without pumping? What were the odds? And that wave at that moment, a hundred to one? A thousand? A million?

There were too many zeros for Jode to put together. He couldn't figure the odds. He did know that the tragedy that befell

Tripper was at least one in a million, maybe one in a billion. This fact gave him no solace. No matter the odds, Tripper was gone and Old Moe was wounded.

Suddenly Jode felt the boat shake and shudder. Not the rapid vibration of a bent shaft or broken propeller. No, this was more like giant soft hands pounding on the boat. The windows and hatches rattled. He felt it more in his ears and lungs than through his hands, clenched hard against the wheel. Having never experienced such a sensation, he looked wildly about trying to determine the cause.

As he looked out the starboard window, his heart stopped and his body froze rigid with fear. The building concussions were coming from a waterspout not two hundred yards away. There was no time to react. Old Moe had neither the speed nor agility to escape such a powerful phenomenon. As quick as it came, it melted away in the distance. Jode's heart couldn't stop pounding. His fear caused his knees to buckle. He clutched the tiller for support.

Two hundred yards. Had it been any closer, Old Moe would be nothing but shattered timbers floating on the surface. The engines, Jode and the treasure, no doubt joining Tripper on the bottom.

Regaining his composure, another horrifying thought crossed Jode's mind. The conditions that spawned a sailor's most dreaded foe could certainly produce more. He couldn't see them coming, he couldn't run out of the way if he did. He would have to depend on luck and luck had not been on his side, not today, not ever.

Looking back over the stern he saw the black, rolling clouds that gave life to the waterspout. They were following him, chasing him, closing in with each second. Joe had no choice, there was nowhere to run and nowhere to hide. He turned the boat to keep the wind at his back. If he could keep the wind and seas directly on his stern, Old Moe just might be able to handle the angry storm.

The sea grew dark as the black clouds closed over the tiny boat. It was as if night had fallen many hours too soon. The winds grew stronger. Later Jode would learn that they were a steady 60 knots with gusts over 80. Hurricane force winds without the hurricane.

His course to Fort Myers Beach was just a memory. He now would go wherever the winds would push him. One moment he would be watching the waves in front of him. The next he would turn to see the flag on his stern. He fought to keep the flag, now held stiff by the winds, pointed directly ahead. If the boat turned even slightly catty-wampus to the driving seas, it would capsize.

Cold rain pelted his back like BB's while sweat poured down his face onto his drenched shirt. It was not the temperature, but the fear that made the salty perspiration that stung his eyes.

No longer going north, the storm had forced him to turn due east. There was no time to look at a chart. It mattered little anyway. Jode's destination was in the hands of the storm. Could he make Marco and find sanctuary behind the barrier island? Would he be beached on Cape Romano Shoals? How far had he come? Not that far. The coast somewhere among the 10,000 islands. The storm would decide. He couldn't out run it, and it was not outrunning him. He could only endure it and hope. Hope was something he had damn little of.

Hours passed. How many, he didn't know. The sky grew darker as the sun dropped below the horizon. Jode could no longer see where he was going. He just focused on the flag dancing in the glow of the running lights. He would go where the winds pushed him.

He watched the depth recorder as the sea bottom rose to meet him. It was nearly a hundred feet deep where Tripper lay. Soon it was only thirty. The numbers continued to drop. The shallow waters made the waves steeper and even more dangerous.

Jode had to be ever more vigilant as Old Moe approached the coast.

With only seven feet between the props and the bottom, he turned on the searchlight. The reflection from the falling rain made it nearly impossible to see. The shadows in the distance had to be mangrove islands. He must be near Everglades City. This was an area he knew well. Countless times he and Tripper had run drugs or Cubans from the Keys to this God-forsaken town of smugglers and derelicts. If he could just navigate between the little islands, he would be safe until the storm passed.

Ahead lay Tiger Key. The pass to the south was wider and deeper but the winds were pushing the crippled old boat more to the north. The pass north of the island was narrower and much more treacherous. As Jode entered the pass, the waves were breaking, any turns caused the boat to roll violently, threatening to capsize with each passing swell. Jode swung the wheel violently from port to starboard and back trying to keep to the middle of the channel. With just the starboard engine, as he passed close to Lulu Key he couldn't turn back into the surf. A loud scraping sound followed by a thunderous cracking brought fear into his eyes. Seconds later Old Moe lurched to port and slammed to a stop. Jode was flung into the wheel, his head slamming down into the instrument panel. His eyes rolled back into his head and the world went black.

Sometime later Jode stirred to life, not knowing how long he had been unconscious. His chest felt like he had been run over by a truck and he had a splitting headache. There was blood on the dash. He raised his hand and felt his forehead, it was bloody but it had dried up and stopped bleeding. It wouldn't kill him.

The rain had dropped to a drizzle and the winds had died down to a stiff breeze. He realized that the boat was still, not rocking even with the waves crashing into the stern. He was hard aground. At least the boat couldn't sink . . . any more than it had. With that thought in his head, he laid down behind the helm and passed out.

Chapter 5

The following morning, Jode awoke to a blazing sun burning his eyes. His head still hurt and he had a huge bruise across his chest but he was alive and more or less ok. Old Moe, on the other hand was perched bow up on the beach with a couple feet of water in the bilge. The only thing Jode knew for sure was that there was no way to walk or swim to civilization and that there was no way he would be leaving the treasure behind unguarded.

The first order of business was to get the water out of the bilge and figure out how bad a situation he was in. He couldn't use the bilge pump to empty the boat. Draining the batteries would strand him here just as assuredly as the sand under the hull. So, he grabbed a bucket, climbed down into the bilge and began bailing. It was a lot more work than he thought. After filling the 5 gallon bucket, he had to climb back out to the back deck and dump the water overboard. It was exhausting labor but he had nothing else to do so he took his time and rested often.

By late afternoon the bilge was as dry as it was going to get but the boat was still laying hard against the sand. The next task was surveying the damage and what stores he had on board to either effect his escape or survive until he figured a way out of his predicament. The hole in the boat was just below the waterline. If the boat was in the water, but only about 6 inches wide and a foot and a half long. He'd think of something.

He still had 3 or 4 days' worth of food on board, longer now that Tripper was gone. The water tank was still intact and about half full, so he had about 50 gallons of fresh water. Plenty for a couple of months if he used it just for drinking and cooking. If he was stranded here that long he would go crazy long before he died of thirst.

The sun was low on the horizon and he was dog tired from bailing out the boat so he opened a can of beans and one of spam, ate both cold, laid down in the salon and crashed. Sometime during the night he awoke to the constant buzzing of mosquitoes feasting on any exposed flesh. He got up and closed the boat, lit his last Pic coil, covered himself with an old blanket and tried to fall back to sleep in the oppressive heat and dampness of the closed up boat. The sunrise and breeze off the gulf couldn't come soon enough.

With the sun coming up over the mangroves the thought of a cup a coffee drew Jode awake. Unfortunately, with the boat half out of the water and tilted at such a severe angle there was no way to use the stove. Coffee would have to wait. After a large glass of water and a trip out to the woods, it was time to figure a way out of this mess.

The hole in the side of the boat definitely needs fixing, but with the hull so far up on the beach it won't be until the next king tide that any escape will be possible. With that realization Jode decided that making his prison in paradise more livable was the order of the day. A fire at night should keep the bugs away so he set about collecting firewood. While that sounds easy, dry firewood is another story. He spent the morning scouring the area. Any dry sticks and twigs were piled where he planned to have the fire. Damp driftwood and branches were laid out above the tide line to dry in the sun. He would need firewood for a long time, he feared. With the noon day sun beating down he found some shade by the boat and napped.

When the sun was lower in the sky and the sea breeze kicked up it was time to think about dinner. While there was still food on the boat, it wouldn't last for long. Being a lifelong fisherman that shouldn't present a problem. He grabbed a fishing pole and the bucket off the boat. Walking down the beach he soon spied a mass of fiddler crabs scurrying along the shore. Reaching down he scooped up a hand full, tossed them in the bucket and ambled over to where the mangroves touched the water. A short cast and a couple of minutes later Jode reeled in a nice sized sheepshead. As much as he liked to fish, there was no way to store fresh fish so enough for dinner put an end to his fishing for the day. Dumping out the rest of the fiddlers, he scooped up some seawater and tossed the fish in the bucket. Back at the boat he strung a small line through the fish's gills and dropped it into the water. After tying the line off to the dive platform, he went about starting a fire to cook dinner and keep the bugs way overnight.

After digging a shallow fire pit and getting the fire started, Jode set about cleaning the fish. Usually he would cut off the fillets and remove the skin and scales, but cooking over an open flame required a different technique. After cutting off the head and cleaning out the stomach cavity, he cracked the fish flat and attached it to a piece of mangrove root that wouldn't burn. Before placing it over the fire, he rummaged through the galley and found a tin of Old Bay seasoning. He sprinkled some over the fresh fish, positioned it over the fire and opened one of the few remaining cans of warm beer. While the fish cooked, he took the fish head, still attached to the stringer and threw it back in the water. With a little luck, tomorrow's dinner will be steamed blue crabs. It had been another long day so sleep came easily after a very tasty and satisfying dinner.

Once again, he was awakened by a swarm of mosquitoes. The fire had died down and they came back with a vengeance. Bundling himself up in the blanket, he lay there sweating and swearing. Tomorrow he needed a better idea to keep the bugs away.

Awakening to the soft breeze and sunrise, it was another day in paradise . . . almost. After a trip to the woods and slowly drinking a tall glass of water, it was time to tackle the day's chores. First he spent some time on the hole in the hull. It wasn't really a hole as much as a broken and crushed in section of planking. Not sure how to start, Jode crawled into the bilge and worked the broken plank with a hammer until it was mostly flat with the rest of the hull. It certainly wouldn't hold water but looked a lot better. Not sure how to proceed, he left it at that and contemplated how to better keep the bugs away at night.

The fire had worked well while it burned but didn't burn all night. Building a fire big enough to burn through the night wasn't practical either. That big of flame would certainly draw the attention of the park rangers or other lawmen. Never a good idea. Also, he wouldn't be able to find enough wood nearby to dry and burn to last more than a few nights. What he did have that would burn all night was diesel fuel. Even a small flame would put out some light and enough thick black smoke to discourage even the hungriest mosquito.

Jode set about making a smudge pot for tonight. Again the bilge was the place to search for what he needed. Unfortunately, most stuff nowadays comes in plastic not metal. Oil cans are a thing of the past. Almost giving up he spied an old oil filter laying in the gunk at the bottom of the bilge. His years of slovenly living might just be paying off! The oily old canister held about a quart of oil and had a hole in the top more than an inch in diameter. Grabbing the old filter he held it under the water separator, opened the little spigot, and let the diesel fuel slowly fill the old filter.

Tearing a strip off one of Trippers old t-shirts, he stuffed it into the hole leaving just a couple of inches sticking out the top. Outside near his "sleeping quarters" he dug a small hole and carefully placed the filter in the sand so it couldn't tip over. Tonight will be the test of his ingenuity.

While scrounging through the bilge, he noticed several items that he could use to fix the hole in the boat. It was passed noon and that side of the hull was being assaulted by the blistering afternoon sun. That job would have to wait until the cool morning breeze and shade made the hard work tolerable.

Thinking about dinner, he checked the line with the fish head tied to the dive platform. Pulling it in slowly so as not alert his pry, he grabbed the fish net and scooped the unsuspecting crab into the bucket. With the tide going out there were probably more blue crabs to be had, so he tossed the carcass back into the current. In addition to the crabs, boiling up the last two potatoes would make a proper dinner. Maybe add some fresh oysters with a dash of Tabasco to get the meal going. Smiling to himself, he thought of how much that same dinner would cost at Key West's premier restaurant the Pier House. Not that he had ever eaten there.

If he was going to boil potatoes he would need a hot fire that would last at least an hour but the wood nearby was still damp from yesterday's afternoon shower. He needed some dry kindling to get it started. Maybe it was time to start getting rid of some of the junk in the boat, especially Trippers stuff. Might be hard to explain all his old clothes that were obviously too small to fit Jode, even with the weight he'd lost due to his mostly seafood diet and limited ration of beer, he wouldn't fit into his deceased friends clothes. He might find a pair of shorts or two that could come in handy. He made a few trips inside and hauled out some of the old clothes, some magazines and a couple of moldy books. Should be plenty to get tonight's fire started.

As he sat in the shade wiping away the sweat, it came to him that he would need to remove what he could from Old Moe. While she was mostly in the water, at least at high tide, there was still a lot of weight stranded on the beach. Every pound he removed would make it that much easier to float her off the hard and if she rode higher in the water it should reduce the amount of seawater that might leak around his rigged up patch job. Jode wasn't very industrious, to say the least, but this was another job that needed to be done before he continued on his journey. So in true Jode fashion, he remained sitting on the moist sand, shaded by Old Moe, and thought about it.

As the sun approached the horizon, it was time to get the fire started and cooking his fancy Pier House dinner. Once the fire had burned down to hot coals with just a little flame he placed the pot with water and potatoes on to boil and headed out towards the mangroves to hunt up his fresh oysters.

The sun had set by the time the potatoes were soft and he had finished his oysters. After removing the potatoes he dumped the blue crabs into the boiling water. When the pot began to boil again, he removed it from the fire and let it cool. Sitting in the sand with the half-moon rising in the east he picked at the crabs and thought to himself how nice an ice cold beer would taste with the fresh seafood. Unfortunately there was only a splash of rum and 4 warm beers left on board and no way to cool them without killing

Old Moe's batteries. While delayed satisfaction was a philosophy of life Jode had never subscribed to, his current situation left him few choices and even fewer alternatives. Yearning for that beer and no hope of drinking it, he covered himself with his old sheet, reached out for a burning stick and carefully lit his homemade smudge pot.

Sleep wouldn't come easily, as he laid there watching the small dark orange flame spewing black smoke into the night. His thoughts were on tomorrow and how he was going to bandage up Old Moe to make her seaworthy for one more voyage.

He awoke to a rising sun. Well rested from the best night's sleep since leaving the Marquesas and running low on beer. It could have been from the lack of mosquitoes or a hangover but Jode felt good and looking forward to getting to work for the first time since that last day diving for treasure. He reached over and placed an old bean can over his smudge pot smothering the flame and headed out to the bushes.

While the boat was still cool from the night air he crawled into the bilge to collect what he needed. First thing he grabbed was one of the floorboards that had floated loose during the near sinking. He also found an old tube of 5200. A while back, he was trying to stop one of the many leaks that plague Old Moe and bought it, thinking it was caulking. He quickly found out it wasn't.

3M 5200 is a slimy white goo that once it is on something it never comes off. That includes wood, fiberglass, clothes, skin and anything else. He once heard an old sail boater referred to it as "white death" because it ruins and kills anything it touches. If the tube is any good it is just what he needs to seal the broken plank. Next up was finding any wood screws that were scattered throughout the boat. Some were too short, some too long and some just right but they all went in his pocket. He would separate the wheat from the chaff later. Before he left the bilge to collect his tools he took a minute to uncover the treasure. He knew it had to still be there but just looking at it gave him motivation and lifted his spirits. He held the cross in his hand, then picked up one of the short chains. Sitting quietly, he thought of Tripper and how he would never enjoy the fruits of his long hours of labor recovering it. Carefully returning the gold back to its hiding place he grabbed a small handful of silver coins and put them in his pocket. A reminder of what he was working for.

The tools on Old Moe were few and in poor condition, Jode was not a Mr. Fixit by any stretch of the imagination. 'If it ain't broke don't fix it' was his mantra. He cobbled together a rusty hand saw, a couple of screw drivers and in an epiphany of creativity an old ratchet and socket.

The first order of business was cutting the board to fit the hole. With the dull saw the less cutting, the better. After holding the board up to the side of the boat he figured if he cut one strip about 8 inches wide from the narrow side of the floor board he would have what he needed. Making a two foot cut in a half inch thick board shouldn't be that difficult but between balancing the board over a 5 gallon bucket and the rusty old saw it turned into nearly an hour of hard labor.

Now he needed to put screw holes around the outside edge of the patch. An easy five minute job with an electric drill. Of course, Jode didn't own a drill and didn't have any electricity if he had one. This is where his great idea paid off. While looking for wood screws, he found a really big one, about a quarter inch thick and 3 inches long with a bolt type head on it. Placing the wood against the hard-packed sand he lined up the bolt and gave it a good whack with the hammer to get it started, then screwed it through the wood with the ratchet. Once it came out the other side he backed it out leaving a hole big enough for the smaller screws he had collected. Again, the small job was a long and tiring task but he was finished before the sun was overhead.

If worst comes to worst, once the board is screwed on the boat It would stop most of the water and a working bilge pump should keep Old Moe afloat. The irony of that thought was not lost on Jode. Placing the tube of 5200 into his caulking gun he soon found that it had hardened up and no amount of pressure on the trigger was going to get it to squish out. Taking the tube out of the gun Jode squeezed the tube up and down. It felt a little soft at the bottom so he took out his fillet knife and cut off the bottom of the 5200. The white slime started to ooze out so he quickly held it over the patch. Using a cockle shell that was in the sand nearby, he smeared the goop over the patch and pressed it over the hole in the hull. Grabbing one of the shorter screws and a screwdriver he started it in one of the bottom holes in the middle of the patch. Once it started he began adding screws towards each end, then began the same process on the top going back and tightening the screws as he added more. He saved the biggest and longest screws for the end of the patch, using them to pull the wood tight to the hull while squeezing the nasty white slime out to run down the hull to the sand. It must have been just pasted noon as he finished as the sun was overhead and beginning to beat down on the side of the boat where he had just been working.

He tapped the patch with his hammer and it felt and sounded as strong and solid as anything else on Old Moe. Not a resounding indication of quality but as good as it was going to get. Stepping back several feet, Jode admired his handy work. The wooden patch from the bilge was stained with rust and old oil and had several dings and scrapes. From a distance, it blended in so well with the dirty and worn side of the boat, that if it wasn't for the bright white slime oozing out around it, it would be barely visible.

Tired and proud of his accomplishment, it was time to celebrate. He climbed onto the boat and went below to retrieve one of his last four beers. Leaning against the hull a few feet from the patch he popped the top and took a big swig of the 85 degree beverage. Swallowing the warm beer brought him back to Key West, walking down Duval St. listening to the music pouring out from the tourist traps. Of course they all played Jimmy Buffet songs. "Warm Beer and Bread they said could raise the dead" was playing over and over in his head. A cold beer would have been great but as Jode had said many times, "the warmest beer I ever drank was cold enough" as for the bread, it had been nearly a month since he and Tripper had finished off the last crusty. Even that sounded pretty good right now.

Dog tired and relaxed, Jode leaned back and dosed off, it had been a lot harder work than he'd bargained for. The hot sun moved behind the clouds and a breeze kicked up waking Jode from his slumber. He looked out the pass towards the gulf and saw two boats heading south towards Indian Key then up the channel to Everglades City. They were going fast to out run the approaching afternoon storm. While Jode wasn't breaking any laws that he knew of, he preferred to remain incognito. The boat could be seen from the gulf but at this distance Old Moe would appear to be just another old abandoned derelict washed ashore during one of the many storms that plagued the area. Unless someone came right up the pass he would be left alone and even then most boaters would go on by not giving him or Old Moe another thought. At some point he might need to find help to pull Old Moe off the beach but waiting another week or two for the full moon tides was still his plan.

Hot, sweaty and covered with salt and sand, he looked forward to the rain. It didn't disappoint what started as a light shower soon turned into a real gully washer. The big drops pounding down on the deck and a torrent of water pouring out the scuppers into the narrow bay. To conserve the remaining fresh water, he hadn't had a real shower in days. He went through the salon to the head, grabbed a bar of soap and a towel and headed outside for a refreshing combat shower. Clean and dried off, he sat beneath the bimini watching as the rain and clouds continued their trek inland. His hands and arms ached from the strenuous and repetitive labor and his back was sore from stooping in the sand at the base of the hull but it felt good. Add to that a slight buzz from the first beer in days and he felt happy and content. Hunger overtook him so he headed into the galley to see what was left to eat. With the rain there would be no fire tonight. Finding the last can of spam and a can of corn he sat at the small table in the salon and consumed his disappointing meal. Even though he was hungry, the cold greasy canned meat was hard to choke down so he set it aside hoping it would make a better breakfast sizzling over the open fire. With no refrigeration it might spoil, but the stuff was meant to last a thousand years, it should at least make it until tomorrow. With that he collapsed on the filthy couch and soon fell fast asleep.

Another sunrise, another long day on the beach waiting for the tides to take him away. Jode climbed out of the salon grabbing a dry magazine as he went. After his trip to the woods he lit a small fire and cooked up the rest of the spam. As the fat began to sizzle in the can it almost smelled like bacon, almost. He fished out the now crispy meat with a fork and had breakfast. Even though he was still hungry after last night's disappointing meal the cooked spam was not very tasty or satisfying.

After yesterday's accomplishments he had a renewed sense of purpose to get Old Moe ready to cast off. Today's job was replacing the worn seal in the port engine's raw water pump. He had done the task many times over the years so he finished in about an hour, loaded up another bucket full of crap from the bilge and climbed out onto the deck before the sun heated the interior of the boat to an unbearable level. Throwing anything that would burn next to the fire pit he carried the rest into the bushes where he had started a pile out of sight. Jode wasn't a neat freak by any stretch of the imagination but leaving trash on the beach was a no-go. If a boat came by and saw his lifeless carcass being feasted on by buzzards no one would bat and eye but a pile of trash on the beach would necessitate an immediate call to the authorities!

With the most important job out of the way, or as he liked to say put the big rocks in first, it was time to figure out what he was going to eat for the rest of his time on Lulu Key. Fresh fish, crabs, oysters and maybe some clams for sure but that was getting pretty boring and with the food he and Tripper bought in Key West down to a couple of cans of beans it was time to supplement the menu.

Jode took the bucket down to the water and used wet sand and seawater to scrub it out. After rinsing it out one last time to remove the sand he stuck his head in and sniffed. Smelled clean enough so he headed into the bushes searching for something new to eat. Once he was away from the beach and the salty sand the plant life began to change. Palmettos were replacing the mangroves and sea oats, a few scrub oaks were in the distance indicating higher ground. In south Florida swamp cabbage, the heart of the sable or cabbage palm, is a local delicacy but without an ax or chain saw there was no way to remove it from a 20 foot tree. Palmettoes are a lot like cabbage palms and grow low to the ground. By grabbing the newest shoots coming out of the center of the plant and pulling as hard as you can, the heart of the palmetto comes out. Once he pulled the sprouts out, he took his knife, cut the soft white meat from the hard green stem and dropped it into the bucket. In no time he had a nice layer of swamp cabbage at the bottom of his bucket. Further from the beach, the shade of the tall sable palms and scrub oaks made for a comfortable and enjoyable walk. With nothing else to do Jode decided to spend the day exploring the island.

Soon he spotted a beauty berry bush. Its bright berries looking like purple gems covering the stems like the cornmeal on a corn dog. He sat and ate his fill while adding more to his bucket. Next he found a small patch of wild or Brazilian coffee plants. Their berries were red and not as plentiful as the beauty berry. He had heard that the fruit could be roasted to make a beverage similar to coffee but without the caffeine it seemed like a lot of work without the rewarding kick. Even so, he ate a few of the bitter and slightly tart berries and added some to his growing collection of groceries. Continuing on into the woods became more and more difficult as the vines grew across the ground and up into the oak trees. Some of the vines were wild grapes. Unfortunately Florida's grapes are mostly thick vines and lots of leaves. Every now and then there would be a few grapes. Not the bunches of grapes like in the store but just five or six loose berries less than a half inch across. There weren't enough to deal with but when he saw any he popped them in his mouth and savored the sweat taste of the juice. With a couple inches of veggies in the bottom of the five gallon bucket, he headed back towards the beach. Soon, the vegetation changed back to only the most salt tolerant plants. Among them he spotted a sea grape tree and some coconut palms. He had plenty of experience with both. As kids he and his friends would take the ripe coconuts and slam them down on the road, pointy end first. After several tries, the husk would begin to split away from the nut and with a lot of tugging and prying it would let loose, exposing the hard nut within. It would be a lot of work to husk the coconuts but he picked up a couple of fat brown ones, shook them to confirm they were still full of milk and added them to the bucket.

Next up was exploring the sea grape tree. They're not really grapes but they grow in clusters so that's where they got the name. They have a tough skin surrounding a thin layer of fruit over a big pit. Like most things on the island, a lot of work for little nourishment. To make matters worse, the berries don't ripen all at once. You could have an over ripe berry clearly past its prime right next to a hard green newbie. But when ripe they were tasty so Jode began picking and eating with some making their way into the bucket. As he made his way deeper into the bushy tree, he heard a loud screeching, Akk, Akk, Akk, that startled him and hurt his ears. Looking around he saw a small green parrot maybe a foot tall at the most. Must have been one of the many escapees that populated the area after hurricane Andrew released many pets from their homes and cages. The bird was going from cluster to cluster taking a bite out of any ripe fruit it found than moving on to the next without finishing what he started. Ruining the berries for anyone or anything else. The waste aggravated Jode so he grabbed a stick and hurled it at the pest. The bird fluttered away but not far, landing on a branch just a few feet away squawking and muttering something Jode couldn't understand. It was saying something over and over, probably two words "damp turd?", "dim bird?", who knows but it wasn't happy about having company at his tree! Tired of exploring and listening to the nasty bird he made his way back to the beach and Old Moe.

After diving into the water to cool off Jode picked up his fishing pole and headed down the beach to catch dinner. Soon he had two mangrove snapper on his stringer so he headed back. One might be under the size limit but that had never bothered him before and under the circumstances it didn't even cross his mind. As he approached the boat he heard some scratching come from the bucket he'd left in the shade. A green bird head popped up and looked his way. He picked up a stick off the beach threw it at the little thief. When it hit the bucket the bird flew out squawking and yelling "damn bird, damn bird" as it dashed back into the bushes. "Damn Bird, I guess that seems fitting enough!"

With nothing else to do and it being too early for dinner, he set about opening one of the coconuts. After placing the nut in a small indentation in the sand he used the hammer to pound on the point until the husk began to split apart. Turning the hammer around, the claw made easy work of ripping the husk from the hard shell of the nut. Shaking it to confirm it was still full of milk he had an idea. Getting a cup off the boat he carefully bore a hole in two of the "eyes" with his fillet knife turned it upside down and let the watery liquid drain. Soon the cup was almost full. Smelling the coconut water gave him an idea he should have thought of days ago. He got up and soon returned with the open bottle of rum. The label had washed off during the almost sinking but he knew it was his favorite brand, On Sale. After adding a scant ounce to the coconut water and throwing in some beauty berries he settled down on the other side of the boat to watch the sunset and enjoy a much deserved happy hour.

Once the sun sank into the sea it was time to make dinner. The snappers yielded four nice little fillets. He put a frying pan in the fire and tossed in the swamp cabbage. Seeing the congealed grease in the bottom of the spam can he added that and some salt and pepper for taste and let the fire do its job. Once the palmetto hearts were soft he pushed them aside and added the fillets. After the satisfying supper he leaned back thinking that despite all the hardship, his life wasn't that bad. Wishing Tripper was here to enjoy it, he put his hand in his pocket and rubbed the silver coins together and smiled. Yup, he would have enjoyed this.

The next morning seemed a little anticlimactic. It was the first day in a long time when there was nothing that had to be done. Old Moe was ready to go, except for being stuck in the mud, that is and other than fishing or foraging for food the day was empty. After his trip to the woods Jode ambled down the beach surveying his domain and picking up any fire wood he came across. He was inspecting the high tide line and while it was slowly advancing every day as the full moon approached he had his doubts it would be high enough to get Old Moe floating free. He stuck a stick in the sand at yesterday's high tide line and figured he'd use it to keep track of how much it changed day to day. With nothing else to do he boarded the boat and went down below. There was still a lot of crap to be tossed out and with the boat closed up most the time, the mildew smell was getting worse not better. He decided to haul the damp cushions and bedding topside and let it dry in the sun. Making sure he brought them back in before any afternoon storm or the evening dew.

He then went through a few junk drawers in the galley. Who's he kidding all the drawers on the boat were junk drawers. Dumping anything broken or useless, which was most everything, into the bucket thus lightening the load for the day he would float off his island prison.

Following an afternoon siesta it was time to go pick some berries and go fishing for dinner. He started by harvesting some more palmetto cabbage as he now called it and headed over to the sea grape tree. Before he got there he heard Damn Bird squawking an alarm announcing his arrival. Jode quickly picked the ripest grapes in a race with the bird then headed back to the beach. The bird soon followed. The next day was much the same as his life slowed down and eased into the boring restless routine of waiting for the day the water came and freed him.

Chapter 6

couple of days later he was startled awake by Damn Bird's loud obnoxious squawking, Akk, Akk, Akk. . . Akk, Akk, Akk. . . Akk, Akk, Akk, if he had a hangover like in the old days his head would have most assuredly exploded. He tossed a piece of firewood at the damn bird but it continued to yell. Then he saw what it was all upset about. Just on the edge of the brush not thirty feet away was a big snake out warming itself in the sun. Jode picked up the largest piece of firewood he had nearby and hurled it at the serpent. He missed of course but it was frightened enough to slither back into the woods. He didn't know whether it was poisonous or not and didn't care to find out. The excitement over, he walked far down the beach in the other direction before relieving himself.

On his way back he took out his tide stick and moved it up to last night's high tide line. It hadn't moved much. In fact he noticed that a strong westerly wind had more effect than the moon. Large thunder storms in the everglades also effected the tide levels as all the water that fell from the skies filled the creeks before flooding out to the gulf. Sitting there watching the smooth waters of the inlet slowly moving out with the tide he realized his predicament was worse than he had first thought. The situation that lead to his stranding was a big thunder storm, gale force winds pummeling the coast at a flood tide. It would take a combination of all three to lift Old Moe off the mud and it could just as easily make his situation worse. It wasn't that the boat was that far up on land but more the gradual slope of the beach or more accurately, the mud flat. Old Moe was nearly level but the stern had sunken down into the mud. The keel was out of sight, the rudders stabbed down into the muck and the props were more than half underground. Even if he had more water, putting the engines in gear with the props still buried would break something, or more likely everything, immediately. Depressed at the realization of his dire circumstances he decided to open another coconut and finish off the last couple of ounces of rum.

The next day he was still in a funk but tried to get motivated to do something to facilitate his escape. When low tide came he crawled up under the dive platform and began digging out the props. At first, he used what was left of the old bilge board to drag the sand back then as the hole got deeper, he scooped more away with the old saucepan he used for cooking. After a couple of hours he was exhausted and the tide was rising making any more progress impossible. He collapsed in the shade beside Old Moe and took a siesta. When he awoke he rinsed off in the salt water picked up his bucket and went to collect his dinner. Damn Bird had taken up the habit of sitting in the shade under the bimini during the heat of the day. He flew up and followed him into the woods. When the duo returned Jode got his pole and headed down the beach to fish. He wasn't in a hurry even doing a little catch and release to pass the time. Finally he settled on a nice mangrove snapper and a small sheepshead for dinner.

As he approached the boat he waded to the stern to inspect his handy work now that the tide had risen. What he saw made him feel like screaming. In fact he let out the loudest AAUUUUUG he possibly could. With no one to hear except the bird who instantly flew away, he sat down in the sand and held his head in despair. The tide and current had washed the sand back in the hole he just dug, the props were just as buried as they were before he had started. All the hard work was in vain and hope for an escape from his prison was nearly gone. Soon his hunger pains were enough to get him to move. He started a fire and cooked his meager supper.

The next day was much like the last. However, Jode found just enough hope to at least continue halfheartedly lightening the load from Old Moe and drying out what items still needed it. As he went through Tripper's berth he found some of the books he had read. Tripper was the reader, not Jode. The titles ranged from spy novels to funny, local detective stories by authors like Rodney Riesel. Tripper's reading list was based more on what was on the free bookshelf in the marina day room than anything else. Jode started loading the old books into the bucket. The first to go in was 'The Perfect Storm'. Jode had experienced enough perfect storms to last a life time. Next to it was a copy of 'The Confederacy of Dunces', the book that flew off the shelf and hit the head of the captain in the Deadly Storm. Jode thought back to when he and Tripper would sit on the back deck having beers and Tripper would share what he had read. Some nights his quotes from the Confederacy were so funny they spit out more beer then they swallowed. He decided to keep that book and 'The Edge of Honor', a story about some navy guy during the civil war. Tripper did reenactments when he was reading it. He would grab the gaff or landing net and commence a swashbuckling duel or pantomime lighting off an old fashion canon. It was hard to tell how much of it was the author's words and how much was Tripper's over active imagination. Jode smiled at the memories and absentmindedly rubbed the old coins. The smile soon faded and only a deep loneliness remained.

There was nothing else he could do and nothing else to do. A couple more days passed. The moon was almost full and the tides had risen but nowhere near enough to free him. With nothing to do, his siestas got longer and his work infrequent. It was during one of those siestas that he was awaken by Damn Bird's squawking. Not as loud as when the snake invaded his space but squawking none the less. Jode, now awake listened carefully and heard an outboard motor in the distance. This could be good news or bad so he snuck around the bow of the boat and peered out to the channel leading to the gulf.

Staying hidden he looked over at the interlopers. There were two teenage boys in the boat. One a little taller with blond hair, the other had black curly hair, definitely not brothers, probably best friends. They both were very tan. The dark haired one almost looked colored except for his white ass peeking out from above his baggy bathing suit. The tans and the confident way they handled the boat made it obvious they spent much of their free time out on the water and in that boat. The boat was what Jode was most interested in. It was an 18 or 19 foot runabout with a big motor, maybe 90 or a 115 horsepower. Not real fast but perfect for fishing and exploring the back waters of the ten thousand islands. It was also perfect for what Jode had in mind, but first he had to get the boys to go along with the scheme he had planned.

He jumped out from behind the bow and yelled in his loudest and best pirate voice. "What are you no good scallywags doing in my creek? If you don't get out of here and away from my beach in two seconds I'll keel haul the both of ya and send ya to Davey Jones's locker!!!"

The boys jumped at the sudden charge and loud yelling. Then looked at each other, nodding in agreement they started. "It's not your beach," Ya, the younger added. "You can't tell us where we can and can't go. This is our beach, you get out of here!"

A small smiled crossed Jode's lips well hidden by his scraggily beard as he yelled, "You Get out of Here!"

"No, you get out a here."

"You go!"

"No you go!!!"

"You better leave NOW!"

"You can't make us."

"Yes I can", "Cannot", "Can"

Jode knew he had them now, just needed to reel them in. One boy might leave but two or more never. Neither was going to be the first to back down or turn tail and run. The embarrassment would be too great and they would be called a chicken forever.

"You're not even a real pirate."

Jode couldn't argue with that. He looked more like a washed up Robinson Caruso than any pirate he ever heard of. Leaving his Pirate voice in the past he held up his hands in surrender saying, "You're right. I'm no pirate but I have seen them and I know where they buried their treasure."

"You're crazy old man. There aren't any pirates anymore."

"Well let me tell you what I have seen and if you don't believe me. Then it's on you." He now had their interest and the boat drifted towards Jode but the taller one bumped the throttle now and then to keep them safely off the shore and out of Jode's reach. Always one to spin a yarn and not having anyone to talk to for nearly a month, except the damn bird, he was not going to give them the abridged edition. No siry, they are getting the whole enchilada. Every good lie begins with the truth and every good salesman knows the sooner you get the prospect nodding and agreeing, the sooner he becomes a customer and Jode desperately needed the boys to buy what he was selling.

"I grew up on the water just like you two. I can tell by the expert way you handle that there boat that you know what you're doin'. Why I figure you boys know the waters around here like the back of your own hand. Everything from Goodland clear down to Shark River." The boys looked at each other, how did he know?

Jode smiled just a little. "Now I know you never told your folks you went that far and I won't tell 'em neither but when I was your age I was the same way (identify with the mark, er, customer) I spent most my time out on the water exploring and looking for new adventures. Just like you guys (They're not "boys" anymore, no sir). I spent my whole life out on boats and most of that time I spent looking for pirates and their treasure. Now I've seen a lot of treasure in my time but none of it was mine."

"Did I mention I'm from the Keys? Darn near my whole life. There's been pirates in the keys for hundreds of years and there are pirates and treasure hunters there still today. Now I know you guys know the keys bet you even been down there for lobster season" They're nodding again. No doubt their folks have headed to the keys probably every summer. "Did you know the keys don't end at Key West?" More nodding, of course they do. "Goes past a lot more islands all the way to the Dry Tortugas."

"We been there with Billy's dad," the young one pipes in.

"Doesn't surprise me, adventurers that you guys are. That huge fort was built for one thing and one thing only. . . to stop and catch pirates! That shows you how many pirates were out there and there are still some left. I know it 'cause I saw 'em." They let the boat drift a little closer to shore as they got wrapped up in the story. Their imagination filling in any blanks. To draw them in closer, Jode pulled his tide stick out of the ground and started drawing in the sand.

"Here's where we are. This here is Goodland and down here Shark River. But you know all that," more nodding. "Here's the keys and way over here is the Dry Tortugas, but that's not where I saw the pirates, no siry, I saw 'em right here on Boca Grande Key." Scrapping an X between Key West and the Tortugas and with as much flourish as Salvador Dali, he stabbed the stick in the center of the X. The boys leaned over and starred at the mark.

"Was anchored out on the gulf side of the key. Beautiful night just a slight breeze off the straits. I was relaxing on the back deck sittin on that deck chair right there." He pointed and their eyes followed. "Then I smelled some smoke. You usually don't smell smoke during the rainy season, specially that far off shore" More nodding. "So that got me wondering what was up, so I peered through the night and saw an orange glow coming from the middle of the island. Listening real hard I thought I heard voices or more like singing. I got in the dinghy, that one right there (pointing again while watching their eyes follow along), and real stealthy like rowed to shore. After silently pulling the dink up on the beach, not far you know, just enough to keep it there but easy enough to push off and get going in a hurry."

"Then I snuck up through the mangroves and over the bank to where the singing was coming from. You could have knocked me over with a feather when I saw maybe 50 pirates singing and passing around a big jug of rum. In the middle of the scurvy lot was the fire and next to the fire was a huge chest full of treasure!" I had there undivided attention now. They never heard such a tale. "Well there were at least fifty of them and only one of me." No need to bring Tripper into the tale. "So I laid down in the brush and waited. Quiet as a mouse. Soon, one by one those old pirates stopped singing and passed out. The moon was high in the sky when clouds swept by and blocked it out. This was my chance they were all snoring, even the one closest to the chest, so I crawled real slow and quiet like, over to the treasure. When I got close I reached over real carefully and put my hand in. All I felt was hundreds of coins and jewelry. I couldn't resist taking some so I grabbed a handful and started to bring it to my pockets. But luck wasn't with me that night, nope, lady luck was on the side of the pirates, one coin slipped through my fingers and fell back in the chest with a clink that only gold and silver make."

"Well that was it. The pirate next to the chest eyes popped open and looked me straight in the face! No matter how much rum he'd drunk he knew someone was stealing their gold! He jumped up and yelled to his mates. I jumped and ran even faster. Before you knew it we were in a foot race to the shore. Now I might not look that fast of foot but with 50 pirates chasing you, there is no limit to how fast you can run!" More nodding. I'm thinking these boys have been chased after getting caught doing something they shouldn't too.

"I got to the dinghy first but they were close behind. I pushed off, glad I didn't beach the boat too hard. With all the strength I had, I pulled at the oars like my life depended on it, 'cause it did. I got to deeper water but those pirates dove in behind me and swam like dolphin. I never knew pirates could swim so fast. Even the pirate captain dove into the water, his parrot not wanting to get wet flew up and landed on my boat just about where he's sitting right now." Once again accentuating the tale by pointing at Damn Bird sitting on the railing and once again their eyes followed the stick to the bird.

"But like I said, I was pulling on those oars like there was no tomorrow and made it to the dive platform while the pirates were still behind me. I wrapped the painter around the cleat then bounded up the ladder to the helm and started the engines. I thought I was in the clear but then remembered the anchor was still holding Old Moe and it wasn't going to let go. There was no time to haul it in. I jumped down to the deck and with one motion I took out my knife." Suddenly Jode's hand reached in his back pocket and in the blink of an eye, he held the shiny blade pointing right at the two boys. Their eyes went wide and they fell over each other trying to get to the far side of the boat. Nearly capsizing the small craft in their haste. Before they could react he swished the knife through the air like a sword and said, "I cut the anchor line with one feld swoop and made my escape!" Putting the knife away to calm their nerves, he pointed again for them to see the anchor line indeed cut through and hanging limp at the bow of his boat. "With all the pirates in the water and their boat on the other side of the island there was no way they could catch me so I made my way north. A fierce storm hit that night, you probably remember it about three weeks ago, give or take. With no anchor to hold me off shore, the storm pushed me on to this beach and that's were I've stayed ever since."

It took a while but the oldest boy was first to speak. "That's a good story but that doesn't mean it's true."

"You don't believe me?" Jode said with indignation. Now that the boys were only a few feet away, he could tell they weren't quite as sure of themselves as before. He jammed his hand into his pocket and flung it open right in front of their young faces. They jumped back until they saw the silver coins laying in his palm. Now they were hanging over the side leaning closer to see the coins. "These are the very pieces of eight that I took from that very chest," Jode added smugly as he snapped his hand shut and put the coins back in his pocket. Well, it was clear the boys were dumb founded and believers now.

Letting the moment sink in, Jode went in for the close. "Now I only have this treasure but I'm going back to get the rest as soon as I get this boat back in the water and for that, I need your help."

"This boat will never pull that old tub of a boat back into the water." The oldest protested. The dark haired boy nodded in agreement. "Besides why should we help you to go get all the treasure for yourself?"

"Oh, I'm sure with your help Old Moe will be floating and underway by this time tomorrow. Once I'm on my way back to Boca Grande Key, I'll split the pieces of eight I already have with you both. Even Steven."

"What do you mean?" The young one asked, feeling a little braver now.

"Well you come back here tomorrow about two o'clock. High tide is around three or so. We'll have time to put my plan together. When Old Moe is free, I'll give each of you two coins and I'll keep two for myself, deal?" He held the coins out and took his right hand to move them around so they could see them and count the six coins. Their eyes were glued to the coins. There was no way they would let them escape their greedy little hands.

"Deal," they both said at once.

Jode put the coins back in his pocket and offered his hand. He shook both their hands to seal the deal. "Now don't tell your Ma or Pa or anyone else for that matter, or the deal is off. Besides, if your dad finds out you been talking to pirates, you'll be grounded for sure and never get the coins."

Nodding again and with smiles on their faces, they turned the little skiff towards the gulf and went off as fast as the boat would go. Jode stood there smiling. Those were good kids and they would be back tomorrow. He just knew it.

Paraphrasing Mel Fisher, Jode thought to himself, "Tomorrow is the Day." His prison sentence had been commuted and he would be on his way to Fort Myers Beach with a haul of treasure in his bilge. In the best mood since Tripper brought up that cross, it was time for a celebration. He went in the galley and came back with one of his three last beers. The other two he would save for the big celebration tomorrow. He sat on the dive platform with his feet dangling in the water. Savoring every slip of the warm brew and watched as the sun began to set.

He was hungry but didn't care to go fishing or foraging for another meal he didn't want to eat. He couldn't sleep either. His mind was full of plans for tomorrow. Everything he needed to do, to prepare for the boy's return. How he was going to get Old Moe out of the mud and back in the water and most of all, the adventures in front of him with money in his pocket for the first time he could remember.

He finally fell asleep in the middle of the night but was wide awake as soon as the sky began to lighten. He knew what he had to do first. He recalled a puzzle an old guy once told him. How do you put two gallons of rocks, two gallons of gravel and one gallon of sand in a five gallon bucket? If you put the sand or the gravel in first, the big rocks will be over the rim. No, there is only one solution. Put the big rocks in first. Then the gravel will fall around them and the sand will fill the crevasses in the gravel. The lesson is that, with any project or task, put the big rocks in first. Do what must be done. Then what should be done and finally, if there is time, energy or money left, do what would be good or nice to be done. Jode was definitely a big rocks kind of guy. He seldom went beyond that and the gravel and sand rarely made it into his bucket.

The biggest rock was controlling the boat as it went into the water. To fast or too far and things could break or bad things happen. To keep that from happening, he needed to tie off the bow so he could release the boat into the water as fast or slow as was safe. He took what was left of the anchor line and pulled it out of the locker and tossed it on the ground in front of the bow. He climbed off the boat, took the end of the rope and started walking up the beach towards the woods. He needed to find something to tie it to that was within the reach of the line and as straight in front of the bow as possible. He saw a bush straight ahead. It was about 10 feet tall but mostly a bunch of branches coming out of the ground, none of which were strong enough to do the job. As he looked more closely he saw that at the base, it had one trunk but the branches started out a few inches from the dirt. He crawled on all fours under the bush, fed the line around the stump twice, then tied it off with a couple of half hitches. The stump looked stout and the branches wouldn't allow the rope to ride up and come loose. He wasn't sure if it was strong enough but he did know that if his intention was to pull out the bush, he would have a heck of a job doing it. He retraced his steps to the bow, climbed aboard and pulled in the line as tight as he could. Holding it with his fingers against the cleat, he let out another two feet and secured the rope to the bow cleat. Now if the boat slid back, it could only move a couple of feet before the bush stopped it. The biggest rock was in the bucket.

Once the boat is back in the water, he will need an anchor. If not immediately, then soon. Bad things happen when something goes wrong and there is no anchor to set. This Jode knew all too well. He climbed down into the bilge and lifted out the spare anchor. Then the bucket with the chain and 200 feet of line. After hauling them both to the bow, he set the anchor in the chocks and attached the chain to it using the turn buckle. Now, he could take out all the chain and rode and feed it into the rope locker but that was sand and it would be much easier to accomplish when the anchor, chain and a hundred feet of line were in the water. Jode seldom dealt with sand and in his mind, easier was always better.

It was getting hotter as the sun rose and he was getting tired. He needed to get the strenuous tasks done before it was just too hot to move. He climbed down on to the sand and inspected the raw water inlet on the starboard side. At some point he would need to start at least one engine and he needed to make sure it could draw in cooling water and hopefully not too much sand and mud. Some mud could make it through the engine and out the exhaust and some sand could be trapped in the sea strainers but too much of either and he was done for. The inlet was above the water but the tide was still low and should come up at least another foot or more before the boys returned. Grabbing his trusty sauce pan, he began scrapping away the sand beneath the inlet. In no time, he had a hole about a foot deep and two feet long. It would be nice if it was longer and deeper but it should let in enough water without drawing in too much sand. Maybe he'll do more later if there is time.

One more big rock and he'll be ready. Not done but ready. Digging around the boat he came up with some old dock lines that weren't too worn and not too big to tie off the runabout. He also got out his old fenders. Jode wasn't concerned about damage to Old Moe, those days were long gone, but he didn't want the runabout or its engine to get scratched up in the process. If Blondie returns home with any damage to the boat his dad will no doubt put some serious wupass on him and that just wouldn't be right. With the most important tasks completed, it was time for a rest and to figure out what else should be done before shoving off.

After a couple of glasses of stale water from the tank and a few minutes resting in the shade, Jode was ready to continue preparations for his escape. Today is the day! The countdown was on and there were less than two hours until lift-off. Next up was packing up his outdoor "kitchen," the pile of pots, pans and utensils he'd been using to cook and eat by the fire. First, he scrubbed off the soot with wet sand then rinsed them in the saltwater before carting everything on to the boat and dumping them in the galley sink. He even loaded up his homemade smudge pot. It worked reasonably well at keeping the mosquitoes and no-see-ums at bay and he was confident that wherever he ended up there would be bugs.

Everything was coming together and there wasn't much left to do. Against his nature he took some time policing up the area around the boat. Even though he was leaving a lot of junk up in the woods he felt that the beach had served him well and shouldn't be left looking like a pig sty.

As he was filling in the fire pit and smoothing it over with sand he heard an outboard motor running flat out in the distance. The boys were a little early. A very good sign. With the damn bird squawking in the background, he stepped out from behind the boat and sure enough, the small craft came screaming around the point and into the inlet. This time the boys were smiling and waving. He returned the gestures and hopped up on the dive platform to catch their boat and tie it off. Jode could tell they were itching to get on with the task, collect their loot and head back to Everglades City to show it off.

After they tied off and shut down the motor, they looked at Jode with skepticism. In the clear water they could easily see the props and rudders buried in the sand. "No way can we pull you out, dude."

"No worries dudes," he replied mocking them. "We'll be out of here in an hour, just you wait and see." They still didn't look convinced.

Jode took command and started giving orders. They turned the boat around facing out into the inlet and tied it off to the aft cleats on Old Moe then crisscrossed the lines to the cleats on the runabout. Leaving enough slack, they wedged the fenders between the stern of the small boat and the dive platform. After checking everything one more time, Jode had them startup the outboard.

"Now, here is the important part. When I tell you, put it in gear and leave it idling so we can make sure everything is tight. Then I want you to slowly, I mean real slowly increase the rpms to about a quarter throttle. After checking the lines again, I want you to SLOWLY turn the wheel a quarter turn to starboard then back over to quarter port. If everything is going our way just sit there and turn back and forth for about 15 or 20 minutes or until I tell you to quit. If anything starts shaking or you feel anything at all, shut her down. Got it?" The older boy at the controls nodded yes with a very serious look on his face. Then put the engine in gear and did as he was instructed.

Jode climbed up on the back deck and watched from a safe distance. He had prop dredged docks many times. If it is too shallow for your boat at the dock because of too much sand or silt just tie the boat off real tight, put it in gear and let it do its thing. Before you know it there will be plenty of water under the keel. Of course, your neighbor might end up with the same problem when you're done but that never seemed to worry Jode. He even did a little dredging out on the water. With a good anchor, he would set up over a small ledge in shallow water out in the gulf and within an hour he would have a deep hole and a new secret lobster condominium filled with bugs in just a couple of days. Jode continued to watch the boys and day dream until the big swirl of mud and sand drifting up the channel from behind the boat began to lessen. He waved to Blondie and gave the universal sign of a hand across the throat and he pulled back on the throttle and shut down the motor.

"Now we just have to wait and let the tide clear out the silt and we'll see how we're doin."

The dark haired boy lifted up the seat behind the wheel and dug out a drink and handed it to his friend. Then, looking over to Jode, asked. "Want a drink Mister?"

"Sounds good." He responded a little too quickly and a lot too eagerly as the boy tossed over the beverage. At the sound of drink, Jode's mind went to an entirely different place but the cold plastic bottle felt good in his hand, opening it he drained half of it in two big gulps. It was some Gatorade kind of thing packed up by one of their moms no doubt but to him it tasted terrific. It was the first cold drink he'd had in at least three weeks and tasted way better than the stale tank water he had been living on.

After savoring the last of the drink, he bent over the side to evaluate their progress. The boys leaned over the back of their boat as well. The incoming tide had washed away the silt and you could see the props and rudders were out of the sand and about six inches off the bottom. A few feet further back where the shaft of the outboard was there was still a wall of sand deeper than what had been under Old Moe but too high to get the props over. Now came the hard part.

"Ok guys, time for part two. I'll have you start up the motor and put it in gear like we did before. Then I'll go up to the bridge, start the starboard engine, put in gear and see if we can get the old girl to move. Now I can't let the engine run very long because of all the mud so when I get up there I'll give you a thumbs up and you give it a little more throttle, not much, just a little more than before. As soon as we start moving you pull the throttle back to an idle. Got it?"

"Got it, but won't you just run aground again?"

"I've got it covered. I tied off the old anchor line so we can only move a little bit. But it might jerk some when it takes the slack out, so I want you guys sitting in that seat and hanging on until I give you the all clear. Ok?" They both nodded and climbed behind the helm looking serious and holding on. Good. This was the moment of truth. If the batteries are dead or the engine doesn't start, the show's over.

Jode climbed up to the bridge and turned to the boys. Their eyes were wide with not just a little concern on their young faces. He gave the thumbs up, and heard the outboard spool up as he turned and hit the starter. The diesel came to life and he pulled the shifter into reverse and gave it a little more throttle. Black smoke belched out the back as the big prop moved tons of water up and under the hull. It took only a few seconds until the boat started moving back and just like that the rope came tight and it came to an abrupt halt. He shut down the engine and turned with a huge grin on his face and gave the cut sign to the boys. They high fived each other and seemed as happy as Jode that the boat moved one step closer to freedom.

They all looked over the side to see what happened but there was a huge cloud of silt all around the boat and down the beach. Now that the tide was almost high, the current was approaching slack so it would be awhile before they could evaluate their progress. The boys sat next to each other and exchanged stories as Jode got off the boat and checked to make sure nothing had gone wrong. Everything checked out and the props and rudders were off the bottom but there was still a wall of sand blocking his escape. He told Blondie (he would hate that I referred to him as that in my head but I either didn't ask or didn't remember their names!) to start up the motor and begin prop dredging like we did before.

This time with less sand to move and a lot more area under the boat to move it into, the process went much quicker. After just a few minutes, Jode went back up to the bow and loosened the rope. Almost immediately, Old Moe moaned and slid ever so slightly back. Looking at the boys to confirm everyone was safe, he loosened the line and let the boat creep back from the strain of the outboard. Two more feet and he cleated off the old rope and went to the stern and gave the cut sign once more. When the water cleared, the props were free and between the bow coming down and the sand washed away, there was no longer any fear of hitting anything as he backed out. He gave the boys a high five and felt like hugging them for saving him. Of course he didn't. Instead he reached in his pocket and took out the coins he had promised them. Holding them out, they both had big smiles on their faces as they snatched the coins and stuffed them into their pockets.

"Sure want to thank you guys. I knew you were the right men for the job. Now if you could pull me out into the channel so I don't get any more crud in my engines, I'll start 'em up and be on my way back down south to Boca Grande Key to dig up the rest of that treasure."

He walked to the bow, unhooked the old anchor line and tossed it over board. They started up the outboard and when it went into gear, Old Moe moved ever so slowly out into the channel. Jode stood at the stern and helped untie the lines and bring them aboard. As he did, the young one tossed him another drink. After saying thanks again Jode got real serious and said, "Now you don't go tellin' nobody about our little adventure today and certainly don't tell anyone about all that treasure down on Boca Grande Key. Don't even tell about me." They looked at each other, smiled and nodded. Then as they turned the boat to leave the older boy looked back and asked. "What's your name? We never asked."

"Just call me the Pirate."

"Ok, Mister Pirate we won't tell a soul." Waving good bye one last time he hit the throttle and the boat flew out the inlet heading south. The boys slugging each other, pointing and waving in animated conversation.

Jode couldn't help but smile. Before sunset everyone they knew in Everglades City will have heard the story of the pirate . . . at least once, and by this time tomorrow, Old Moe will be a three-masted schooner with fifty canon and a hundred pirates on board. Smiling even more, he bent down, flipped the breaker for the fridge, found the two beers in the galley and tossed them in the freezer. As he cleared the inlet, he looked south to make sure the boys were out of sight. Then turned to starboard and headed north towards Goodland and Fort Myers Beach. Back on the water he couldn't be more content until he heard that familiar squawking and Damn Bird landed on the rail.

Chapter 7

There was no hurry to get to Goodland. Coon Key Marina would be closed by the time he got there and there was no good place to anchor once you got behind Marco and into Goodland Bay. As he approached the inlet south of Goodland, Jode slowed to an idle, found a nice protected spot in about 10 feet of water and dropped the anchor. After letting out all the chain and another 70 feet of rode, he cleated it off and headed to the galley for the first cold beer in nearly a month. He sat on the back deck, the cool sea breeze keeping the bugs away, as he watched the sunset. Damn Bird was still perched on the rail all puffed up and content as well. He had almost forgotten how peaceful the gulf was at anchor in the evening after all the day boaters had returned to their slips and it was quiet except for the splash of a pelican or the heavy breathing of a dolphin as they pursued their last meal of the day.

Rubbing the two coins together, he couldn't help but think of Tripper. They had been friends for years, no decades, and had seldom been apart during the entire time. Even Old Moe as small and cramped as it felt with them both living aboard was now big and empty without him. It had been their home for nearly 12 years. Now it was just him. Feeling both relieved to be free of the Ten Thousand islands and melancholy about the loss of Tripper, Jode sat silently and slowly drank his second and finale beer. Maybe it was coming down from such an exciting and productive day, the two beers on a stomach that hadn't seen food in almost two days or his solemn mood but he soon passed out or fell asleep so soundly that even the noise of the last empty beer can slipping from his fingers and clattering to the deck didn't cause him to stir.

Jode awoke to the sun rising over the glades and the water as flat as a sheet of glass, or butt ass calm as they used to say. He was well rested but hungry and thirsty. The stale water in the tank wouldn't cure either one but he drank some anyway then took his first shower in weeks. No need to save water now. There was as much as he wanted or needed just three miles away. After drying off with a damp musty towel, he rummaged through the aft cabin to find his cleanest dirty cloths. "Today is the day," he thought to his self. The first day back to civilization since he and Tripper snuck out of Key West under the cover of darkness.

The diesels started right up. Luckily he had turned off the fridge when he grabbed the last beer. It might not have made any difference but not knowing the state of the batteries or how much the bilge pump needed to work keeping the boat dry it was a precaution he was glad he took. He went to the bow, fished the remaining line into the rope locker, pulled up the rode and chain and did the same. Finally he pulled the anchor out of the muck and rinsed it by pulling it up and down a few times before bringing it up and securing it in the bow pulpit.

With the ground tackle aboard and stowed he put the engines in gear and headed to Coon Key Marina. A few minutes later the fuel docks came into sight and he carefully approached. Before he got to the dock the dockhand was out on the seawall, arms crossed and glaring at him and the dirty old boat he was on.

"Can't dock here, move along, this is for customers only."

"I need fuel and supplies two hundred dollars of diesel should do it."

"Got a credit card?"

"NOooo, Cash," Jode was getting a little pissed at the condescending little prick.

"Well it's pay in advance. No fuel and fly at this marina!"

"Ok, with me. Now toss me a line and help me get tied up. Fuel fill is in the bow and I need the water tank filled, it's on the back deck port side."

The dockhand relented and tossed a line and Jode cleated it off and stepped onto the dock. Reaching into his dirty old shorts, he took out two crisp new C-notes. Silently thanking Big Carlos for the cash. Seeing the bills the dock hand's attitude changed immediately. "Ok, I'll get right on it. Anything else you need?"

"Got a grocery store around here that I can walk to?"

"Nope, nothing in Goodland and the Publix is about four miles away. Got a ship's store behind the dock master's office," he added pointing.

"Got beer?"

"Yup, and most everything you need for a day out on the water. Go check it out and I'll take care of the fuel and water."

"Thanks," what a difference a little cash makes he thought while heading to the small store.

His welcome at the ship's store was just as warm. The kid behind the counter glowered at him as he walked in. First thing Jode spotted were cheap styrofoam coolers stacked by the door next to the beer cooler. A good start for sure. He grabbed a cooler, opened the door to the beer and lifted out a six pack, then put it back, bent down and grabbed a cold twelve pack, set it in the cooler and brought it over to the checkout counter.

"Will that be all?" the little snot hissed. Jode just ignored him. The smell of fresh coffee now had his undivided attention. He headed over to the urn and filled the biggest cup they had, added three of the little creamers then raised it to his lips and took a big sip. It burned his mouth but was terrific none the less.

"You know you got to pay for that."

Snarky little piss ant, "I Knooowwww." He responded. Seeing a rack of donuts next to the coffee urn, he reached for a big frosted one and took a big bite. Turning and smiling, he stuffed the rest into his mouth. Then picked up another, brought it over to the counter, put down the coffee and placed the donut on top.

"Is that all?"

"I'll tell you when, that's ALL." Jode was losing his patients but then he realized he hadn't been around people other than Tripper and the boys in almost a month and a half. Looking at his reflection in the window let him know that wasn't the only problem. He looked like the typical grab and go vagrant. "Don't worry I have money to pay. They're fueling up my boat at the dock right now", he added. The kid relaxed a little and Jode went about his shopping.

Another cooler held premade sandwiches all wrapped up and ready for a picnic out on one of those rent-a-boats that were all over the place. He looked in and spied one thick with thin sliced roast beef. His mouth watered as he picked it up to examine. Cheese stuck out between the bun and the meat, lettuce and mayonnaise were squished up against the clear wrapper. A feast wrapped in cellophane. He had to have it and spotted a ham and cheese to go with it. After putting them on the beer in the cooler he went up and down the short isles grabbing chips, slim jims, and a variety of snacks. Just as he was heading to the counter to pay up, he saw some packages of crackers, thinking what the hell, he tossed a couple on the pile for Damn Bird, if he was still around.

Having made peace with the clerk the checkout process went smoothly. He asked if there was anything else Jode needed. "Couple bags of ice."

"It's outside, it's locked up. I can get it for you on the way out. That will be $47.28 total."

Jode took out another hundred and put it on the counter. While the tension between the two had subsided that didn't stop the kid from giving the bill a complete and thorough inspection, ending with a swipe of that funny pen they use.

After getting his change Jode loaded up this stuff and went outside for the ice. He placed one whole bag in the bottom of the cooler, dropped the other on the sidewalk to break it up, dumped it in, opened the twelve pack of beer put them in and the sandwiches on top. Should stay cold for a couple of days.

He put the bags of snacks on top of the cooler and headed around the building to the fuel dock. When he looked up he stopped dead in his tracks. There was the dockhand spraying the hose across the deck. Following the water with his eyes, there was Damn Bird on the rail. When he got sprayed, he tucked his head into his wings and closed his eyes. As soon as the spray moved away, he puffed up and shook off the water. The routine repeated until the dockhand noticed Jode watching. Sheepishly he said, "He landed on the boat so I thought I'd chase him way with the hose. Wouldn't budge though, not your bird is it?" He added in his defense.

"More like a hitchhiker from my stay in the ten thousand islands. Seemed to be enjoying the bath anyway," putting the young man at ease.

"You're all fueled up and the water tank is full, let me give you a hand with that and I'll help you shove off." He took the supplies from Jode and handed them over the rail after he got aboard. The snacks went inside. The beers and sandwiches up by the helm. Before starting the engines, Jode reached into his pocket and took out the two ones and change and gave it to the dockhand as they shook hands. "Thanks for the help, not much but appreciate you taking good care of me and the bird," he said with a smile. Then he climbed up to the bridge and started the engines while the young fella cast off the lines, gave Old Moe a push and waved goodbye.

The sun was up and warm and with just a slight breeze, a perfect day to be out on a boat. Jode sipped his coffee and quickly finished off his second donut as he motored through Goodland bay and under the San Marco Bridge. The channel was narrow and weaved around the mangroves and sandbars, requiring constant attention. After he passed under the State Road 951 Bridge and by the Marco Island Yacht Club the channel opened up into the bay. Next on the port side was Factory Bay where all the waterside bars and restaurants were located. It was too early for the lunch crowd but he could smell bacon sizzling and it made his stomach growl, donuts or not. Finally, he rounded the point, passed all the condos and headed out Big Marco pass. Once he was in twenty to thirty feet of water he turned north towards Fort Myers Beach. With the wide open gulf in front of him and little to no boat traffic, he leaned back in the helm chair, opened the cooler and popped open a beer. Life was good.

The shore north of Marco was miles of white sand and uninhabited uplands. Beautiful old Florida. Soon that serene landscape was replaced by condos and civilization. Reaching its worst around Naples north of Gordon Pass. Bored with watching the development go by, Jode reached in the cooler and opened another beer and brought out that tantalizing roast beef sandwich. Before he had it unwrapped, Damn Bird flew out of nowhere and landed on the wheel. Shrugging, he tore off a small piece of bread and tossed it on the helm. The bird hopped down grabbed the bread with his claw and started to peck at it. Jode took a big bite of the sandwich and the two enjoyed a leisurely lunch at sea.

By the time the sandwich was gone, he could see the water tower on Bonita Beach and the shore was once again deserted and beautiful as they passed the bridge over New Pass and Lovers Key. Originally he had planned to take the easy way around the north end of the island down Matanzas Pass into the Back Bay behind The Beach but after the warm welcome he got in Goodland, he thought it might be better to sneak in from the south and follow the channel up to the south end of the anchorage. While there wasn't anyone looking for him and he didn't expect any problems, the locals and especially the resorts wouldn't be happy with another old boat and boat bum cluttering up "their" community.

With his new route decided on, he turned east around the tip of Lover's Key and under the Big Carlos Pass Bridge. He chuckled and wondered if Big Carlos knew he was named after such a little known and seldom used inlet.

The trip behind Estero Island, the real name of Fort Myers Beach, was much like behind Marco. The channel was all over the place, weaving around the many sandbars. When the bay opened up around mid-island, he stayed along the northeast bank and the mangroves. Almost a mile wide at this point he could make his way up towards town with little chance anyone would notice him from their mansions on the island.

He chose an out of the way spot a good distance from any other boats, put the engines in neutral and dropped the hook. After setting the anchor, he shut down the engines, opened another beer and admired the scenery around his new home. When that one was finished he reached for another but first headed down below to grab a bag of chips. Back on the bridge he popped the top on the beer and took a swig, then went to work opening the bag of chips. As soon as it made a rustle, he heard a familiar squawking. In seconds the bird flew out of the nearby mangroves landed on the helm and began pacing back and forth muttering "damn bird, damn bird", "damn bird, damn bird" as he went. Jode stuffed a big handful of chips into his mouth and tossed a few down for the bird. Both satiated, they enjoyed the late afternoon in silence.

Jode's thoughts soon focused on his recent past. Just over 24 hours ago he was stuck in the mud near Tiger Key.

A smile crossed his lips as he thought of the boys and the pirate story. Rubbing the coins in his pocket together, he thought of Tripper and how he would have loved the story and its telling. He would be there, standing in the back, pantomiming every pirate sneer and thrust of a sword. Adding a perfectly timed "Aaarrg" or "Shiver me timbers" to compliment the action. Yes it would have been one heck of a performance. Worthy of a tin bucket full of tips at the Malory Square sunset party. But he wasn't there.

The sun was just falling behind the Matanzas pass bridge and would soon set. He opened the cooler and took out his last sandwich. As he began to open it, Damn Bird jumped down from the bimini and demanded his cut of the take. Jode tore off a piece of bread for the bird and finished the rest. How his life had changed in barely two months. He recalled the happiest day of his life. The day he first laid eyes on that gold coin on the reef off the Marquesas. His lungs almost exploded at the sight of it. Even better was seeing Tripper's face when he saw the sun glinting off the gold in Jode's dripping wet hand. They had such plans. More money than they could spend, a new boat, cars, wine, women and song, or at least beer, broads and adventure. They didn't even get the chance to tell their tale to their friends in the keys before being run out of town by Carlos' thugs. Diving everyday collecting the treasure was hard work but rewarding. Tripper will never get a chance to enjoy the fruits of his labor or the fun and excitement of telling his stories. No, his best friend ever, was lying dead at the bottom of the gulf and Jode was sitting here on a patched up wreck of a boat. A hundred miles away from what he called home and the people he called friends. Not knowing a soul in town. Dirty clothes hanging loosely over his shrunken frame. Eating a mass produced, prepackaged sandwich like it was a gourmet feast. All the plans and dreams they had were just a fog blown out to sea. The sadness weighed him down. He couldn't bear to even think about it. So he just sat in the dark and felt it.

Soon the full moon rose above the mangroves. It lit the eastern sky, its moonbeams danced off the small ripples in the bay, sparkling like diamonds. But the sight had no effect on Jode. He got out of the old deck chair, went down into the boat still hot from the sun and a long day of engines running. He crawled up into the V-berth beneath the open hatch, pulled a dirty sheet, thankfully dried by the sun, over him and let the gentle rocking of the boat and waves lapping at the hull, lull him to sleep.

Chapter 8

The sun was high in the east when he awoke. Still sad from last night's realization of his plight, he had little motivation to get up. But he had a lot to get done today. Most importantly going to shore and finding groceries to eat and beer to drink. Not necessarily in that order. After that, he would go up town. He and Tripper had been this way a long time ago and any friends they had met were no doubt long gone. The bars were probably still there just different names, faces and vibe. It will be the first time going to a strange bar by himself in years. He and Tripper were pretty much inseparable. Jode, the introvert, not much for starting conversations with strangers, would say, "We don't know a soul in this place." Tripper, the exact opposite would respond "Come on, the place is full of friends. We just haven't met 'em yet" and in we'd go. Within minutes of entering the bar he would have a crowd around him, bending their ears with some wild tale of adventure. Doubt anyone believed him but they enjoyed listening. Soon they would be buying him a beer and egging him on to tell more.

New town, new bars, new people, Jode wondered if it was worth it, but he couldn't sit on the boat by himself forever. He washed his face. Halfheartedly brushed his teeth. Put on the same cleanest dirty clothes from yesterday. Climbed into the dinghy and rowed across the bay to the Tropical Shores canal and up to the dinghy dock behind Topps Groceries. It took him about 20 minutes and in the heat and humidity he worked up a sweat.

The dinghy dock was crowded with small inflatables. He nudged them aside and got close enough to tie off and climb out of his little row boat. His was the only one without a motor. He stood there surveying them with a lot of jealousy and a tad of larceny when suddenly a gruff voice called out, startling him back to the present. "Hey you, what ya lookin' at? Haven't seen you here before?"

He turned to see a guy a little younger than himself, sitting on the ground, leaning against the bike stand with his hand out. "How about a little help here?"

Even though Jode had done his share of pan handling he didn't appreciate it in others. "No handouts from me dude." The guy just shook his head in disgust.

"Not asking for a handout, DUDE, just a hand up" as he pointed at his right foot. Jode followed where he pointed and saw a metal rod or tube about an inch and a half in diameter running from the cuff of his pants into his shoe. It took him a few seconds to catch on.

"Oh, sorry man, I just thought, well here let me help you up," as he reached down and offered a helping hand.

"Thanks, names Luke but most folks around here call me Sarge. What's your name and what brings you to our fair city?" as he shook Jode's hand.

"Jode, but most folks call me Jode," he smirked. "I just got here from Key West and need to get some supplies. Got sort of delayed and I'm out of most everything."

"Did you row that boat all the way from the Keys? You look rough dude."

"I got kind of stranded in the Ten Thousand Islands for a few weeks. Just pulled into the Back Bay yesterday afternoon. I'm gonna head up to the grocery store and restock."

Luke held up his hand like a crossing guard. "Wait just a minute, there's no freebies in this town and you try a snatch and grab around here and you'll get yourself an all-expense paid vacation in the county jail."

"Hey, I got money DUDE. I'm not stealin' nothin' I just need to do some shopping."

"Hey no offence, I just wanted to warn you that you go up there lookin' like that, they'll toss you out in a New York minute if you're lucky, or call the cops on you if you're not. Before you know it you'll be dumped off across the bridge on San Carlos and told not to come back . . . or worse."

"What do you mean the way I look?"

"Ok, if what you say is true, you've had a rough few weeks. I get it. But dude look at yourself. You're rail thin, dirty clothes hanging off ya, you have a particular aroma about you and for Christ's sake you're wearing a piece of rope for a belt. Not to mention that wild hair and scraggily beard will make women scream and children cry. . . Just sayin! Now, if you have the money you say you have and promise you'll listen to me, for your own good, I'll go with ya up to the store and try to run interference for you so you can get what you need and get out safe. Just trying to help out a friend when they need it. Deal?"

"Geez, when you put it that way it sounds pretty bad. Deal but what's in it for you?" Jode responded dejectedly.

"Nothing, so let's go get you squared away," Luke said as he placed a hand on Jode's shoulder and guided him up to the entrance.

Jode was first through the door. Both his feet hadn't crossed the threshold before a big fat guy came barging out of a cubicle towards him. He had on a white collared shirt and a name badge that said Jerry something or other, Manager. Pointing a finger at Jode's face he shouted, "Hey, you just turn around and get the heck out of here. We don't tolerate shop lifters around here!"

Luke stepped in front of Jode and held up his hands in surrender. "Just hold on Jerry. Jode here has had a tough trip up from the keys and needs some groceries. He assured me he has money to pay and I believe him. Just let him pick up his stuff, pay for it and we'll be gone. I'll even keep an eye on him while he's in here."

Jerry was exasperated but couldn't rightfully deny entry to a paying customer. "All right Sarge, but if things go bad it is on you! And don't think I'm not watching, Got it!"

"I GOT IT, now come on Jode, let's do some shopping." As they entered the store Luke leaned over and whispered, "Here's the rule, you touch it, you bought it. No fingering the merchandise and whatever goes into that cart you better have money to pay for, Ok?"

"Ya, I got it. Ya think he's really gonna watch us the whole damn time?"

"Dude, you're gonna have more eyes on you than a stripper in boot camp!"

As they started down the right side of the store, the first department they came to was produce. As they passed the grapes, Jode reached out to try one. Before his fingers touched the bag, Luke smacked them away and gave him a dirty look. Next item of interest was the apples, Jode put one in the basket, picked up another and brought it towards his mouth. The dirty look returned. "What? I'm going to pay for it."

"This is a grocery store, not a restaurant. You pay first then you can eat whatever you want."

Jode placed the unbitten apple in the cart added potatoes, onions and a green pepper before moving on to the meat section. He knew he wouldn't be able to keep the fridge going if he stayed at anchor more than a few days. He would at least have a cooler to keep his beer cool so he just got prepackaged ham, hot dogs and some lunch meat. After adding a loaf of bread and some snacks, he tossed in peanut butter, jelly, coffee, some of that fake powdered creamer stuff then some mustard and miscellaneous items. As an afterthought, he tossed in a box of crackers for Damn Bird if he was still around. The can goods aisle was where he usually stocked up but after his ordeal, nothing looked good except for a couple cans of baked beans, he was only a short distance from the store so no need to worry about the long term. He was heading to the beer when Luke pulled his cart to the left towards the soap and personal care aisle. Then stopped it while he tossed in off brand shaving cream, disposable razors, a couple bars of soap and some laundry detergent.

"What are you doing?" Jode protested.

"You really need this stuff dude. If you don't have the money put something back."

"I said I have the money."

"Ok." To make his point even more obvious, Luke picked up a container of deodorant, held it high over the cart and dropped it in like a plane on a bombing run. Jode just glared.

Finally at the beer cooler, Jode reached for a twelve pack then thought better of it and lifted a case of PBR cans into the cart. Luke gave him a look, but he just shrugged and moved on.

As they approached the deli and bakery the aromas became unbearable. Jode couldn't help himself. Fresh bread, blueberry muffins and cookies flew into the cart. The deli had boxes of fried chicken that he just couldn't resist, so in it went. The cart was nearly full as they headed to the checkout counter.

The girl or women behind the register smiled, "Hey Sarge, got a new friend?"

Luke returned the smile and added a little wink, "Hey Janice, This is Jode. Just met him. He's from Key West."

She gave Jode a once over then looked at the full cart. Concern crossed her face and she looked back at Sarge. He just gave her a shrug and nodded ok so she went to work ringing up the groceries. After a few stressful minutes, she finished up and hit the total. "That will be $121.62, cash or charge?"

Every eye in the place was on Jode. He reached in his pocket, peeled off two hundreds and put them on the counter. Janice, Sarge, Jerry and everyone else paying attention were both surprised and relieved to see he had the money. "What?"

"Nothing, here's your change. Thanks for shopping at Topps and have a nice day."

As they left Jerry called out, "Don't leave the parking lot with that cart."

Sarge just turned around and said, "Don't worry about it JEERRRY. I'll bring it back myself!"

As soon as his feet hit the sidewalk, Jode reached down tore open the case of PBR and popped open a beer. After a long pull, he looked over at Sarge and held out one for him. Sarge just shrugged, took the beer. "It's noon o'clock somewhere," and took a swig.

"Thanks man, you were right they would have tossed me for sure."

"Don't thank me just yet."

They headed back to the dinghy dock but before they got there, Luke or Sarge, pulled the front of the cart to the right and headed it through a gate towards a baseball field. "Where we going? Thought we couldn't leave the parking lot with the cart? Should I leave it here?"

"You leave it here and it will be empty when you get back. Don't pay any attention to numb nuts Jerry and you'll see soon enough where we're going." Jode hesitated but Sarge just kept on so he just followed.

"Head over to that dug out and have a seat on the bench on the left," Sarge said as he pointed the way.

"What's up?"

"You'll see." Sarge said as he set down his rucksack and rummaged through it. Soon he brought out electric hair clippers and plugged them into an outlet at the back of the dugout.

"What do you think you're gonna do with those?" Jode asked with a little fear in his voice.

"I'm going to get you squared away solder. You can't be walking around town looking like some crazy guy from the lost lagoon. Now hold still." In no time there was a pile of hair at Jode's feet. Then Sarge grabbed his nose tilted it up and ran the clippers over his face. "Now, police up all this hair and put it in the trash can over there."

"Why?"

"Cuz I said so and besides when those kids get here to play ball you don't want it to look like a dog was murdered in their dugout." Jode picked up the hair and started towards the trash. "Wait just a minute. You missed some back there. Ok, now we can go."

Jode couldn't believe how bossy the guy was. Not my dad, not my boss, he thought but he seemed to be used to barking orders and Jode was just a little afraid to argue. Ok, a lot afraid!

They were finished loading everything into the dinghy, but Sarge wasn't finished giving orders.

"Now when you get back to the boat wash out some decent cloths to wear, shave your face and get cleaned up. I'll meet you at the Mexican restaurant on Old San Carlos at 1600 hours, that's four o'clock."

"Why?"

"Cuz I said so, you need someone to show you around town before you get in trouble. You go around dropping C-notes and you'll get all the wrong attention. Cops or robbers, either way, you'll be in trouble. Besides, it's Margarita Mondays. Two dollar margaritas and fifty cent empanadas, best deal on the island." Jode just stood there, not knowing what to do so he said, "Yes sir!"

"Do I look like and officer to you? Do you see any bars on this collar?" Jode just nodded no. "Then I'm no SIR. Got it?"

"Yes Si. . . . . Sarge." Jode stammered. Then hopped in the dinghy and started rowing as fast as he could.

Before he was out of the canal, another dinghy came up behind him. It had a 15 horsepower on the back. Nice, he thought.

"Hey, you want a tow? Rowing that thing looks like a lot of work."

"Oh, man. That would be great. That's my boat at the very back over there by the mangroves." He tossed the guy the bow line and before he knew it, he was leaning back enjoying a beer as he was pulled across the bay to his boat.

After loading all the groceries onto the boat and stowing them away, it was time for a break. He sat in the old deck chair thinking about what just happened. That Sarge was a bossy SOB but he had a point. If anybody saw somebody looking like him dropping C-notes, the first thing that crossed their mind would be criminal if it was a cop or an easy mark if they weren't. Jode hadn't been to a bar in nearly six weeks and an icy margarita did sound inviting. Not sure what an empanada was but he liked Mexican. If he was going to town and meeting Sarge, he better do what he was told. That guy is kinda scary.

He went below and looked through his clothes. His pants were way too big so he took a look at the few things left of Tripper's. He'd tossed all the shirts. Even skinny they were still too short and while the chicks looked good with a bare midriff, it definitely wasn't his style. He found a pair of Tripper's favorite cargo shorts. They were long and baggy on him and he liked the look. On Jode they would be a little short but would fit around the waist. He picked up a couple of his better t-shirts and brought them all on deck to wash. He had plenty of fresh water but getting more would require a lot of work so he dipped a half bucket of brackish water off the swim platform added some of the laundry detergent and got to work. The water was nowhere near as clear as in the keys or even Tiger Key but with the tide coming in it was clean enough. When the soapy water was dirtier than his clothes, he dumped it overboard, refilled and rinsed them out. Finishing off with fresh water from the wash down hose. After hanging the shorts and shirts up to dry, he headed down to shave and cleanup. When he looked in the mirror to shave he didn't recognize the guy looking back at him. His beard was reduced to a patchy stubble and his hair was shorter than it had been his entire life, nearly to the bone on the sides and barely an inch of flat top left on his head. Looked a lot like Sarge's he thought and he didn't like it!

After shaving and showering, he grabbed a beer, picked up the box of fried chicken and headed back on deck. On queue Damn Bird flow over squawking so he tossed some breading on the deck for him and they had lunch. After a little nap, he was awakened by the boat rocking as the tide began to turn and it swung around pointing south into the bay. That was good. An outgoing tide would bring him right to the dinghy dock under the bridge. Rowing against the tide would be almost impossible and he couldn't depend on hitching a tow this far back in the anchorage.

At about 3:30, he got dressed in his clean clothes, put on his old deck shoes and Tripper's belt and headed to the dinghy dock. As he figured, there was no free ride but the tide was running fast through the narrow anchorage so he just needed to row enough to steer around all the boats on the mooring balls and soon was at the dinghy dock. Once again it was packed with inflatable boats and they all had motors except his. The thought of pinching one crossed his mind but he knew he'd be caught immediately because anyone would recognize their own boat or motor even from across the bay.

He pushed his way between a couple of boats, tied off and headed up Old San Carlos. As soon as he turned the corner by Nervous Nellies, he spotted Sarge leaning against the wall in the shade across from the Mexican place. He waved Jode over and waited. When Jode met him, there was no hello or how ya doin', he looked him over, grabbed his chin and inspected his face, looked him up and down, raised his t-shirt to see the belt and continued down his scrawny legs to the big old boat shoes. He felt like a prize bull being judged at the county fair.

"Well you won't win any beauty pageants but you look a damn site better than this morning. Getting rid of the rope belt and miss matched flip-flops makes the outfit. Let's get ourselves some drinks . . . . and remember what I said about those C-notes."

As they entered the hostess greeted them. "Hey Sarge, the bar as usual?"

"Hey, yup, got a wing man with me today so you better warn the ladies things might get out of hand." He said with a smile and wink. She returned the smile and blushed just a tad.

They sat down at the end of the bar. Sarge put his rucksack under his chair as the bartender walked over. "The usual? Rocks with salt?" Sarge nodded then the bartender turned to Jode. "You?"

"Same."

"Separate checks?"

Sarge shook his head no. "No, we can figure it out. This guy here is a math genius." He added as he nudged Jode. The margaritas arrived in no time. Jode grabbed his and downed half like he hadn't had a proper drink in weeks. Cause he hadn't. "Whoa slow down. This isn't a race. If it has been three weeks since you tied one on, you'll be under the table before the sun sets."

"Closer to six weeks," Jode responded. That got Sarge's attention but he didn't react and let it slide.

When the bartender returned with a second round Sarge ordered four empanadas each. Jode said he never had one before but Sarge assured him they were great and the best he had ever tasted. They shared small talk. Neither seemed to want to tell their life story to someone they just met. Every now and then they were interrupted when someone came up to say hello to Sarge and ask how's things going. He seemed to know everyone in the place and everyone was friendly. After the third margarita, he asked for the check. Jode was enjoying himself and wanted to stay but was feeling the effects of the drinks and besides happy hour was almost over.

As they nursed their last one, an older guy came up to the bar to pay his bill. He reached over and picked up the one in front of Sarge and handed both to the bartender. He turned to Sarge and said, "Semper Fi."

Sarge turn to him with a smile and said, "Hey, I'm not a jar head!" He pointed at his shoulder where a patch use to be and added, "Army, 1st Cav."

The old guy smiled. "Air Force. From 30,000 feet can't tell the difference, Jar head, ground pounder, ya'll look alike!"

"Don't care what you call us. Just make sure you drop your load on the bad guys!"

The old guy smiled, "Most times we do." Handing the two checks to the bartender he said, "Add another round for my friends here and cash me out." "What about your friend here, army?"

"No he's a sailor."

"Squid huh? Too bad for him. Carry on soldier," as he touched the bill of his hat in a mock salute. Sarge returned the gesture as he walked away.

Watching the exchange, Jode asked what he meant by squid. "Navy term, not the most complimentary."

"Why'd you tell him I was in the navy?"

"Never did. You're a sailor aren't you?" Jode kind of nodded agreement. "Just let him jump to his own conclusion. You kind of look like one now. You got a couple of ones?" Jode dug in his pocket and handed over the singles. Sarge put them in his pocket and left a five on the bar.

When they were out on the street Jode said "Pretty sweet gig. That happen often?"

"More often than not. Meet me at the dinghy dock a little before 1600 tomorrow. Bring your laundry. If you don't have a lot of quarters, give me a five and I'll get change." Jode hesitated. "There's a washer and dryer you can use over at Matanzas Inn. You can do your laundry while we have some beers upstairs at Petey's. It's Twofer Tuesday there tomorrow, and don't tell me you don't have any dirty laundry."

Jode couldn't argue with any of it, so he handed over the fin. "Where you live?"

"Here and there. See you tomorrow."

They shook hands and parted company. Jode headed towards the dinghy dock, Sarge up towards the beach and Estero Boulevard. As he was rowing and riding the tide back to Old Moe, Jode wondered about Sarge as the old Roger Miller song kept playing in his head. "Every handout in every town and every lock that ain't locked when no one's around." Four margaritas were defiantly over his new limit. So when he got back to the boat, he tied off the dinghy, crawled into the boat and passed out.

Tuesday began with a pot of coffee relaxing on the back deck watching the sun sparkle off the waters of the Back Bay. Jode had slept in after yesterday's visit to the bar. No seeing the sunrise today. With his second cup of coffee he opened the blueberry muffins and had a leisurely breakfast. Damn Bird was on the deck beside him sharing in the spoils. It was hard to believe this was only his second day at the Beach. So much had happened over the last few days and so much seemed to have changed, not the least of which was his appearance. He still hadn't decided how much he disliked his new hair cut but he didn't know anyone here, other than Sarge and besides, he didn't have to look at it. He had to admit it was cooler and more practical and if it meant free drinks, what's not to like?

With the tide coming in until midafternoon there was no reason to leave the boat and a lot of reasons to wait until the current was going in his direction. He took his time getting the laundry together and picking up around the boat. He fished a while but this wasn't the keys or even the ten thousand islands. Only thing he caught was a slimy sail cat. He opened the cooler for a beer and found mostly water and very little ice. After popping open the beer and having a swig, he went about transferring the last bit of ice and the almost cold contents to his old igloo cooler. He'd bring the little styrofoam one with him to get ice while he was in town.

When he got to the dinghy dock Sarge was already there waiting. He gave Jode a hand unloading the laundry then handed over the bag of quarters. "Follow me through the parking lot and passed the pool and we'll get the washer going." After putting the clothes and quarters in the machine they headed up the stairs to Petey's. Jode saw several open seats at the bar and headed that why. Sarge grabbed his arm and steered him to the railing overlooking the harbor instead.

"Why aren't we going to the bar?" Jode asked.

"You'll see, we need to wait here a few minutes." As they looked out over the water, Sarge noticed his gaze locked on one of the motorized dinghies plying the mooring field. "You're not thinking of stealing one of those are you?"

"Nah, never get away with it. I do need a motor though. With the tides and current I'll be stuck on the boat most days without one. Where we were anchored in Key West we didn't have to fight the current all the time to go to shore."

"We? I thought you were alone on the boat."

"Am, now," Jode said as he subconsciously rubbed the silver coins together in his pocket.

Sarge noticed the distant look in his eyes and the subtle sadness as he starred out at nothing in particular. He had seen that look many times before in Iraq and even in the mirror.

"What happened?"

"Ah, long story. Not a happy one."

Sarge knew enough to not push for any details and instead looked over to the bar. The barmaid, Lila, just put a pizza stand in front of an older couple sitting at the bar. "Come on, let's get that beer." He walked over and asked the guy if the seat was taken, when he nodded no and gestured to sit, he did and motioned for Jode to sit down beside him.

"Hey, Sarge."

"Hey, Lila. Meet my new friend Jode, I call him Sailor. How about a couple of beers. Don't back 'em up just keep 'em coming one at a time. Don't want them getting warm."

"Ya, I've had enough warm beer to last a lifetime," Jode added.

She returned with the beers set them down and gave Jode a good looking over. "Sailor huh? Most not be a very good one. You're so skinny you look like you've been shipwrecked on some deserted island. You know like Gilligan or that Tom Hanks guy in Cast Away."

Sarge nearly chocked on his beer. Might have even come out his nose. "You're something Lila, fact is, if what he told me is true he was shipwrecked on his boat down in the ten thousand islands for the last few weeks. Just got into to town a couple of days ago."

"Really?" Jode nodded confirmation. "Well I'll be damned. That sounds like a story I'd like to hear. You come in sometime when we aren't so busy and tell me all about it. Might even be worth a few complimentary beers just to listen." Then she turn around and brought the pizza over to the couple next to them.

They drank their beers in silence as the couple served up slices of pizza and talked among themselves. After they each had two slices the old guy turned to Sarge and asked if they would like a slice. "We can't eat all this and we're staying at the motel so no way to take it home. Honey, can you get another couple of plates for these guys?" Lila dropped off the plates and he served up the rest of the pizza and handed it to Sarge and Jode.

As they were finishing off the pizza, Lila brought them another round of beers. Sarge's watch buzzed. "Better finish off that beer and go put your clothes in the drier. Based on how much was in the load I'd put $2.50 in to make sure they're dry. I'll hold down the fort until you get back." Jode did as instructed and headed down the stairs to the laundry room.

By the time he was heading back up the stairs there was a new beer waiting at his empty seat.

"You serious about buying a motor for your dink?" Sarge asked. Jode nodded in the affirmative. "How much ya willin' to pay?"

"I think I could get an ok 5 or 10 horsepower one for a couple of hundred bucks. Don't want to spend any more than that. Got to watch my cash for now."

For now. An interesting way to phrase it Sarge thought. "Let's ask Lila. She knows all and sees all from her perch up here." Hearing her name she came over giving Sarge a snap with the bar towel. "Hey, Sailor here needs a motor for his dinghy. He's afraid he'll get too bulked up for the ladies if he keeps rowing that thing against the current", as he reached over and squeezed Jode's skinny but muscular bicep. "Thought you might have some idea where to look. Being as you know everything going on in this town."

She rolled her eyes up and to the right like she was thinking. "Don't want to send you over to the competition, but a lot of the fisherman hang out at Bonita Bill's. Most the guides are over on the mainland at Hurricane Pass. They have a lot of contacts. Best bet might be to talk to Steve. He's the forklift driver over at Moss Marine stack storage. He sees every boat and owner as he takes them in and out. He'd know if anyone is selling or replacing a motor."

"Thanks, that's a real good start." Turning to Jode he added, "I have a lot of errands to run tomorrow. Be by most those places. How about I see what I can find and meet you about 1500 hours at the dinghy dock Thursday. If all goes as planned I should be able to put together a deal for you."

"Ok, but two hundred max."

"You got it, bring some small bills in case it's less or you can talk down the price."

"Not my first shot at wheeling and dealing." Jode responded a little too sharply.

Business out of the way, they ordered another beer. Then Lila brought by a tray with two more pieces of pizza on it. "Folks over there said they were full and wondered if you'd like it. I told them Sailor here was starving after being on a desert island and would appreciate it." She said with an evil grin. They both nodded thanks to the folks across the bar and dug in.

Sarge's watch buzzed again. "Duty calls. Hey Lila how about one more than cash us out. Sailor here has laundry in the dryer. You know how people get if you leave it there too long."

She dropped off the beers and returned with the check. Not much for pizza and beer for two. They drank their beers and dug out cash to split the bill and tip. As Jode was fishing through the remaining quarters, Sarge noticed an odd looking coin. "What's that?"

"Oh, nothing much. Just a little reminder of Key West. After Mel Fisher found the Atocha they were all over town. Not worth much but brings back some good memories." Sarge let it lie. "Oh ya, I need to pick up some ice before I shove off. Almost forgot,"

"Hey Lila, any chance you can help out a struggling castaway with a little ice for his cooler?"

She let out a false exasperated sigh. "Let me see if I have any old plastic grocery bags." She returned in a couple of minutes with the ice doubled bagged and tied shut. "Now remember, you owe me that story sweetheart." Jode just smiled and they headed down the stairs.

"Give me the ice," Sarge said as he reached for the bag. "I'll put it in the cooler while you go get your laundry." After Jode got to the dinghy dock, they were saying their goodbyes when Sarge added. "If you are going to the grocery store tomorrow it's a good place to change a C-note. They know you now. You also might want to stop by that big church down the road, Chapel by the

Sea. They have a thrift store in the back where you might find some clothes that fit better. The Kiwanis also have one you can check out. A couple words of advice, if you see anything military that fits buy it and if there is a lady working there, I don't care if she is 17 or 75 ask her for help picking out some clothes, she'll do a whole lot better job then you or I would. See you Thursday at 1500. Bring cash. I have a good feeling about finding that motor."

Chapter 9

Jode waited until mid-day to row across the bay to the dinghy dock behind Topps. Even though he wasn't rowing against the tide, waiting until it was almost slack helped. The first stop was the church thrift store. It was small without a lot of stuff. Looked more like the kind of place where donations are given away to those in need. He was pleasantly surprised to see an attractive woman in her mid-thirties behind the desk. She was dressed in business work clothes and had a nice, friendly smile. "Hello, welcome to Chapel by the Sea. My name is Shelly. How can I help you?" Taking Sarge's advice to ask for help was a lot easier than he had expected.

"Hi, names Jode. Just got in town a few days ago. Lost most of my stuff in a boating accident on my way up from the keys, so most anything will help."

"You're tall and so slim I doubt we have much that will fit you, but let's take a look. How'd you hear about our little store?"

"Met this guy and he told me about this place and another thrift store on the island."

She stood up and came towards him with her hand out to welcome him and shake his hand. Then she reached up and brushed her left hand over his bristly flat top. Made him a little uncomfortable, but he liked it anyways. "That guy wouldn't happen to be Sarge, would it? You have the same haircut." She smiled when she mentioned his name. Must be friends.

"Ya. You know him?"

"Yup, he's a real nice man. Comes to service most Sundays. Comes in late after everyone's already seated and sits in the back. Leaves after the Message or Sermon. That's the most important part anyway. I think he is a little self-conscious, the leg or maybe his circumstances. Shouldn't be, everyone likes him and as I said he's a real good man. Now let's see what we can find."

She rooted around the store and found a couple pairs of shorts and a pair of pants. She held them halfway around his waist to see if they fit. "These look to be a little big but I expect you will be putting on a few pounds if you're hanging around with Sarge."

"Ya, I lost about twenty pounds recently and expect your right about filling out some. Do you have any old military clothes?"

"Let's see, I think we have some old fatigues in the back. Too short for you but they would make good work shorts as cut-offs. Heavy material and a lot of pockets. I have a couple of fishing shirts that might fit you too."

Soon they had gone through everything that he might be able to use and Shelly added everything up. "That will be $16.50, but if you don't have the money that's ok. You can just take it. We give away most stuff here anyway."

"No, I have the money and you have been a great help. Here you go, exact change." In the past, Jode would have just taken it but he had a feeling Sarge would disapprove. He did have the money so why not.

"Thank you. Here are the directions to the Kiwanis Thrift store. They have a lot more stuff, not just clothes if you need anything else. Tell Sarge, Shelly says hello when you see him."

"Will do. Thanks again."

He headed up to Estero Boulevard, took a right and followed the directions to his next stop.

When he went in he received an equally friendly greeting from an old couple in their 60's or 70's. "Well you're a tall, thin drink of water, young man." The old guy said. The woman shushed him and got up to welcome Jode in. "What can we help you with Honey?"

"Just got some clothes over at the church and Shelly sent me over thinking you might have a few more things that fit. Also could use a new pot and fry pan if you have anything."

She took his hand and led him around like a kid in a candy store. She gave him another pair of shorts, one of long pants, a fishing shirt and three t-shirts. Then she stopped next to the dress clothes. "These just came in and the fella was about your size, tall and thin. Should fit real good."

"I don't need any dress-up clothes. I just live on a boat." He protested.

"Honey, everyone needs at least one good outfit. Now, I don't know if you go to service on Sunday or not and it isn't any of my business but even if you don't you need a proper wedding and funeral outfit." She wasn't going to take no for an answer so he just agreed and added them to his growing pile. She then led him across the store to the pots and pans and picked out a couple of nice ones, added some utensils and a salad bowl before letting him loose. She went back to the counter. Rang up the merchandise and said. "Comes to $36.00, but if you don't have the money, you can just pay whatever you want. We're here to help folks out as much as raise funds for charity."

"No, not a problem. I have the money and all this stuff would be a lot more at the Walmart, that's for sure." He paid the bill, loaded up all his purchases and headed back to Topps. It turned out to be quite a load to carry in the heat.

When he got to the store, he placed all his stuff under the cart and went in to pick up a few groceries, more beer and a couple bags of ice. Unlike last time, no one gave him a second look as he entered. Even the manager guy, Jerry, didn't even lift his head. In a couple of minutes he was heading to the checkout counter. He saw Janice and got in her line.

When it was his turn, he began placing his items on the conveyor belt. "Hey Janice. Nice seein' you again."

She looked up with a blank stare on her face. "Do I know you?"

"Ya, met you just a couple of days ago." No reaction. "It was Monday. I was here with Sarge."

She looked at him again. Closer this time. Suddenly her eyes sprang wide open and with a big smile on her face she pushed both hands into Jode's chest and shouted, "Get Out. That's you!"

Everyone within ear shot turned to look. Even Jerry was lifting his substantial bulk out of his chair. Janice's face turned beet red as she sheepishly gave a little wave and said. "It's ok, just a friend I haven't seen in a while."

"Friend huh? That sounds nice to me." Jode responded.

She looked him up and down and even gave a little sniff. "Looks like you put all those cleaning products to good use, no offense. No one would recognize the new you. Did Sarge give you that haircut?"

Jode nodded in the affirmative. "Thought so, army regs all the way." She totaled up the sale and Jode handed over a hundred dollar bill.

"Any chance you can cash another one for me?" he whispered. "Sarge told me not to be seen around town with any big bills."

"Good advice. Those bums by the dock would roll you in a minute if they knew and the cops would think you stole it or its drug money if they saw you flashing all that cash. It's not drug money is it? No cocaine on it, is there?"

"No it is not stolen or drug money. As for the cocaine, I got them in the keys so can't say for certain." He added in a conspiratorial tone. She smiled, took the bills, swiped them with that pen thing and counted out his change. They said their goodbyes and he headed back to the dinghy dock and rowed out to Old Moe.

He took his time unloading all his booty and carefully packed everything away. Before repacking the cooler, he dumped the cold water and what little ice was left from what Lila gave him into the syrofoam cooler, added a few beers, packed up his regular cooler and put it in the shade. Should be good for two or three days if he doesn't open it too often. He lifted the little cooler with the beers up to the bridge, grabbed some snacks and settled in for a relaxing afternoon. The bag wasn't even open before his resident freeloader flew over to join him.

Thursday was the day he got a new motor and freedom from the tides. If Sarge was successful. If not, he would have to bum a tow or wait until after 8PM to catch the incoming tide. Stuck on Old Moe until at least two, he decided to crank up the old huka rig and inspect the bottom of the boat. He was pretty sure everything was ok. There hadn't been any new or serious leaks but better to be safe than sorry. He wasn't looking forward to jumping into the tannic brown water. Last time he was underwater was in the Marquesas. There you could inspect the bottom of the boat while standing on the sandy bottom. Not here. With visibility only a couple of feet, it took him almost an hour to cover the whole boat but everything looked as good as could be expected so that was one less thing to worry about.

After some lunch and a beer, he showered and shaved. Didn't want to fail Sarge's inevitable inspection. He put on his new fatigue cutoffs. Luckily, Shelley offered to do the cutting. She held them around his waist, there was no way he could have gotten into the short pants, made a mark and cut them off right above his knees. The length was perfect and the cut much better than he could have ever done. He reached for one of his "new" fishing shirts then thought an old but clean t-shirt would be a better choice for today's business. The tide changed and he waited another half hour for the current to pick up and headed over to the dinghy dock.

As he was tying up, an old compact pickup truck pulled into the parking lot. Sarge got out of the passenger side and another guy stepped out the driver's side. A wave and hello were exchanged. Sarge introduced them, "Jode, Nick, Nick, this is Jode." they shook hands a little reluctantly. Jode walked up and looked in the bed of the truck. There laid a clean, black, six horsepower mercury, two stroke out board with an integral fuel tank. He had to fight back a smile. It was perfect! "Looks like it has been used a lot. How much you asking for it?"

"Two-twenty-five."

Jode gave Sarge the stink eye. "I don't have that kind of money."

"Hey, it's worth every penny and a lot more," Nick countered.

"Don't care what it's worth. It's what I can pay. I'll give you a buck fifty, cash."

"No way, I'd just as soon keep it for that chump change. How bout I throw in the 2 gallon gas can and that open quart of two cycle oil? Take you a month to use it up, going back and forth to your boat for two-bills?"

"I'll give you one-seventy-five right now. . . . . IF it runs good."

"I guess that'll work. Sarge said you weren't rolling in dough and don't you worry, it runs like brand new."

Jode choked back a smile and held his poker face. "Well let's put it on the dink and see if it runs as good as you say."

"Let's see some cash in my hand before it leaves my truck," Nick said holding out his hand palm up.

"If it runs like crap. You high tail it out of here and I'm screwed."

"Or, you take my motor and leave me high and dry! No way that's happening!!" The volume of both of them was getting a little too high.

"Children, children, children," Sarge broke in. "Jode give me the cash. Nick, help him put the motor on his boat and let him do a test drive. He doesn't come back. I give you the money. If Jode doesn't want the motor we load it back in the truck." The two men looked at Sarge then each other, nodded in agreement and got to work mounting the motor on the dink. They were like an old married couple, each telling the other how every little thing should be done but done it got.

Finally it was mounted and ready to start. Nick gave Jode detailed instructions of the starting process, being that all motors are a little finicky. "There's gas in the tank so just open the vent, give that little rubber thing, Ya, that one, looks like the bulb on a weed whacker. Give four or five pumps. Pull the choke out and pull it once, and only once." Jode did as instructed and the motor coughed and died. "Now push the choke back in and give it another pull." The motor started right up and Jode was untied and gone in a flash.

When he came back he had a big smile on his face. "You're right Nick this is a sweet little motor." Everyone was good friends now. Jode tied up the dink as Sarge handed Nick the cash. They all shook hands and before he got in the truck, Nick handed Sarge a bill.

Seeing the exchange Jode waited until Nick was gone and approached Sarge. "Hey what's that?" pointing at the five. "I thought you were on my side."

Holding the fin between his two fingers, he waved it under Jode's nose and with a big smile said, "I'm on everybody's side. I can't help it if everyone loves me. Besides, it might not be Twofer Tuesday but it is happy hour and this little baby will get us each a beer." He put his hand on Jode's shoulder and turned him towards the bar. Jode hesitated and looked back at his new purchase. "I know what you are thinking and no, no one is going to steal your shiny new motor. Look around, you still have the crappiest ride at the dock." He gave a big smile and added, "Let's go get those beers."

When they got to the top of the stairs the place was busy. With the weekend just a day away, the crowds were coming out. With the bar full they found a table in the back around the corner overlooking the bay. Soon the waitress came by. "Hey Sarge."

"Hey gorgeous, how about a couple of drafts for a couple of thirsty old boaters?"

"You're no boater," she said as she poked him in the ribs.

"No I am not but my buddy here is and he just got himself a new motor for his dinghy and we're celebrating." He said with his award winning smile.

As they waited for the beers to arrive, Jode said, "Thanks man. That motor is just what I needed. No more being a slave to the tide chart. Oh, and Janice and Shelly said Hi. Do you know every girl in town?"

"Not yet but I'm working on it," he grinned. "I like your new shorts, by the way, seems you took my advice. They didn't have any decent shirts?"

"Didn't want to get all fancied up when there was wheeling and dealing to be done. Would have cost me more for sure. Thanks again. That motor was worth two bills for sure. Beers on me tonight, until we get to the twenty-five dollars I saved anyway. You seem to know everyone in town. How long you been here and how'd you end up on the Beach? There's no military base or anything around this area. Closest would be a hundred miles north in Tampa."

The waitress brought the beers set them down and after smiling again at Sarge, she left. "Well I guess since we're friends and all now and you did say you were buying, I guess I can tell you my story. The short sanitized version that is."

"I grew up in a little rural town in central Michigan. Typical kid, mowed lawns for money, played sports in school. I was pretty good but not college scholarship good. Out of high school I took some classes at the community college in the next town over. Worked construction during the summers, and other odd jobs. I got bored and didn't see any future in what I was doing and decided to join the army. You know, see the world shit, do more before dawn, blah, blah, blah. Anyway, I liked the army. Shooting up stuff and blowing shit up, what's not to like?

Did a tour in Iraq. Kept my nose clean and made Sargent. Next tour I made E-6 and became the squad leader. Went through a lot of hairy shit. Patrols in enemy territory, getting shot at, typical grunt army life in the sand box. Met some great guys. Made some great friends, lost a few too. That sucked. Was near the end of my second tour. We were in a Humvee. As squad leader I was in the passenger seat, Sandman, he was our long gunner, he could drop a rag head at a thousand yards, was in the back seat. Greaser was the gunner on the 50 cal. He could fix anything. Got us out of a lot of "jams" for sure. Tubbs was at the wheel. That bastard could drive. Used to say "If you're going fast enough nothing can stop you" and he did. Behind him was Wilson, strangest guy I ever met. He could shoot the eye out of a squirrel at a hundred yards and never used the sites, just point and shoot. Said he got a used BB gun as a kid that had the sights broken off so that's how he learned to shoot.

Saved our ass more than once. One time we got ambushed by two rag heads. One fired at us from behind, must have been only 50 yards back. Bastard missed us but Wilson rolled over and dropped them both without even lifting his rifle off his lap. Missed his own toe by about an inch. We called him Woody. When he was in grade school and the little kids learned the names of the Presidents they started calling him Woodrow. He hated that."

"Figures, what were you good at?" Jode asked.

"Me? Everything, I was THE Sarge, but mostly telling everyone else what to do."

Jode rolled his eyes, "I heard that!" Sarge glared at him, then shook his head in disgust.

"Moving on, suddenly all hell broke loose. The front right wheel must have hit an IED. I don't remember shit. I woke up in a field hospital missing a leg," as he pointed down to his fake foot. "Sandman and Greaser were banged up pretty bad, so they were in there too. Tubbs and Woody were patched up out in the field and carted back to base. They got me stabilized, the guys came by to say so long, and then I was airlifted to Germany. A couple of weeks there, then back to the States for a new foot and a several months of rehab."

"When that was done they gave me my walking papers," he let out a sarcastic chuckle. "Put me on a bus and sent me back home. By then my folks had moved to the Florida Panhandle and what friends were left in town had moved on with their lives. Nothing to keep me there, I decided to hit the road and see the country as they say. I had saved up a pretty good amount of cash. Nothin' to spend your pay on in the hospital or rehab. Wasn't anything to spend it on in the sand box either for that matter, so I had maybe twenty grand and my disability. They only gave me 25 percent. Guess they figured you have four limbs and I only lost one so 25 percent. The DAV is appealing it. They say I will get at least 40 percent and probably 50. All that crap takes time so I'm still waiting. If I get it, I'll have a lot more each month and the almost two years back pay should replenish my savings."

Jode seemed to lose focus and looked over to his right. Sarge saw what he was looking at. The waitress was clearing the table that just came open and there was a half full plate of wings left. As he started to raise his hand with his index finger up, Sarge smacked it down faster than a cobra strike.

"What!" Jode snapped.

"I know what you're thinking. Just be patient Grasshopper. Lila's got our six." Jode had no idea what he meant.

"Well, as I was sayin', with money in my pocket and what little they sent me every month, I hit the road. Visited some of my old army buddies, saw the monuments in Washington, even went out west to Denver and the Rockies. Finally went to see my folks. They have a little place in Niceville near Eglin Air Force base. But all their friends are old and I didn't want to stay in a military town so I just kept heading south."

"When I got here I just sort of fit in. The locals are real friendly and the tourists aren't too bad. After a few weeks I decided to stay. Found a little two room apartment on Fairweather Lane, I guess three rooms if you count the bathroom. It was cheap and I could catch the trolley to anywhere I needed to go. When my lease was up, that was last spring, they wanted to raise my rent guite a bit and I was getting low on my savings. I wasn't sure I wanted to reup for another tour here, so I let it go and did some house sitting for some of the snowbirds I knew. I move around from time to time. Every now and then I'm kind of out on my own, but compared to sleeping in a ditch in the sand box with bad guys shooting at you, anyplace around here is good enough. I know I can't do this forever. But it's working for me right now. When the Veterans Administration pulls their head out of their ass and fixes my disability I'll have some hard decisions to make."

Just then their waitress came back with a big plate of food. There were a bunch of wings, some covered with sauce some plain, three slices from a large pizza, two from a small. "Here's the appetizer assortment platter you ordered from Lila. You guys need a couple more beers to go with that? It's last call for happy hour prices?" She had the cutest smile.

"That would be great, and you can cash us out all one tab. Thanks," Jode responded. The story came to an abrupt halt as both men tore into the pile of goodies. She brought the beer and the check after they polished off the food and drinks, Jode dug out his cash to pay the bill. "I got this. Thanks again man. My life is going to be so much easier with that motor. I can come and go when I please and won't get all stinky pulling on those oars."

"No problem, glad it worked out. I'll get the tip." As he smiled and waved the offending five in front of Jode's nose one more time.

They headed down to the dinghy dock. Jode proud as punch as he looked at his new ride. "What's next?"

"Well I got to find a new place tomorrow and the bars are packed on the weekend. No happy hour deals. Everything is top dollar. So, I'm thinking Margarita Mondays is next."

"How about I pick up some beer and something from the deli at Topps and we have happy hour on the boat Saturday? I can pick you up most anywhere that works for you." As he proudly stuck a thumb over his shoulder towards the dinghy dock.

"Hey that would be great. I can meet you on the dock at Salty Sam's about 1500 hrs."

"Deal, See you then." They shook hands. Sarge threw his rucksack over his shoulder and headed up the street as Jode started up his new motor and with the biggest smile in weeks, headed back to Old Moe.

Chapter 10

The next morning Jode was sitting on the back deck enjoying his second cup of coffee and a blueberry muffin. Damn Bird was beside him enjoying the same. Well not the coffee, just some muffin. He looked proudly at his new dinghy set up and decided to do some exploring of his new home. After he finished breakfast he started up the motor and took Matanzas Pass south. It soon widened out considerably. Across from Mid-Island Marina there was a big opening leading off into the mangroves. He took a left and soon was surrounded by nature. A few fisherman were here and there in shallow draft flats boats but no buildings were in sight. He passed Dog Island and headed back into the little creeks and crannies of the mangrove forest. He didn't worry about getting lost even though there were no land marks. He could follow the current either with it or against it to find his way back. Growing up in the keys he spent most his days and all his free time exploring the gulf side of the islands. With a boat not much different than the one he was in, he could get anywhere he wanted. Who needed a car in those days? While the mangroves were the same the water was totally different. No crystal clear water, no way to see the bottom, no lobsters and different species of fish but it brought back good memories none the less. Just winding through the maze of waterways made him happy until he thought of Tripper. They had spent most of their growing up together doing just this. He found the coins in his pocket and gave them a rub. Life sure was different without Tripper by his side. Feeling melancholy, he headed back to the pass and turned north towards Old Moe.

When the old boat came into view he didn't want to end his expedition quite yet, so he passed by Old Moe and continued up the harbor. He passed Salty Sam's and took a look at the dock where he was to meet Sarge tomorrow. Then passed the fuel docks and shrimp boats before going under the bridge. He felt a twinge when he went by the Coast Guard Station. He wasn't doing anything wrong but they were still law enforcement, no need to poke the bear. He decided to run all the way around San Carlos Island so he took the channel over to Hurricane Pass. At the base of the bridge was a bar and he was getting thirsty.

The place was busy and it took a while to find a place to tie up his little boat. When he got inside he was surprised how crowded it was. Sarge was right. Even this far from the beach and off the beaten path the weekend crowd had taken over. He noticed a sign about happy hour specials but it made clear they only applied Monday through Thursday. He had money in his pocket so he went to the bar and got a beer anyway. One beer and a modest tip and five dollars were gone. He'll be drinking on the boat on weekends that's for sure!

He moved away from the bar and watched the patrons. Small groups were spread out across the place, engaged in animated conversation. Jode wasn't the type to barge into a group of strangers and join the fray, so he stood and watched while nursing the overpriced draft. If Tripper were with him, they would be in the thick of it. He would pick a group talking about something that caught his ear and before you know it, they all would be listening to him telling some crazy tale. Probably buy him a beer too. Be the same with Sarge, he figured. Hell he would probably know them all and be invited right into the mix. Jode stood off to the side and thought about how much he missed his buddy, rubbing the silver coins together as he did.

He finished his beer, put the glass on the table, and retreated to the dock. Soon he was around the south side of the island and back to Old Moe.

He didn't want to admit it but he was looking forward to sitting around drinking beer with Sarge. The downside was he would most likely do an inspection, whether he admitted it or not, so Jode got to work putting things away and cleaning up. A little bit anyway. No one would confuse him with a neat freak. Even when he was done, the place was a mess. Just not as big of a mess.

Around two o'clock he hopped in the dink and headed over to Topps with his styrofoam cooler. He didn't plan to do much shopping. Just what he needed for today. A case of cold PBR, ice, some chips and a visit to the deli. There were so many choices and he still felt deprived after the weeks on Lulu key. He couldn't make up his mind so he tossed in a box of fried chicken that was so good and had the lady at the counter make a big Italian hoagie and cut it in half. He knew Sarge liked the chicken. He had a piece with the beer when they first met. If he didn't want the hoagie, it would leave more for him. He wasn't holding his breath. Sarge seemed to eat whatever was in front of him.

When he headed to the checkout he looked around but didn't see Janice. Resigned to the fact she wasn't there he got in the closest line. "Hey, good afternoon, is Janice here today?"

"No, she has weekends off. Is there something special you need?"

"No, just wondered. She was here the last few times I was in." He placed the groceries on the conveyor belt and waited for the total. Digging in his pocket he took out a couple of twenties and a ten to pay up. If Janice was here, he would have broken a hundred but after what Sarge told him he thought it was best to wait until next time.

Back in the dinghy, he headed across the harbor and up to Salty Sam's. Sarge was standing in the shade by the forklift. When he saw Jode he walked down the dock to an open finger pier, tossed Jode his rucksack and climbed in. "Hey, thanks for the invite. Hope you got plenty of beer. It's hot as hell out here in the sun."

"Don't worry I got you covered. Do you carry that everywhere?" He asked pointing at the army backpack.

"Yup, except when I was in the hospital or rehab, it hasn't left my side."

In no time they were sitting on the back deck in the shade drinking a cold beer and shooting the shit. Jode grabbed the bag of chips, tore it open and handed it to Sarge. Before he got his hand in, Damn Bird was streaking out of the mangroves squawking, "damn bird, damn bird".

"What the hell is that? Does it bite? What the hell is it saying?"

"That's Damn Bird. Must be his name. That's all he says."

"He your pet?" Sarge asked as he tossed the demanding bird a chip.

"Na, more of an uninvited freeloader. We met down in the ten thousand islands. He followed me up here. Comes around anytime there is food or hears the rustle of a chip bag." Jode added with a smile. "He saved my life once so it's not all bad."

Sarge raised an eyebrow and gave him a skeptical look, "Really?"

"Ya, I was sleeping on the beach when this huge python came charging out of the brush towards me. If Damn Bird hadn't woke me up with his squawking I'd been a goner for sure."

"Really?"

"Ok, it wasn't that big a snake and it was kind of just sunning itself on the beach but hey, it could have been poisonous and it could a bit me," Jode said with a grin.

They had a couple more beers and some chicken and talked about nothing important. Sarge got up and asked where to take a piss, off the back or down below. Jode told him where the head was. Peeing off the back is usually ok, but around here they were looking for any reason to kick out boats and boaters like him. When Sarge left, he reached over, picked up the backpack and started examining it.

"What the hell you doing with that!" He barked as he came back up the steps.

"Sorry man, I was just interested in what was so valuable you kept it with you all the time. I wasn't going to take anything, just wondering, honest." Jode held up his hands in surrender.

"I got nothing valuable in there, but it is important, especially to me. If you're so damn nosey I'll show you, not a big deal." He sat down, opened another beer and pulled the rucksack over to his lap. "Mostly what's in here is clothes. When in country you might have two or three uniforms, plus tee shirts, skivvies, socks that's about it. You carry a clean set to change into while you wash the dirty ones. Sometimes washing is letting them rinse on the floor while you take a shower. On base they'll wash everyone's at once. Then you pack up the clean ones and you're ready for next time."

"How do they keep all that straight? Doesn't everything get mixed up?"

"Na, first thing they give you in boot camp is a rubber stamp with the last four of your service number and a pad of indelible ink. Every damn thing you own gets that number tattooed to it." Sarge explained as he rolled over his waist band to show Jode the faded black numbers.

"What if someone has the same number?"

"Well the odds are 10,000 to 1, even in a squad that makes it plus or minus 2000 to 1, guess it could happen, but I've never seen it." After he dug out the clothes he reached in and brought out a heavy belt, holster and pistol. "This is the important part. Been with me since I arrived in Iraq, except for the hospital and rehab. M9 Beretta, I call it Bret. Best friend I got. No offense."

Jode's eyes bugged out. Didn't expect that! "They let you keep that?"

"Not exactly. Best I can figure is when the medics showed up, they took this off and cut off my uniform did some triage before medevacking me out. One of my guys probably stuffed it in my rucksack. Back on base, one of the guys was tasked with packing up all my shit into my duffle bag, not that there was much of it, and it followed me around until I was discharged. Guess no one ever asked and no one looked. When it showed up I was as surprised as anyone but I wasn't about to give it back. I take it out, clear it and clean it regularly but haven't had a reason to shoot it since then." As he pointed at his leg. He cleared it, double checked, and handed it to Jode. "Take a look?"

Jode held up his hands and shook his head no. He had no interest in it.

"No? Ok, thought you would have a weapon on board with thieves and pirates and shit."

"Look around, what would anyone steal? The boat? If you got nothin' there's nothin' to steal. Besides, I hate to say it but we operated on the edge of the law. Having a gun could change a night in the drunk tank and a warm meal in the morning to something a whole lot worse. That being said I did pick up a gun a couple months back," Jode added in his defense.

"Well I showed you mine. Why don't you show me yours?"

Jode just nodded and got up and rummaged through his hidey hole and brought up the to-go box.

Sarge was intrigued and somewhat amused. "You get that at the drive-thru? Let me take a look."

Jode handed him the box. Sarge carefully opened it, lifted out the rag wrapped package and carefully set it on his lap. First he spread out the rag, picked up the pistol, opened the cylinder and pushed the plunger to eject all the shells. Then he spun the cylinder, peered through the barrel and slapped it closed. Certain it was safe, he held it at arm's length and sighted at something in the distance. "Nice weapon. Ruger security six 357. I really like the sites on these. Got some serious stopping power too. Hell you pump off a round down below and it would be like a flash bang going off. Even if you miss, no one is going to be seeing or hearing anything for a while." He dug around in his rucksack and brought out a little plastic bottle of gun oil, put a drop on the trigger mechanism, hammer, cylinder and plunger, then ever so carefully caressed the pistol with the old rag. When he finished he cleaned each shell and loaded the gun being careful to wipe off every fingerprint. He wrapped it up and placed it back in the styrofoam box. "That is a fine pistol. If it was stainless it would be a perfect boat gun, but if you keep it oiled and never leave your salty fingerprints on it, it should be serviceable for life. How much did you pay for it, if you don't mind me asking?"

"Two bills, cash," Jode responded. No need to lie about it. He didn't know how much such a thing would cost anyway.

"Two-hundred!! That is a GREAT price dude! That thing must be hotter than a firecracker. I got to hear the story behind that and why all of a sudden did you buy a gun?"

Jode fidgeted in his chair, not sure how to respond or how much to tell. Sarge was looking at him with curiosity and anticipation. He had to say something. "Like I said I got it a couple months back. We were out in the boat doing what we usually do, fishing, diving for lobster to sell, cruising the islands around Key West when we came across something of value. There was no one around and no way to get it back to its rightful owner so we took it aboard. Thought we could sell it through a guy we knew that handled such things years ago when I lived in Marathon."

"You aren't talking about drugs are you?" Sarge asked accusingly.

"No, not saying we never ran pot up from the keys to Everglades City or fished for square grouper, hell everyone on Stock Island that owned a boat did a little of that from time to time. This wasn't one of those times. We took the boat up to Marathon and looked up my old fen . . . friend, Carlos. Back then, he was small time. I guess things went well for him cause he was big-time now. I asked around, then went to see him. He liked what we had and offered half what it was worth. Didn't have much choice so we took it. Thought everything was cool. We both walk away winners, but when he started to count out those C-notes I could see it in his eyes, he wasn't giving us the money, he was just loaning it to us. Got a chill just watching him. You're right about them notes. Don't know why, but they have a hold on folks that a whole pile of twenties can't compete with."

"Like I said he put the fear in us so the first stop was back to the bar. I needed a drink and knew the cook could help out with some protection, so to speak. A couple hours later he came back with that, all bagged up like a sandwich to go. I was right, not a week later we saw one of his goons snooping around Key West, going into the same bars we drank at. We high-tailed it back to the boat and left town in the middle of the night. Haven't been back since."

Sarge was at the edge of his seat, he hadn't expected a story like that. "Wow, that's quite a tale. Glad I wiped my fingerprints off that pistol. No telling what kind of trouble it might have caused. I recommend you keep that hidden and not take it out unless you plan to use it, and if you do, you might want to toss it afterward. They might trace that thing to some bad shit."

Jode looked surprised at that but got the message. He cracked open another PBR and handed one to Sarge then brought out the food and they ate in silence, except for Damn Bird who came over to collect his share.

The sun was down near the bridge and would be setting soon. Jode didn't want to be out in his little boat in the dark with no lights. Some go fast boat could run him down like nothing. He started packing things up when Sarge cleared his throat. "Hum, I got to ask. I noticed some things while I was below deck, the boat looked like it was meant for two. Two coffee cups, some stuff that doesn't look like yours, two beds with laundry piled on each and then you using us and we more than I and me. Who's we and why are they not here?"

Jode didn't know what to say. He just stared off into the distance, his hand reached for his talisman, sadness filled his eyes.

Sarge picked up on it all. He'd seen it too many times before. "Hey it's ok, no need to tell me. Maybe some other time."

Jode came back to the present, "Ya, I'd need something a lot stronger than beer to tell that story."

Sarge gave his shoulder a squeeze. "Well, story or not how about something stronger like margaritas, Monday at the Mexican place?"

"Ya, sounds good." With that they loaded into the dinghy and Jode dropped him off at Salty Sam's.

Chapter 11

Monday, Jode took the dinghy to town and walked down to the Mexican restaurant. He didn't see Sarge outside so he went in and looked over the bar for him. He was about to turn around when the hostess pointed to a small table in the back. "Looking for him?" Jode nodded, thanked the girl, and headed over to greet Sarge. He was sipping his margarita and had one waiting for Jode. "What if I hadn't shown up?"

"I knew you would, besides I think I could choke down another if I had to." They said their hellos and chatted for a couple of minutes until Jode was comfortable and started his story.

"Figured I might as well tell you what happened. No big secret. I guess you're my best friend now. Except for the bird." He smiled.

"Well at least I'm up there with a loud, obnoxious, freeloading bird. I guess that's something," he smiled.

Jode got on with it. "Grew up in the keys Stock Island outside of Key West, just a poor little fishing village back then. I hung around the boatyard and marina when I wasn't in school. That's where Tripper and I met. Nowadays, people think Tripper is about drugs and shit, but that wasn't it at all. When he was a kid he had some kind of problem, eyesight, incoordination or something, but he could trip over his own shadow. We all teased him about it, by junior high it had stuck. He and I hung out together. Collected soda bottles, fished for bait to sell to the bait shop and did about anything anyone asked us to do to earn a few bucks."

"We were about ten or twelve when we found an old wooden dinghy in the scrape pile. We were about to become boat owners! We were dragging it out of the trash when an old guy came up and gave us grief. "What you doing there? What ya think, you're gonna fix that up and sail the seven seas?" We told him that's exactly what we were gonna do and he couldn't stop us. He gave a hardy laugh at that. Then he got down to business telling us every little thing wrong with that boat. Look here at this rot, you'll need to clean all that out with a hammer and chisel. Then you'll need wood to replace it. Not just any wood, has to be proper boat wood like over there." He pointed to another pile of trash. Once he got going, he didn't stop. He went over that boat from stem to stern telling us how much needed to be fixed and how much work we would need to do, every damn detail. We just listened, getting madder by the minute. Finally he said, if we did all those things it might just float. Then he really ticked us off, said we were too dumb and too lazy to do the work. We gave him an earful even though he was an adult. We'd show him, yes siry. He just walked away laughing to himself. We didn't know it then but he just told us everything we needed to know to fix up that little boat and gave us the motivation to do it and do it we did!"

"We worked after school for about two weeks getting the rotted wood replaced. We scavenged the boards and bronze screws from the junk pile just like he told us. Finally, we were ready to do some fiberglass patches and paint, but that cost money we didn't have. A few days later, one of the men was patching up the superstructure on his boat with fiberglass so we went over to watch. He ignored us and talked to himself while he worked. He talked about every step as he did it. Gotta spread the resin on real thick, place the glass over it and make sure there are no bubbles. On and on he went. When he was about done, he stood up, stretched and complained about his back. "You there, you boys, I'm dog tired and heading over to the bait shop for a beer. I'll give you each a dollar if you cleanup this mess and put my tools away, but you better do a good job or you get nothing!"

We just nodded, too afraid to argue. Well, wouldn't you know it, all those scrapes and left over resin was exactly what we needed to finish our boat. Couple days after that, he was finishing up his job with caulking and paint and we got the same offer, except we each got a soda instead of cash."

"After we were finished we put that boat in the water, tied it off to the dock with an old line from the trash and just sat in it proud as could be. Then a miracle happened. The next day there was an old set of oars on the dump pile! We were in business. Soon we wanted a motor so we saved every penny we could all summer. We bought an old Evinrude ten horse and were free to travel anywhere we wanted. At first we stayed within a third of a gas tank from the marina like our folks told us. Then we scavenged up some plastic gallon oil jugs filled them with mixed gas and ventured further out. Before long, we were going all the way to Key West and fueling up at the marina there before heading back to Stock Island."

"After high school we worked around the boat yard and on the lobster and crabbing boats. Did a little lobstering on the side. More a back door kind of business cause we didn't have a license.

About twelve years ago we heard about Old Moe up in Bradenton. We could have it if we could get it running. Well Tripper was a lot like your buddy Greaser. He could get most anything fixed and running. Not necessarily by the book but it worked. Took us almost three weeks to get it ship shape and we headed back to the keys. Stopped here for a while on the way through." The waitress came by and they ordered another drink and some empanadas.

"Since then we lived on the boat, got odd jobs, caught lobsters and hustled tourists on Mallory Square." Jode was telling him about the various scams they ran when the food and drinks arrived so they got to work polishing off the tasty appetizers.

"Everything was going good until the run in with Big Carlos. Like I told you, we grabbed what we could carry and headed out. We spent a couple weeks in the islands between Key West and The Dry Tortugas until our food and beer got low. Then headed up here. That's when everything went down the crapper." He told Sarge about the boat almost sinking and when the hatch cover killed Tripper. He got a tear in his eye and his voice dropped to almost a whisper as he described rolling Tripper off the deck and into the sea.

Sarge reached across the table and put a comforting hand on his shoulder. "I know how you feel. No soldier left behind. But you did what you had to do. You had no other choice."

"I still have nightmares about it, not sure which is worse, those nightmares or the ones where I didn't bury him at sea and he was with me on the island. I don't know what I would have done then." Jode was tired of thinking about it and quickly summarized his wreck on Lulu Key, living off nothing and getting the boys to help him escape. "I bet they're still showing off those coins and telling pirate stories," he said in conclusion.

"Coins huh? Sarge asked.

Jode looked as if he had just gotten caught with his hand in the cookie jar and wondered if he had let the cat out of the bag. "Like I said those silver coins are all over Key West and not worth much. I had six and told the boys I would split the treasure with them so, I kept two and gave each of them two. You would have thought they were pure gold the way they looked at them."

They had a couple more margaritas, talked about nothing for a while and headed out. "Twofer Tuesday tomorrow?" Jode asked.

"You betcha," was the response and they both went their separate ways.

Sarge was waving and smiling as Jode approached the dinghy dock. "You still have that smile on your face. Enjoying that little motor?" Jode waved and his smile got even bigger as he nodded an emphatic yes, while he tied up his boat. A brief handshake and they headed up to the bar. When they got to the top of the stairs, Sarge hesitated and perused the bar. Then walked in and sat next to an older couple with an empty pizza rack in front of them. Jode just shook his head and smiled as he sat down next to him. Lila brought them each a draft, then leaned over towards Jode, "You owe me a story about a shipwreck Sailor."

"Why don't you come out to my boat and I'll give you the deluxe edition?" He teased.

"Sorry, I'm a kept women." She teased back with a devilish look.

"Now that's a story I'd like to hear."

She snapped him with the bar towel, gave a big grin and went back to serving the rest of the patrons.

They visited with the other customers and had several conversations going. Along the way they scored a couple of pieces of pizza each and a guy with a haircut like Sarge's bought them a round. Some people were standing around the bar waiting for a seat so with two beers each backed up, they thanked the gentleman for his hospitality and moved to a small table in the back overlooking the bay. After they got settled and the waitress brought them their first draft, Sarge asked. "Not that it's any of my business but now that Tripper is gone, what's next for you?"

"Well, we had plans to ditch Old Moe, get a car and drive to Texas or maybe even Mexico, but now I don't know. I didn't think about it much while I was stuck in the everglades. Just getting by used up all my creativity. I'm just kind of drifting. That's not always a bad thing." He added in his defense. "Sometimes drifting can be great. Sometimes when the seas were really calm, the doldrums the sailors call it, we would drift along the weed line near the Gulf Stream, the water butt ass calm, couldn't tell the water from the sky. A boat a mile or two away would look like it was floating in the heavens. That kind of drifting clears your head and mends the soul but most of the time drifting isn't good. Drifting in rough seas can be deadly. I know all too well, get catawampus to the swells and they can roll you right over. Next thing you know you're in a capsized boat heading for the bottom. Drifting near a jetty or reef can be just as dangerous. That sharp coral can rip the boat and you to shreds in seconds. I guess the drifting I'm doing now is like out there in the bay." He paused and thought awhile as he pointed out to the boats at anchor.

"That kind of drifting can be the most dangerous. It can get you before you even know you're in trouble. You're sitting there enjoying the peace and quiet, everything seems fine. You don't even notice you're moving slowly towards that sand bar out there. The tide comes in, pushes you up over the mud. You don't feel the keel settling into it. Before long, the tide goes out and you are stuck in one place for good. Kinda like that old sailboat on the bar near that mangrove island in the back." He shook his head and stared out over the water, "I'm getting to like it here and I worry that I might just be runnin aground. If I don't do something soon I might be stuck for good."

Sarge nodded like he understood. He started to speak when the waitress brought the second of their two for one drafts. He took his time to collect his thoughts before responding. "I feel the same way, without all the maritime metaphors of course. I always used the famous Alice in Wonderland quote when talking with my men. "If you don't know where you're going, any road will take you there," or something like that. I found, if left to their own devices, most folks will choose the easy road, but the easiest road is always downhill. You stay on that road too long and you either hit rock bottom or have a hell of a tough hike back up to the ridge, where you can see what direction you should be heading. I think I've been taking the easy road for too long now."

That left them both quiet and melancholy while they finished off their beers. Sarge broke the silence. "You're going to have to get along unsupervised for a few days. I got a gig the next couple of days. A guy I know got some new guns and wants to try them out. Asked me if I would go with him to the firing range to check them out and give him some shooting lessons, right up my alley of expertise. Should be sweet, I get to stay in his fancy house for a couple of days, he buys the drinks and feeds me good and I make a little money. All that for doing what I like to do the most. Blasting the crap out of stuff with a big rifle."

"Sounds good. When do we get together for drinks again?" Jode asked.

"Well that brings us to the weekend and it's getting pretty busy with the residents getting back from their summer travels. How about Margarita Monday?"

"Or we can meet on the boat Friday. I'm going to try my luck fishing. It's been long enough, I think fresh fish would taste good again."

"Sounds good, pick me up behind Topps Friday about 1700?"

"You got it."

Chapter 12

Jode saw Sarge heading for the dinghy dock as soon as he got off the trolley. If he wasn't mistaken it looked like he had a little skip in his step. "Judging by the smile on your face, I'd say you had a good time."

"What's not to like. We had a long drive out to the firing range so we stopped for an early lunch, blasted the crap out of the targets, must have fired 300 rounds at least, stopped for dinner and drinks on the way back. Most fun I've had since the army! I stayed at his place and we spent most of today cleaning the weapons and did an after action report over lunch and beers. Hope you had a productive time as well."

Jode had just finished stowing the few supplies he had picked up while on shore. "Also had a good time. Caught a few fish, nothing like the keys but good enough. Janice told me about a liquor store in the plaza just up the road, so I picked up a bottle of rum to celebrate."

"What brand?" Sarge asked.

"My favorite, On Sale." Jode joked.

"Mine too!" He agreed as he climbed in the boat. Jode handed him a cold beer, went through the usual routine to start the motor, grabbed a PBR for himself and they idled out the canal and over to Old Moe.

Once they were back on board and relaxing in the deck chairs under the bimini, Sarge told the story of his visit to the shooting range. He rattled off a list of rifles and pistols, few of which were familiar to Jode. "We started with the hand guns. He had a Glock 9, Smith and Wesson 29, pretty much the same as your Ruger, and a 45. I shot a few rounds through Bret as well just to stay sharp. Moved on to the rifles, HK-93, an AK-47 and my favorite an M-14. We were able to move the targets out to 300 yards. No problem with the 14, I still got the touch."

When Sarge had talked himself out, they grabbed another beer and Jode told fishing stories. "Like I said the fishing isn't as good here but I wasn't trying to fill a freezer. Caught a couple of keeper trout yesterday. They cooked up real nice. Caught one more and a snapper for dinner tonight. Most fun was the snook. Hooked a big lunker over by Dog Island. Fought it for almost an hour. Couldn't horse it in with the light tackle I was using, had to play 'em and ware 'em out. When I finally got her to the side of the boat, she was a beauty, must have been three feet long. I knew that was some good eating but even if I ate fish three times a day, half would spoil before I got to it. Just couldn't see any reason to do that. I took out the hook, held her in the current until she rested up, congratulated her on a fight well fought and let her get back to getting her own dinner."

To celebrate their good fortune, Jode opened the bottle of rum and poured two shots. They raised a toast to "Good times," knocked back the rum and chased it with another beer. Jode dug out the skillet and some veggies, fired up the little gas camp stove and began cooking dinner. As soon as he got going, Damn Bird showed up so he tossed him a couple of crackers to keep him busy and out of the way.

The fresh fish was excellent and they both had their fill. There was plenty to eat but not a scrap left on the plates. The sun had set and it was getting dark as they sat contentedly watching the harbor slowly empty of day boats and skiffs. "I know you don't like taking that thing out in the dark so I guess I should be heading out," Sarge said as he adjusted his pants and reached for his rucksack.

"No worries, I have a flashlight if I need it. Where you staying tonight?"

Sarge kinda shrugged, "There's plenty of spots. I have my favorites."

"Well if you got no plans and nowhere you have to be, why don't you just stay here? There's always been room enough for two. You can sleep in the V-berth. Besides, we still have beer left and that bottle of rum is still about full. Not a Four Seasons but the view is great." Jode held up another cold beer as an enticement.

"Well I have slept in worse places. No sand and no one shooting at me is a bonus. If you don't mind, sitting here under the stars having another drink sounds pretty damn good. Anything I got going can wait until tomorrow. Thanks," He said as he accepted the offered PBR. They mostly just sat, enjoyed a few more drinks and cherished the peaceful evening before going below to sleep.

Jode awoke to bright sunshine and a bit of a hangover. Rum shooters have more kick than the beer and watered down bar drinks he was used to. He hit the head, put on his shorts and headed up the steps to the back deck. The smell of coffee brewing got his undivided attention.

Sarge looked around, "Hope you don't mind. I scouted out the kitchen and found the coffee pot and grinds. A cup of coffee sounded good after that rum last night."

"That sounds like just what I need, Thanks. You'll make someone a wonderful wife someday." Sarge gave him a dirty look. "Ok, Ex-wife," Jode added with a devilish smirk. "How'd you sleep? Ever sleep on a boat before?"

"Unless you count a troop transport, no, first time. I thought those little waves slapping the bow would keep me awake, but the more I listened to them the less my mind was thinking of other shit. Next thing I knew, the sun was beating in that hatch at me."

Jode took the offered cup of coffee and settled into a deck chair. After thinking a while, he said, "Why don't you just stay here when you're not house sitting? I thought it was tight with Tripper and me but now by myself it feels big and empty. Between the two cabins, the bridge and deck, there's plenty of space to get away from each other if the need arises. We never had any problems. Hate to admit it but it gets kind of lonely out here in the anchorage. When you're in a boatyard or marina everyone is friends in no time. There is always a meeting place for sunset or happy hour, a spot under a tree where everyone brings a deck chair, wide area on the dock or just a picnic table. The anchorage is different. Everyone is spread out and other than a smile and wave there isn't much interaction. I might look for a marina, but there's nothing around here I can afford. Besides, that's like running aground; once you do that, you're staying and I'm not ready to make that decision."

Sarge thought a while before responding, "That's nice of you to offer. I don't have much but I get my disability every month so I can pitch in some. I guess we could give it a try until either or both of us decide what's next and if it doesn't work out, we go our separate ways, no harm, no foul."

He held out his hand to shake and Jode took it. "Well I guess we better go get your stuff and get you squared away in the V-berth." He said using Sarge's favorite admonishment.

"Got everything right here," He shot back, holding up his rucksack.

Jode gave him a sideways look. "If that's all you got then we need to go visit Shelly. I know you like your army clothes and they work like a charm in the bars but out here, you'll either die of heat stroke or if you fall over you'll drown trying to swim in all that fabric. Not trying to be the fashion police but you need some boat clothes."

Sarge slapped him on the back. "Ya, guess you're right. When in Rome and all that shit."

After coffee and a days-old muffin, Jode asked him if he fished. "Not much, the family would go to the lake most summers, either west to Lake Michigan or east to Huron. We would fish and play on the beach but I never caught much," Sarge admitted.

"Well, why don't we take the dinghy over to the grass flats and see if we can catch a couple of trout for dinner? The tides running, so it might be good fishing." Jode grabbed a couple of rods and artificial lures and they loaded into the little boat. Casting and retrieving was a lot more work than just drowning bait but it was all he had. They caught mostly trash fish, pinfish, puffer even a small flounder but Jode did manage to hook two keeper trout, not a record but they were big enough.

As the sun got higher in the sky, it was too hot to just sit and fish so they headed back to Old Moe. "I got a few bucks from my gig last week. If you want to head over to Bonita Bill's for a cold one I'm buying? A lot of fishermen hang out there, so you can regale them with your fishing prowess," Sarge joked.

"A beer sounds good. Let me fillet these whoppers and we can head over." As he was cleaning up after putting the fillets in the cooler, Damn Bird came over to play in the fresh water. To get him out of the way, Jode filled the top of the five gallon bucket with fresh water and let him have a bath. As the bird flopped and flung water everywhere, they loaded back in the dinghy and headed to the bar.

The place was crowded but Sarge was slapping backs and shaking hands in no time. He prodded Jode into telling stories about his ordeal on Lulu key. Everyone especially liked the pirate story that got the boys to help him escape. Minus any mention of the coins of course. When all was said and done they had bought a beer each and enjoyed another three due to the generosity of others. It was a great afternoon. Back at the boat, they fixed dinner then watched the sunset while enjoying another beer and a shot. As they were heading below deck for the night Sarge said, "I have some things to do in town tomorrow. You want to drop me off in the morning and pick me up late afternoon?"

"Nah, I have a list of things to do on the boat that I've been putting off for too long. You can just take the dinghy. It will take me most of the day anyway." Jode responded.

"I could help if you want to wait until Monday?" he offered.

"No offense but I don't think you would be much help. Now, Tripper or your buddy Greaser, we could probably talk them into doing it for us if we handed them a beer every now and then."

Sarge chuckled in agreement as they headed to their cabins.

After coffee the next morning Sarge went below deck. Jode could hear water running and some bumping around. When Sarge returned, he had on a clean uniform that if Jode didn't know better, he would have thought it just came off the ironing board. "You look sharp, got a big date?" he asked with a smile.

"Something like that. Oh, and I'll be doing a load of laundry if you have anything that needs it. I don't have a full load here." Jode said yes and went below to pick up his dirty clothes. He helped Sarge into the little boat and cast off the line.

Jode kept busy but was in no rush so he proceeded at a leisurely pace. He checked all the fluids in both engines, drained the water separators and topped up the water in the batteries. To insure everything was in working order, he started the engines and let them run. He relaxed with a cold PBR as they warmed up and charged the batteries. After a half hour he shut them down and waited until they cooled off before checking everything again. He did a reconnoiter of the bilge, checking the hoses, pumps and clamps to make sure everything was shipshape or as shipshape as possible with Old Moe. When he was satisfied everything was good to go, he started to climb out of the bilge then stopped and lifted a floorboard abeam of the starboard engine. He was once again awestruck at the sight of the treasure. He hadn't laid eyes on it for over a month. There were small gold bars and big silver ones. Canvas bags held the coins, one of gold and another of silver. The jewelry was in a plastic box. In the back was a pile of gold chains. He had heard that the rich passengers wore as much gold and jewelry as they could carry to avoid the cost of stowage and the taxes levied for importing the riches into Spain. He picked up a chain and fondled it lovingly as he thought of all the plans and schemes he and Tripper had dreamed about only a couple of months ago. He heard the little motor and just a minute later, felt the boat move as Sarge climbed aboard.

"Honey I'm home." He called out with a laugh. "Can I get you a beer or are you still working?"

Jode put down the chain and reached for the old floorboard. He hesitated before deciding it was time to share the truth with Sarge. He trusted him and if he was going to stay on the boat, he should know the risk. Just then Sarge stepped down the companion way, holding out the cold can of beer. He froze when he saw the treasure, then looked up at Jode and back to the stash. He didn't know what to say.

"You gonna give me that beer or just stand there with your mouth hanging open?"

Sarge snapped out of his trance and stabbed the beer into Jode's hand. "What the hell dude! You're rich!"

"Not so sure I'd say that. Like those farmers where you grew up would say, 'Land rich and dirt poor', or in this case, I'm treasure rich and cash poor. Can't buy a new car or boat with this. Hell, can't even buy a beer!"

"You're half right, definitely can't buy a beer but I'd bet there are a lot of folks that would trade a used car or boat for a couple of those gold bars." Sarge stood there mesmerized. If C-notes got people's attention gold was like seeing the angels in heaven. "You must have thousands, hell, hundreds of thousands of dollars' worth of treasure there. That explains a lot of the holes in your stories. I thought something was up but would never have guessed that." He exclaimed pointing.

Jode casually replaced the floorboard and everything looked as dirty and worthless as before. Sarge turned to go back up on deck before Jode held up a finger. When he again had Sarge's attention, he reached over the port engine and lifted up the corresponding board. There lay a mirror image of what he had just seen, except there was no plastic box of gemstones. Jode took a big pull on the beer, covered up his hidey hole, climbed out of the bilge and shut the hatches. Sarge just watched in stunned silence.

They grabbed another beer and sat in silence for a long time, both processing what just happened. Finally, Sarge spoke,

"So, you want to tell me the back story of where all that loot came from? If you don't that's ok too."

Jode took another swig of beer, poured himself a shot, leaned his head back and thought about it. "Well, it all started when Tripper and I were catching summer crabs out in the Marquesas, that's what we call out of season lobster. . . . " He told the story of finding that first gold coin and how he and Tripper used up every last breath in their scuba tanks searching for more. He had already told him about Big Carlos but added more detail about the gold and his story of a 'friend' who worked for Mel Fisher. Sarge asked a few questions along the way but generally just sat and listened. Jode skimmed over Tripper's death and from there on, he had pretty much told his story before.

"With all that time in Key West between trips to find the treasure, you must have made a lot of plans. Even more after finding so much. What did you have in mind and now what are you going to do with Tripper gone? Seems to me, with him gone and the shipwreck and all, those plans must have gone down the crapper." Sarge asked with genuine concern. Jode just shrugged, he wasn't sure how to answer the question and wondered how much sense their plans even made now.

After they had some dinner they headed up to the bridge to watch the sunset. As the sun passed under the bridge Jode broke the silence. "We figured we'd buy a used car here, then drive up to Port Charlotte and sell some to a shady pawnbroker jewelry guy we heard of. That would give us enough cash to head over to Texas and maybe even Mexico, selling small amounts as we went. Maybe be rich enough by the time we get there to live the good life. Our run-in with Carlos went sideways, way worse than we thought. I'm not sure how often I want to do that. He didn't buy the friend in need story for a minute so I expect the guy in Port Charlotte won't either. Besides with all the delays and what I've had to spend just getting by, I don't think I have enough to even get started."

Sarge thought about it, "Well, you still have some cash?" Jode nodded yes. "And I have a little and I get another check on the first so you don't need to do anything right away. Why don't we give it a little time and see if we can come up with a plan. In the meantime, I know a few guys that would like one of those gold coins. I could use the friend story. It wouldn't be enough money to raise any eyebrows, just a few hundred dollars here and there. Besides, I know these guys. They aren't mobsters or anything, just old guys with a few bucks who would like something different that comes with a story they can tell at the bar. Probably make a necklace out of them, kinda Jimmy Buffet style. Might pick up enough dough for a grub stake, to get things started. What ya think?"

Jode thought about it. "Sounds good. What's your take?"

"Wasn't thinking about a cut," Sarge shot back, a little offended by the remark.

"Hey, no offense, I just thought if you're doing the work, you should get a share of the rewards. How about 20 percent?"

"I'd do it for nothing but it's up to you, ok?"

Jode held out his hand to shake on it. "Well it will buy us some time to come up with a plan and keep us in beer in the meantime."

The next morning they discussed their situation but didn't make any decisions. Sarge said he wanted to stop by the Beach Library and do a little research on the Atocha. If he was going to get top dollar for the coins he needed a good story to go with it. He also planned to talk to a couple of friends he thought might be interested before actually carrying any gold into town. Jode would drop him off behind the grocery store and they would meet later for Margarita Monday. As he was getting out at the dock, Jode told him, "Might want to go see Shelly and see if she has any proper yachting outfits. Those desert fatigues aren't cutting it out on the water." They laughed at the juxtaposition as Sarge stood at attention and saluted, "Aye, Aye, Captain!"

Jode went to the store to pick up ice and a few miscellaneous items and to say hello to Janice. After dropping off the items at the boat, he headed over to the salvage yard behind the shrimp boats on San Carlos Island. He brought a six pack of beer and some cash and hoped to find another anchor for Old Moe. They might have one he could pick up for scrap value.

A few beers and $50 got him a rusty old anchor, chain and rode from a scrapped fishing boat much larger than Old Moe. He guessed that the workers he gave the money to had no intention of turning the cash over to the boss but that was no concern of his. Back on the boat he swapped out the bigger anchor for the spare he mounted in the ten thousand islands and stowed the smaller backup below deck where it belonged. He had worked up quite a sweat so he got cleaned up before heading into town to meet Sarge. He also loaded up his collapsible 5-gallon water bag. If he filled it up on every trip, he should have enough water on board to avoid a special trip to the fuel docks or spending a day going back and forth to the dinghy dock.

When he got to the Mexican restaurant, Sarge was at his usual spot at the bar. As soon as Jode sat down, the bartender slid over an ice-cold margarita on the rocks with salt. He was starting to feel like a regular.

They talked about nothing and visited with the other patrons at the bar. As usual, someone bought them a round. "And a round for the military brats at the bar." He heard an old guy with short hair yell over the din of the crowd. With big smiles they raised their glasses in thanks to the generous old coot. Yes, Jode was getting to like living on the Beach.

After a few too many two dollar margaritas and a slew of empanadas, they decided to amble back down to the dinghy dock and head to the boat while it was still daylight. Sarge grunted as he hefted his overstuffed rucksack over his shoulder. "Looks like Shelly sold you the whole damn store. Are we in for a fashion show tonight?" Jode laughed as he jabbed Sarge in the ribs.

"Not all clothes. I also got a few books from the library, been reading up on that Atocha find of your buddy Mel Fisher, got some ideas that will help me raise a little cash here and maybe make your little trip to Port Charlotte more profitable," Sarge told him as they were leaving to dock. They were both tired from a busy day and too long at the bar, so by mutual agreement, the fashion show and plans for the treasure would wait until tomorrow.

Chapter 13

They were both moving a little slow the next morning, no doubt an after effect of the margaritas. Sitting on the back deck drinking coffee, Sarge pulled out one of the books and was paging through it when Jode asked him what he was reading. "Quite a story about Mel Fisher and the Atocha. Looks like there was a whole flotilla of Spanish ships that left Cuba in 1622. Most were sunk by a hurricane that summer. Says here that there were other galleons that carried as much gold as the Atocha. One was named the Santa Margarita! Be funny if the gold you found was from that one. It goes on about how Mel found another shipwreck years before on the east coast that made him famous or at least gave him enough notoriety to raise money from investors to search for the Atocha. Most folks thought it was just a scam but he found enough stuff along the way to keep them interested. Took about 16 years before he found the Mother Lode, then spent another 8 years in court before he and his investors got to keep what they had found."

"In the book, they have a lot of pictures of the treasure, his boats and the divers that worked for him. Even some from when they brought it into Key West. Here's one of him standing by the docks with a huge gold chain draped over his shoulders." Sarge leaned over and showed Jode the pictures. He took the book and leafed through it briefly. Sarge stifled a grin as he lit the fuse that would set Jode off on a tangent, "Didn't you say you were there The Day they brought in the treasure?" That was all it took. A volcano with a modest amount of facts and a whole lot of youthful imagination was about to erupt.

"You bet I was there, me and Tripper both and I'll tell ya all about it. . . . and it is the Gods Honest truth!" Jode was fully recovered from his hangover and ready to go. Sarge just grinned some more, picked up his coffee, leaned back and got comfortable. Anytime a story begins with "the Gods honest truth," you know it's going to be a whopper and the truth will be the first casualty.

"We were, that would be Tripper and I, out at Malory Square looking to the southwest. We heard something was up and wanted to be the first to see it and we were. In the distance you could see a column of black smoke heading our way. Couldn't make out the boat from that far off but we knew what was coming!

We ran as fast as we could down to the Galleon Marina and out on the docks all the way out to the T-dock. We were waiting as it rounded the breakwater into the Bight. You should have seen it! It was so loaded down with treasure that the wake of a ballyhoo would swamp it, and smoking? Those old diesels were working so hard to push the load through the water that the whole harbor was covered in thick black smoke in no time. Could barely breath and the sulfur burnt our eyes." Finally, Jode stopped to take a breath and a quick gulp of coffee and he was off again.

"They pulled up to the dock near Elizabeth Street and started to unload the loot. There was an army of cops and the row of armored cars stretched all the way to Duval. They lifted crate after crate of gold and silver coins up onto the dock. Another row of men hauled it to the waiting armored cars trip after trip. Soon the place was packed with spectators and news crews. Not just the local TV but from all over, each pushing and shoving to be in front. Then it turned into a pandemonium, that's when Mel stepped up in front of the crowed. He had so many chains on him he could hardly move. When he held up that golden cross, well, you'd thought he was the messiah." Jode was on a roll. "They kept unloading most of the day. There was a stack of huge silver bars that was as high as your head. Must have been using it for ballast. No way could a ship hold all that weight any other way!" He stopped to inhale.

"Says in here that the whole town was celebrating," Sarge said to egg him on even more.

"Celebrate!! Hell, the town went wild! Me and Tripper were just teenagers then but I tell you the beer ran like water. Every bar in town was celebrating a payday and what they weren't giving away for free was paid for by customer after customer buying a round for the bar! Like I said we weren't of drinking age but we still enjoyed a beer as much as the next fella. That day there was no asking for I.D. or how old you were. If you were tall enough to reach the bar you could just help yourself and help ourselves we did. I'll never forget "The Day", still remember it like it was yesterday!"

Sarge just chuckled, he might remember it like yesterday, but not like it was written in any books he had read at the library. He envied Jode having such a happy memory from his youth.

Jode had pretty much talked himself out so they went back to looking at the books and planning what to do with the rest of the day. Sarge wanted to look over the treasure and compare the coins and gold bars to pictures in the books then head back to the library to work on a plan that was growing in the back of his mind. Before they closed up the hidey hole in the bilge, Sarge asked if he could take one of the coins into town. He had an idea who might want to buy it. He figured he could use Jode's 'I got a friend' story to move a coin or two.

Jode dropped him off behind Topps like yesterday and they agreed to meet at Petey's for Twofer Tuesday at 1600 hours.

Jode was filling up his water bag when Sarge showed up. "How'd your day go? Learn anything new at the library? Or that other thing?" Sarge just shrugged and said they'd talk later as they headed up to the bar. They took their usual spot at the bar and also as usual they scored some left over pizza and a couple rounds of free beers along with the ones they bought.

After returning to Old Moe they each grabbed another beer, Jode tossed a few crackers to Damn Bird and they retired to the bridge to watch the sun set. Soon, Sarge fished in his pocket and brought out some bills. He fanned them out and waved them under Jode's nose. "Whoa! Where'd that come from?" was his first reaction.

Sarge grinned, pulled out a C-note put it back in his pocket and handed the rest to Jode. He thumbed through them and counted $700, not including the one Sarge kept. "I think you have this all wrong. You've been looking at the value of all that gold and silver but the real value is in the coins themselves!"

"What do you mean?" Jode asked.

"One of those gold coins weighs what? An ounce? At today's price, that's about $600 and you would be lucky to get half that, but as a historic coin, it could be a couple grand! Now I'm not saying we can get that kind of money; there's no documentation or anything but they have to be worth more than $600. I got $800 for that one and he thought that was a great deal and offered to talk to a couple of his buddies that might be interested. Now we can't sell much without raising suspicions but we might pocket a few thousand, no problem."

He had Jode's undivided attention. He reached in his rucksack and took out a couple of photocopies on plain paper and handed them to Jode. "What the hell is this?" Jode asked as he looked them over, not having any idea what they had to do with the treasure.

"That my friend is a photocopy of your mother's obituary."

"What the hell are you talking about? This says Mildred Collins. Who the hell is she? The name isn't even right! You're bat shit crazy dude!" He exclaimed, shaking his head in disbelief.

Sarge had a big shit eating grin on his face now, he was having way too much fun with this. "Well, Jake, your mom just passed away two weeks ago and you're down here from Indiana to clean out her house and close out the estate." Jode's face was all contorted and had no idea what Sarge was talking about. "You see, your dad, who preceded Mildred in death," he pointed at the obituary, "invested a small sum with Mel Fisher when they vacationed in Key West in the early eighties. Wouldn't you know, he was one of the investors who shared in the Atocha discovery. Took over eight years to settle all the legal fights and when that was done, he elected to receive his small portion in treasure instead of cash. He invested $2,500 and got back over $15,000 of treasure that is now worth upwards of 40-50K!"

"OoooKaaay, I still don't get it," Jode confessed.

"The short answer is you were going to sell some of the gold to that pawn broker, jewelry guy in Port Charlotte. You know the 'I got a friend' bullshit didn't work. So, this is the new shtick. You pretend to be Jake Collins. Mildred lived in Punta Gorda Isles so it makes sense that you would choose a local place to get rid of her stuff. We pick out some gold and silver coins that look like the ones from the Atocha. Maybe some gold chain, a gemstone or two to come up with $40,000 worth in today's value. You go in there and let him talk you down to half price plus or minus and you walk out of there loaded."

Jode thought about it. His head was hurting. He got up grabbed two more beers and the bottle of rum. He took a shot handed the bottle to Sarge and had a swig of beer. "Sounds awful complicated. Can't it just be my gold that I got from Mel?"

Sarge shook his head no, "Won't work, you're too young. No way could you have gotten any of the Atocha gold. Even this Jake guy is a few years older than you but I don't think that is a problem. I can get more information on the treasure, Salvors Inc. and this Collins lady and we can put together a story and a plan. We go up to Port Charlotte, do the deal and haul ass. In the meantime I'll sell a few things to my buddy's friends to get us going then we head out to Port Charlotte. Whatcha say?"

"Fooof, you laid a lot on me. Does sound better than what I tried. If it still sounds good in the morning and you can get all that information you're talking about, I guess I'm in." Jode reached for the bottle of rum, poured some in each of the plastic cups, handed one to Sarge and they toasted to Mildred and Jake Collins.

The next day was much the same. Jode dropped Sarge off behind the grocery store. He cut through the ball fields behind the school over to the library to do whatever it was he was doing, then headed out to pedal a few more coins. Jode was in charge of stocking up the boat. They didn't plan to be out that long but after last time, Jode wasn't taking any chances. There would be plenty of beer, rum and food on board. His frequent trips to Topps even piqued Janice's curiosity, "Why all the groceries all of a sudden?"

Jode told her that he and Sarge were heading up to Boca Grande to fish and might anchor in Pelican Bay for a few days. He couldn't say he minded seeing Janice every day and that she took an interest into his comings and goings. He didn't make any special trips for fresh water. He would fill the tank when he bought fuel on their way out of the harbor.

In the afternoon they would meet at one of the local bars for happy hour. Like in the keys, even though they had more money in their pockets, they weren't going to change their routine or throw money around. When they returned to Old Moe for cheaper drinks and to watch the sunset, Sarge would bring Jode up to speed on what he learned and any sales he made. The cash was adding up pretty fast at $900 for a gold coin and $50 for silver 'pieces of eight.' One guy wanted a short piece of chain to make a bracelet. Sarge could almost hear the stories the old guys would be telling at the bar while wearing the gold around their necks but for the real payday, they needed to get "Jake's" story fleshed out.

There was no need to know everything about Mildred or Jake, mostly what was in the obituary, local address and dates of death for Mildred and her husband. The type of things the pawn guy might check out or questions he might ask while making small talk while he looked over the treasure. To get the maximum price for the items, they needed much more information about the Atocha and Mel Fisher. Sarge found out real quick that the old guys buying the coins, or in one case a short piece of chain, asked a lot of questions. He kept the lady at the library busy making photocopies. He wanted a picture of everything they had that matched what Mel had found. None if it came from the Atocha but it was obviously from the same time period. Having pictures and in some cases, even prices made it look more authentic and legit.

He had started a notepad with dates and facts. He even roughed out some short stories for Jode to use if he had to: where you from, how long was your mom in Punta Gorda, it was like playing what's your favorite color with a little school girl. They would play over a couple of beers but it soon became too boring but with what was at stake, they put the time in, by Thursday afternoon they had had enough. It was time to put their plan in motion. Luckily that required a trip to the bar for happy hour.

Sarge went through his usual reconnoiter of the bar before sitting down, but this time he chose an old guy with his mobile phone laying on the bar in front of him. They ordered beers and after Lila set them down, they began visiting with their neighbors. Just before their glasses were empty, Sarge asked the old guy next to him if he could borrow his phone. "Don't know? Can I trust ya?"

Lila was watching and piped in, "I'd trust him with my life, or at least a couple of hours or three," she added with a lecherous smile on her face. Sarge's ears began to redden as he accepted the offered mobile phone. "It's not like he's gonna run away with it," she added with a wink and a smile.

Sarge got redder by the second. "You just had to go there, didn't you?" Lila just struck a sexy pose with one hip hiked up and both hands turned up out at her sides.

Jode pushed Sarge towards the stairs, while barely choking down a laugh. They walked behind the motel to a table and chairs away from any other guests. Sarge handed the phone to Jode along with a slip of paper with the number on it.

He dialed and waited, "Hello this is Jake Collins, I'm in town to close out my mother's affairs and I have a few items you might be interested in." . . . . . "I appreciate that, it was kind of sudden," . . . . "Well it is quite a story if you have time?" . . . . "Back in the early 80s, my folks were in Key West and my dad got talked into investing with that Mel Fisher guy, Salvors Inc. I think was the company name. My Mom was furious. But when they hit the Mother Lode, my dad couldn't have been happier. Took another eight years before he got his payout. He took a small portion of the treasure instead of cash. No taxes that way. Until he sold it, but he never sold it. He carried one of those gold coins in his pocket every damn day, until the day he died. Anytime my mom gave him any grief about some dumb decision he made, he'd just take out that coin and wave it in the air. They would both bust out laughing. That treasure gave them more pleasure than ten times the money would have!" . . . . "Well I'm keeping that coin, that's for sure, but there were a lot of medical bills with my mom. They were never really well off so I was thinking it would be best to change the rest of the treasure into cash and not tell the lawyer or the government." . . . . . "I guess you do see that a lot." . . . . "Well as best I can figure it was worth about $15,000 when they got it. It must be worth three or four times that now." . . . . . "9 gold coins, not counting the one I'm keeping, almost 3 feet of that heavy gold chain, a small gold bar, a bunch of silver coins, I think they call 'em pieces of eight, and a emerald that is about the size of a nickel." . . . . "No, haven't found the paperwork. I know he had it cause I've seen it but who knows where he put it" . . . "Ya, I'll keep looking but when he put something in a safe place he usually hid it so good even he couldn't find it." . . . "Old folks, go figure." . . . . "Ya, I know we aren't talking retail." . . . "Well my daddy used to say, 'Half of something is way better than all of nothing." Sarge gave him a look with one eyebrow raised. Jode just smiled. "Well, I got a lot going on. You know Salvation Army is coming for the furniture and all, how about Tuesday around 2:30, 3:00 o'clock?" . . . "Ok, I'll see you then. Thanks." He pressed off and handed the phone back to Sarge.

Sarge let out his breath. It was like he was holding it the whole time, slapped Jode on the back and congratulated him on a job well done. They headed back up to the bar to return the phone.

"Well Lila, you were right, they didn't run off with my phone. I barely use the damn thing. At least, the phone company will know I'm still alive. Not that they'd care or stop billing me! Give lover boy and his side kick a beer on me!" The old guy said as he put his hand on Sarge's shoulder and gave it a shake.

Sarge started to turn red again, but that was just the start of it. Lila took a cold mug out of the cooler, held it up to her mouth, and put a big lipstick kiss on the side, filled it with beer and slapped it down in front of Sarge. The bar went crazy hooting and hollering, Sarge was getting redder by the second. Well, that set the stage for the evening. Every time Sarge finished a beer someone would buy them both another round and Lila would deliver it in the same sexy fashion. She lamented that the dish washer was probably going to kill her. Happy hour was long gone by the time they got up to leave, but the show wasn't over. Lila sauntered over to Sarge, grabbed him by the chin, turned his head and planted a big lipstick kiss on his cheek. She must have rearmed because it was thick and red! Everyone at the bar went nuts, hooting and hollering, cat calls and wolf whistles. Sarge turned so red, Jode had to push him towards the stairs before he had a stroke or someone called 911. The laughter was deafening.

"Sarge has a girlfriend!" Jode teased like they were in grade school.

"Shut up or I'll shoot you myself," Sarge barked.

"Hey, at least we got to use the phone, had way too many free beers and I've never seen Lila's tip jar so full. I call that a win, win, win." Sarge just gave him a dirty look and plopped into the dink.

Chapter 14

It was a slow start to the morning. The plan was now put in motion and while the list of things left to do wasn't long, it was important. They would leave Ft. Myers Beach on Sunday, cruise to Pelican Bay near Boca Grande, stay two nights, then head up Charlotte Harbor to Port Charlotte on Tuesday. This gave them an extra day in case something didn't go as planned. After coffee and a light breakfast, they loaded into the dink and headed to the dinghy dock behind the grocery store. Jode let off Sarge. He was meeting with one more guy who was interested in a coin after he stopped at the library, made some more photocopies and returned the books he borrowed. Jode bid him farewell, "If I get done before you, I'm stopping at the Yucatan for beers. Otherwise I'll meet you at the dinghy dock by the bridge about four."

"If you find a decent canvas bag, get two," Sarge responded.

Jode returned to Old Moe to make preparations for the voyage. After lunch he headed over to the dinghy dock under the bridge and walked up town to thc Island Hardware. IIe had a list of items he needed, to make some minor repairs and was looking for a small tool bag that he could use to carry the gold and coins over to the pawn shop. They had everything he needed and it was a lot cheaper than going to a marine supply store. He loaded the stuff into one of the tool bags and headed over to the Yucatan for beers. What's the use having money in your pocket if you can't enjoy it? Soon Sarge showed up and they compared notes and finished off another round. As they were leaving, Sarge said, "We need one more thing, some of that tissue wrapping paper to wrap up the items you're bringing to the pawn shop."

"What do we need that for?"

"It will make them seem more valuable. Besides your mom would have them wrapped up nice and pretty since they were so important to her and your dad." Sarge explained.

"My mom?"

"Ya, Mildred. I think I can get some at that little tchotchke place across the street."

"Do they sell that?" Jode asked.

"No but I'm sure they have some."

"You going to steal it?"

Sarge looked at him like he was insane. "NOooo, they will just give it to me." With that, he entered the store while Jode stood outside and watched. There was a pretty young lady behind the register; she smiled as he walked up. Sarge was smiling as he spoke with her for a few minutes. She reached under the counter, pulled out some tissue wrapping paper, folded it carefully and placed it in a plastic bag. As she handed it to Sarge, she was smiling and they stood there a few moments too long, each holding an end of the little package. Her left hand gently touched Sarge's arm as she left the bag in his hand. He started for the door, turned and said something. The girl smiled and her cheeks reddened just a hint.

"What was that all about," Jode asked.

"Oh, nothing. I told you everybody loves me!" He said with a grin. "Stick with me kid and you too can be a lady's man."

Jode's eye brows lifted, "You think so?"

"Well anything is possible but it would take A Lot of work!" He responded while patting Jode on the back.

"Thanks a lot!"

They headed down to the dinghy dock and got in the little boat. Once under way, they decided to head over to Bonita Bill's for a few more beers. It could be their last hurrah for several days.

Jode took Saturday to finish up his repairs and stow everything away. He didn't expect any bad weather but the Intracoastal can get pretty rough with all the boat traffic and most boaters don't give a damn about their wake. Sarge asked for two more gold coins. "There is something else we need that I want to pick up before we head out. I'll be back late afternoon."

Jode had a questioning look on his face, "Must be something valuable?"

"Not valuable but important," Sarge said as he took the coins. He grabbed one of the tool bags, hopped into the dinghy and headed to shore.

Jode was relaxing with a beer on the bridge when he heard Sarge returning in the dinghy. He climbed down to the aft deck to help him back aboard. First, Sarge handed him the tool bag that was much heavier than when he left and then a package about four feet long wrapped up with an old piece of tarp and duct tape. "Don't know what you spent all the money on but it is heavy, that's for sure."

"Bring it down below and I'll show you." They went below and after Sarge opened a beer and handed a refill to Jode, he unwrapped the package. As he cut away the tape Jode could see a big rifle. It looked kind of rough and military. With questions written all over his face he didn't need to ask, Sarge started giving him the low down.

"M-14, we used these in the sandbox. It is an old design but perfect for open spaces and long distances. Was the main infantry weapon until Vietnam. Too big and unwieldy for the jungle so they brought out the little plastic M-16 but in the desert, it was perfect." He took a box of shells out of the tool bag. They were almost three inches long. "These babies here are dead on at 500 yards. Sandman was good way past 1000 yards with his M-25. Pretty much the same rifle with optics and a bipod to steady it. Figured if we were carting around all this gold, we needed more than those little pea shooters," as he gestured towards his rucksack, "This thing will go right through a fiberglass boat. Hell I could sink any boat out here. Aim for the waterline, small hole where it goes in, big hole where it comes out the other side."

"Really think we need that?" Jode asked.

"God, I hope not but if someone gives us any problems, this should make them think twice. Maybe go bother someone else. Better safe than sorry. I also got a couple boxes of ammo for my

M-9 and one for your 357. Can't hold off an army but like I said, they'll think twice."

Jode was fixated by the hefty rifle. "Can it really shoot that far?"

"This is the one I was shooting at the range the other day. It's all sighted in for 300 yards. Hit a beer can no problem. Any further than that I might have to adjust the sights." He pointed to the adjustment knobs on the rear sight. "Biggest issue is seeing what you're aiming for. That's why the sniper version has that big scope on it. I figure if we can't see them they're no threat to us anyway." With the lesson over, he wrapped the weapon back up and stowed it in the hang-up locker.

Sunday was the day to shove off. Sarge wanted to hear the sermon at church so Jode brought him over to the dinghy dock at Tropical Shores canal. While he was at the service Jode made one last trip to Topps. They would only be gone four or five days but it would be nice to have fresh food and not have to rely on canned goods. With the engines running several hours every day except Monday they could run the refrigerator and not worry about killing the batteries. To be on the safe side Jode picked up two bags of ice, one would go in the freezer just in case and the other in the cooler with the beers and ice water. No need to open the fridge every time they wanted a PBR.

Back on the boat, Jode hoisted the anchor as Sarge worked the controls. Once Jode was back at the helm, he guided Old Moe over to the fuel docks the shrimp boats used, purchased $300 worth of diesel and filled the fresh water tank. The deckhand helped him shove off and they made the slow trip up to Boca Grande.

Other than trying to avoid the go-fast boats and their wakes it was a relaxing and uneventful trip. Dolphin played in the wake at several spots and there were plenty of birds atop the channel markers. Damn Bird would squawk every time they passed an osprey but didn't seem to bother with the other birds. They entered Pelican Bay slowly to avoid the shoals and found a quiet spot away from the other boats to drop the hook. Sarge seemed particularly interested in all the wild life, dolphin and pelicans fishing for dinner, osprey and an eagle overhead, and a sea gull standing watch behind the boat waiting for snacks. Cold beers were consumed and after a leisurely dinner they watched the sunset over the island.

Everything had gone smoothly so there were no plans for Monday. After breakfast they got in the dinghy and went exploring. While the water and mangroves were different than in the keys, much of the wildlife was the same. Jode was in his element and enjoyed showing Sarge his domain. They spent almost three hours poking through the little mangrove creeks and toured several of the bays and coves. One cove was full of big manatees.

There must have been at least a dozen. Several had scars from boat props but they seemed healthy and happy despite of it. After a late lunch they hung out on the boat and enjoyed the peace and tranquility. Sarge was dozing under the bimini while Jode tried his luck fishing. They both appeared to be relaxed and content, but in fact, there was a lot of tension and apprehension just below the surface. Tomorrow was the day of the big score.

Jode had a fitful night but finally fell asleep after midnight. As the sun came thru the hatch, he struggled awake and headed up to the salon. He was met by the smell of coffee and Sarge sitting at the dinette cleaning his guns. "Really think that's necessary?"

"Well good morning to you too. No, not necessary and not even needed. I just cleaned them two weeks ago after going shooting. Had trouble sleeping and decided to do it. Used to happen all the time before a patrol and cleaning my weapons helped me to relax. Cup of coffee?"

Jode nodded yes, got the coffee and sat down across the dinette. He watched as Sarge carefully wiped off each bullet before loading it into the clip. He then put the clip in the pistol, racked a bullet, removed the clip and added another bullet. He went through the same process with the M-14. "Where did you get that?" Jode asked pointing at the long rod with a small handle.

"Oh, that's the cleaning kit that comes with the rifle." He responded while showing Jode the metal cover on the butt of the stock while he stowed it back inside. When he was through, he carefully placed the rifle back in the hanging locker. Jode noticed that he hadn't wrapped it back up.

Sarge poured himself another cup of coffee and gave Jode a refill. "Decided what you're wearing today?"

"Ya, I guess I'll wear those dress-up clothes the old lady talked me into at the thrift store. Not very comfortable but can't go in flip flops."

Sarge agreed, "It does make you look older and it is more like something a guy from Indiana would wear. You go in your regular clothes and you'd look like a beach bum. No offense."

"None taken," Jode said as he got up. "I guess we ought to get going. It's three hours up the harbor and under the bridge. Figure we'll anchor on the north side of the river. It's pretty well protected if we decide to stay overnight. I can take the dinghy back under the bridge and to that canal we saw on the street map you printed off at the library. Take another half hour to get up to the bar on the main drag then it's just a short walk over to the pawn broker. All and all we got four hours of travel plus time for me to get all prettied up. Guess we should get moving."

They pulled up the anchor and got underway. It was a smooth trip up to Port Charlotte but neither man relaxed enough to enjoy it.

After dropping the hook, Jode showered and put on his 'wedding and funeral' outfit. He hoped neither would happen today. As expected, Sarge gave him a thorough inspection before he climbed into the dinghy and headed west under the bridge. He stayed as close to shore as he could without running aground to save time and avoid any boat wakes. It would be hard to explain showing up soaking wet. He passed a little marina before spotting the canal. At an idle, it took almost 15 minutes to reach the dock behind an old bar that faced US 41. He tied off the dink, grabbed his canvas tool bag and headed in the back door and sat at the bar. He didn't want to look too suspicious so he ordered a draft. There were a few other customers, probably regulars, this early in the afternoon. He asked the bartender if he could leave the boat at the dock for a while. After getting an affirmative response he finished his beer, gave the man a five, said keep the change and headed out the front door to his appointment.

Jode carried the tool bag and his jacket across the road and over to the pawn shop. He stopped to put on his jacket, got himself straightened up and walked into the business. At the counter was a small man about six inches shorter than Jode, but then again Jode was tall. He wore a flowered collared shirt, shorts and sandals. Seeing his casual attire Jode removed his jacket and set it down on the next stool as he reached out his hand in greeting. "Hi, I'm Jake Collins. We spoke on the phone." Wes introduced himself and the two men shook hands. Without further delay, Jode set the bag on the counter and the pawn broker began inspecting the contents. He lifted out each item, placed it on a small scale, then inspected it closely through one of those jeweler loop glasses. He mumbled and shook his head while evaluating every coin. He had a disinterested look on his face. After a while he started to speak.

"These coins aren't in the best of condition." "Did you find any documentation? Not worth much without that." "Could be stolen," and on it went. Every time Jode tried to make a positive comment or observation it was dismissed as unimportant or unreliable.

"You could make jewelry out of the coins." "That emerald would make a great neckless." "People would come in here just to see Atocha treasures."

Wes continued to ignore the suggestions. "Just what I need, a bunch of looky-loos coming in here and not spending a dime. Worse, they would probably steal something on the way out. . . . Tell ya what, I'll give you ten thousand for the whole lot."

"Ten Thousand? According to what I've read it's worth $50K at least. I'm looking for at least twenty-five large. That should leave you a whole lot of profit," Jode protested, to no avail.

Just then they were interrupted by a door opening in the back. Wes excused himself and headed to the rear of the building. Jode could barely hear a hushed conversation. He couldn't make out any words, but the other person had a deep, scratchy voice. After the door opened and closed, the pawn broker returned. He had a slight bounce in his step and seemed to be in a much better mood. He sat back down, reviewed his notes and looked over the coins again. "Well I guess there are some people that would like a piece of pirate treasure. Maybe make the gold doubloons and silver pieces of eight into necklaces or rings. I'm a goldsmith so I might be able to increase the value that way. Maybe melt down that gold bar and use this coin for a mold to make duplicates. . . . Of course, I'd disclose they aren't authentic but being made from Spanish gold most folks wouldn't care." Jode nodded his approval and was glad things were starting to look up, at least a little. "Tell you what, I'll go 15K."

It was a much better offer but Jode was holding out for more. The phone rang and Wes again excused himself to answer it. "Hey . . . . . Ya, still here. . . . . Maybe another 20 minutes. . . . Ok, see you there." He hung up and returned to the counter. "This all you got?"

"That's it, except for the one coin my dad carried around. I'm keeping that one. Like I said on the phone, I got to take care of my mom's estate and head back to Indiana. Was hoping to get at least, $20,000 to cover expenses before I leave." Jode replied with as much conviction as he could muster.

"Well I guess it might work out," Wes replied. "I'll go the 20K on a wing and a prayer. Hopefully, I won't regret it. Let me get the money. I'll be right back." A few minutes later, he returned with three straps of bills, one of Benjamins and two of Grants. He set them in front of Jode as he began organizing the treasure in a box from under the counter.

Jode could barely control himself. He had never seen so much cash in one place. He picked up the strap of 100's and inspected it, the strap was tight and looked like it came right from the bank. He thumbed through the bills one way then turned it around and did the same in the other direction. All the bills had a 100 on them. He didn't want to insult the man or take the time to count every bill so he went through the same process with the 50's. If a few were missing who cares it was still at the high end of what he had hoped to get. They shook hands and bade each other thanks and good luck. Jode placed the stacks of bills into the tool bag, put on his jacket and left the shop.

It seemed like a much shorter walk back to the bar. The tool bag was much lighter but in Jode's eyes, much more valuable. He entered thc bar and headed for his seat while waving for the bartender to bring him another beer. "Here ya go. Hope your little venture went well?"

"Did indeed," Jode responded as he downed the beer, handed the barkeep another fin and headed out the backdoor to his boat. He hopped in and as he untied the line he looked back up at the bar. The bartender was talking on the phone and looking out towards the dock. Jode waved goodbye and the bartender responded in kind. His business successfully completed, he relaxed and idled down the canal to the harbor and back to Old Moe.

Sarge had been sitting up at the helm relaxing for over two hours now. Things were taking longer than he thought they would but on the other hand, he had no idea how long such a thing would take or whether fast or slow was good or bad. So he just waited looking west under the bridge for any sign of Jode. A little while later he saw a speck of a boat near shore heading his way. He decided he would go below and meet Jode with an offering of a cold beer. In celebration or consolation, either way a beer would be appreciated.

When he opened the cooler he saw that the ice was almost completely melted, it wouldn't keep the remaining six pack cold for long. He took out four beers, wiped them dry and put them in the fridge for later, leaving the remaining two on the counter. Then emptied the cooler and wiped it out before stowing it away. He had just opened the two beers when he heard the little motorboat approaching and felt Old Moe rock as Jode stepped aboard. Suddenly Damn Bird let out his signature, 'Akk, Akk, Akk.' The bird never squawked at Jode before so that got his attention, causing him to stop dead in his tracks. Listening, he heard Jode call out, "What are you doing out here? I thought our business was done!"

"It's done when I say it's done and it isn't done yet. We came to get my money back."

"Hey, we had a deal, fair and square. You got what you wanted and I got paid. So hit the road. I'm not giving you nothing," Jode protested.

"Well I don't see it that way. First off, you're not Jake Collins. That crap you pawned off on me could be stolen. You might be setting me up, so the deal's off. You hand over the cash and I keep the gold. That's how this is going to go down!" The little guy said with total confidence.

Jode was beside himself, "No way, ain't happening, get away from the boat. We had a deal!"

The little guy smirked, "you don't understand, I'm not asking, I'm telling and if you don't do as you're told my big friend here is going to, as they say, feed you to the fishes." With that, the big guy pulled out a very big pistol and pointed directly at Jode's chest. "So we understand each other, you will put down that tool bag and keep your hands where he can see them. We are coming aboard and we will tear this boat apart and make sure you don't have any more of that "Atocha" treasure. You got that slick!"

Sarge had remained perfectly still and quiet before carefully removing the Beretta from his rucksack. His usual habit was to give it a quick press check but he didn't want to make any sounds and knew full well it was locked and loaded. With the gun close up to his face he moved up the steps to the hatchway, careful not to rock the boat as he went. He peered around the bulkhead and saw a 20 foot center console with two guys aboard. One was big and ugly wearing long pants and a dirty ball cap. He was holding a 40 cal. pointed at Jode. The other guy was much thinner and shorter and was wearing a flowered shirt, bright blue shorts and sandals. There was no question who was the brains and who was the muscle. "Now, put down that bag and get the hell out of the way!" Blue shorts barked.

Sarge had seen enough. "Hey fatso, I have a nine mil. pointed right at your big head and from here, there is no way I can miss, you so much as flinch and you're a dead man. I've killed men before so I suggest you don't even think about it." The big guy froze but his face turned beet red. He was pissed. The veins in his neck bulged out so far they looked like they would burst. The muscles in his wrist tightened.

"Ah, Ah, Ahhh, I know what you're thinking. You think you can swing that big pistol of yours my way and take a shot. Don't even think about it. Before the message gets from your thick head down to your hand, I'll put a bullet right through your head and before your brains are chum in the water, that blue-shorted jackass beside you will be just as dead. So, as you so aptly phrased it, this is how it's going down. Fatso there is going to slowly and carefully drop his pea shooter overboard. Then you two are going to leave peacefully and never come back. Got it?"

The big guy was about to explode as he looked over to his boss. Blue shorts looked hatefully into Sarge's eyes, turned a millimeter towards his goon and gave a tiny nod. The big guy hesitated just a second before reaching over the side and dropped the gun overboard.

"Ok, very good. Now you are going to leave and if I ever see either of you again I will not be so magnanimous. Do you understand?" They both gave a slight nod. "Say it!"

"Yes," they said softly in unison.

"I can't hear you!" Sarge barked.

"Yes."

"Yes what!"

"Yes sir."

Sarge smiled just a little, "Now get the hell out of here and don't come back," as he motioned them away with the barrel of his pistol. With the boat leaving, Sarge reached into his rucksack, pulled out the belt and holster and put it on. Then he grabbed the beers and headed up the gangway to the aft deck. One look at Jode and he knew he clearly needed a drink to settle his nerves. He sat on the gunnel, pale and shaking. His white, collared shirt stuck to him like skin with all the sweat. His eyes sized up Sarge top to bottom, bare feet, or more accurately, a barefoot and fake one, desert fatigue cut-offs, a green army tee shirt and that holster and gun. The sight didn't calm his nerves. "You think they're coming back?" he asked weakly.

Sarge looked at the boat racing away in the distance and nodded yes, "That big guy was pissed! Maybe because I got the drop on him. Maybe because I made him drop his weapon over board but one thing is for sure, he'll be back even if he has to swim out here and that blue-shorted jackass with him is not letting loose of whatever you have in that bag." He handed Jode the beer and let him take a swig. The carbonated beverage cut through his dry, pasty mouth and the alcohol settled his nerves, just a little. He closed his eyes, tilted his head back and took a deep breath.

"Shit man I thought they were going to shoot me."

Sarge agreed, "Ya, probably would have. Before we get into the after action report, we need to get the hell out of here. You haul the anchor and I'll get the engines going." Sarge headed up to the helm and started the engines. Jode went to the bow and began pulling in the anchor. Between the physical exertion and keeping his mind on task, he was much calmer and focused as Sarge turned the boat towards the channel and the opening under the bridge. He quickly changed out of the dress clothes and shoes and headed up to the helm. Sarge slid over to let him drive and both men finished off what little beer they had left.

Sarge got comfortable in his new seat before asking, "So, what's in the bag that's important enough for them to follow you all the way back to the boat?" Jode handed him the bag. Sarge opened it and his eyes got big just looking at the bundles of bills.

"Guess that's enough to make someone want it back. So, what went down at the pawn shop?"

Jode took a minute to clear his head and organize his thoughts before beginning. "Everything was going like we planned. No problem getting up to the bar. Bought a beer, asked to leave the dinghy, gave him a five you know, enough but not too much, and walked over to the pawn shop. At first the guy was a pain in the ass, complaining about everything until some guy came in the back door. Then he got more agreeable and offered more cash. Come to think of it, the voice in the back sounded a little like that big guy. Anyway, he was offering more money, then got a phone call about another appointment, seemed to be in a hurry then agreed to the 20K I was asking for and I left. Thought everything was great until they showed up at the boat." Jode looked down in disgust, "Guess I should have seen it coming. Was too easy, almost like Big Carlos. He wasn't giving me the money just lending it until he could get it back along with anything else we got."

Sarge gave him a pat on the back. "No way you could have known. You worked our plan as best you could. Might be that guy's MO to figure out who isn't on the level and rob them. Makes sense, a thief isn't going to report a theft to the cops. He gets valuable inventory for free and the mark is just glad he got away with his life. Guess they didn't count on me and Bret waiting for them at the boat." They had just passed under the two bridges and were heading back to Boca Grande. "I'm thinking they are going to be back with more goons and more guns as soon as they can. What's the fastest way out of here?"

Jode looked over and shrugged, "No fastest way out of here. Only way out is by Boca Grande. There we can go south to the Beach, north in the Intracoastal or out the pass into the gulf. No other choices."

Sarge didn't like what he was hearing. "Anyway to get there faster? They are going to be after us as soon as they can. They know the boat and can spot us from miles away. We don't have any idea what they will be in so they could be on us before we even know it's them."

"Sorry man, no other way out. We could head south at Jug Creek Shoals but that only shaves off about half an hour, beside they could still see us before we got around Useppa. Might be able to go faster but that's only going to save another half hour tops unless we go balls to the wall and I don't think Old Moe would hold up to that for long. If they get back on the water soon no way we're out running them even if they are in that same center console." An uncomfortable silence was the only response. After a few minutes, Jode looked up to the sky and started to think like the pirate he was. "Unless we can hide until they stop looking for us or it gets dark enough to sneak out of the harbor. Not many boats are out after dark and if they come toward us, you can bet it isn't to say hello."

Sarge liked the idea a lot more than a shootout in the middle of the harbor. "I didn't see any place to hide on the way up here and they could be out looking for us in no time. You got any ideas?"

Jode just smiled, he was in his element now. "Matter of fact I do! We keep heading due west as we are now. I know we took the short route down here close into Fat Point but most folks that don't know the waters or just trust the charts would take the main channel almost all the way to the western wall and turn south at Marker 2. If anyone is watching they will think that's what we're doing. But instead of turning to port and heading out the harbor to marker 5, we can make a hard right and head up the Myakka. We'd be pretty far away by then and hard to see even from the bridge. When we make the turn we will be out of sight behind the mangroves in just 10 or 15 minutes. Now we can't escape that way but there is a good hidey hole before we get to the bridge over the river. It's called Muddy Cove. Chart says there's no water but it is plenty deep for Old Moe. We can get way back by the mangroves and even if they go by, it will be hard to see us. Probably look like an old derelict boat from the last hurricane anyway. We wait them out and skip out after midnight."

Sarge agreed, it was a much better plan then just lumbering out the harbor until who knows how many goons or boats catch up to them. With the plan in place, Jode increased to RPMs to get to the cove as soon as possible without putting too much stress on the old worn-out diesels.

After they passed marker 2 Jode continued west for about a half mile before taking a hard right and heading up the Myakka River. As the bridge came into sight, he throttled back to an idle and headed east towards an opening in the mangroves. After entering Muddy Cove he creeped slowly, as far back as he could before the props started to kick up a lot of mud. As they went under the bridge in the Peace River he noticed it was near low tide and the current indicated it was coming in so he wasn't worried about getting stranded for several hours. Worst case they would need to wait until after the next low tide before leaving but even that would be before sunrise. He put Old Moe in neutral and went to the bow to drop the hook. He only let out about 30 feet of chain, didn't want to swing away from the mangroves if the wind changed and the less chain the quicker their escape. With the boat more or less anchored he shut down the engines and they sat on the bridge letting the stress of the afternoon melt away as they watched and listened.

Not even a half hour later Jode heard a go-fast boat coming out into the harbor. The distinctive whine of multiple high horsepower outboards cut through the peaceful calm of the cove. The noise gradually increased until it suddenly changed pitch and got much louder, then faded away. "That's them I'm almost sure."

"What makes you think that?" Sarge asked.

"Shhhhh," Jode hissed as he held his fingers to his lips and continued to listen. The noise was fading away when it changed pitch again and then back after about 20 seconds. A minute later it was gone. "Yup, that was them," he said confidently.

Sarge had a puzzled look on his face, "What makes you so sure? We didn't see anything."

"Want the long version or the short version?"

"Got nothing but time. I'll take the long version," He replied.

Jode sat back in his seat and got comfortable. Sarge did the same. "First by the sound, that was one of those fancy go-fast boats with three maybe four big outboards on it. Probably go over a hundred miles an hour. No reason for it to be out here now. See, those boats aren't good for anything but showing off. Can't fish, can't sleep aboard, can only hold a few people to party. The only thing they're good for is showing other folks how rich and important you are. Sounds like blue shorts to me." Sarge nodded his agreement.

Jode continued. "Well, you were just out in the harbor, nobody out there. No good showing off if there is no one to see you. Besides, it's Tuesday, no beach parties, no sand bar parties hell even the waterside bars are almost empty during the week. Nope, no one's taking a boat like that out today. To top it off, it's getting close to sunset. Now I figure it must be big fun running a hundred miles an hour down the harbor but after the sun goes down that would be pure suicide. Even 30 or 40 miles an hour is dangerous in the dark. Can't imagine how frustrating it would be to be going 20 or 30 in a boat that is made to go a hundred miles an hour faster. No way are those guys out for a joy ride. Ya know what the clincher was?"

Sarge just shook his head no.

"When we were listening it wasn't too loud until they took the corner from the river out into the harbor. Once the exhausts from those big outboards were pointing our way, it got LOUD. Then a few minutes later the sound changed and changed again. That was the clincher."

"How's that?" Sarge wasn't getting the connection.

"Well, if they were out for a joy ride they'd put the hammer down and gone balls to the wall straight to marker 5, but they didn't do that. By the sound of it, they were weaving one way and then the other. You see those boats are low to the water. Can't see very far. Even binoculars don't help cause you're going too fast and the boat is bouncing around like crazy. So, every time they see something in the distance they need to check it out, make sure it's not us. Not a big deal when you're going a hundred. Just takes a few seconds to get close enough to see. Hell, they could get from one side of the harbor to the other in a minute, two max. They were out looking for something and I guarantee it was us they were looking for!"

Sarge wasn't a boater but it made sense to him. "Well, if we know they are out looking for us and what kind of boat they're in, what are they going to do and do you think they'll find us?"

Jode sat back and thought for a while. "No way to know for sure but I'm guessing they know the waters around here pretty good. They can get from here to Naples or up to Sarasota in just over an hour so they probably have been to every beach bar and hang out in the area. With that fast of a boat they can cover a lot of territory and they got to know Old Moe is good for only 10 knots, 15 at the most. Gives them a lot of options to check out everywhere we might have gone, before we had a chance to get away."

"First we know they left after 5:30 and searched the harbor as they headed out. They probably think we would get away as fast as we could and there's only one way out and that is near Boca Grande. From there we could go south towards the Beach, take the Intracoastal north towards Sarasota or head out the pass then north or south. Oh, one more option would be to try to go the back way behind Pine Island but the water is skinny and would be almost impossible in the dark. Quite a few options but with a boat that fast they can cover a lot of ground. Check everything out."

"If they haven't seen us by the time they reach marker 5, they'll start thinking either Old Moe is faster than they thought or we took a detour. I'd take a quick side trip to Matlacha Pass, worth the ten minutes to rule that out then head back towards Boca Grande. To cover all the options they would need to head south in the Intracoastal to maybe Redfish pass then go out into the gulf. Maybe pass Boca and do a loop north ten miles or so. That leaves only the channel going north which they would have to slow down because it's busy and has, no wake and speed zones, if they even care. Not finding us, they would start searching any and all anchorages like Pelican Bay. By then it is getting dark so it would slow them down. I expect we'll hear them coming back in about 9:30, 10 o'clock."

Sarge took it all in, he wasn't a boater but it made sense. "You think they'll check out around here when they get back?"

"Hard to say but probably not. Not a good place to hide. We were stuck like in a burning house trying to escape. Instead of heading for the door we are in the back closet of the back bedroom. We put ourselves in a corner. Don't think they would expect that. Besides, they have probably never been up here, no bars, no parties, no reason to go up the Myakka. Nothin up there except brown water and alligators." Jode took a pause. Then added, "But you never know, sucks if they do, we got our backs to the wall."

With that happy thought, they sat back, watched as the sun fell behind the mangroves and listened.

Chapter 15

Sarge wasn't one to count on luck. Fail to plan means you better plan to fail, and failing was not in his vocabulary. He spent the next two hours looking over every inch of the cove and going over every scenario he could think of. He had little doubt that Blue Shorts and his gang would do everything they could to find them. Based on the boat Jode described, there would be three or four armed men aboard and not carrying semiautomatic pistols like Fathead had, no they would have some serious firepower and wouldn't hesitate to use it.

Neither man spoke as the sunset. Soon the partial moon began to rise and the dark cove took on an eerie calm as the mangroves cast long shadows into the surrounding water. Sarge didn't want to unnecessarily alarm Jode but just to be safe he brought all their firepower up on deck. His M-9 had two 15 round clips plus one in the chamber. The M-14 had two twenty round magazines and again one in the chamber. Jode's 357 was a six-shooter. He didn't bother with the extra boxes of ammo. If what they had wasn't enough there would be no time to reload. Any confrontation would be up close and personal.

The plan Sarge had in his head was simple and hopefully effective. Just like his patrols in the sandbox, he was going on offense. Playing defense when you're outmanned and outgunned not to mention cornered was a losing scenario every time. He thought of briefing Jode ahead of time but with his limited experience with firearms, much less being shot at, he decided to leave that to the last minute if it came to that.

Just as Jode predicted, it was almost ten o'clock when they heard the go-fast boat in the distance. It was going much slower than when it left and sounded like it was heading toward them. There was no tell tail increase in volume indicating they had made the turn back up the Peace River. This could be Showtime.

Sarge handed the M-9 Beretta to Jode. "I don't think it will come to it but if those guys are heading towards you, you need to be ready. Don't show your hand too soon. The range on this thing is 50 yards at best and that is for a trained shooter. Keep down and out of sight until they are 50 yards away, no further. When they are in range, stay hidden as best you can, then aim, fire, aim, fire, aim, fire until you hear the gun click open indicating the clip is empty.

Don't just stick the barrel out and pull the trigger. You won't hit anything and you won't scare them away. If you take your time you might get close enough to discourage them or at least make them think twice before getting closer. When the clip is empty, get to cover and reload. Don't start shooting again until they are within 25 yards. Again, aim, fire, you will definitely get their attention and might even hit something. Keep your revolver in reserve in case they come alongside." Jode had begun to tremble slightly and turned pale. "Now, I don't expect any of this to happen but I want you to be ready and exercise some discipline. Just pulling the trigger and making noise isn't going to help anybody." Sarge had no illusions that his instructions had fallen on deaf ears but it might keep Jode from wasting all the ammo before he had a hope of hitting anything.

"What are you going to do?" Jode choked out.

"I'm taking the rifle in the dinghy and heading over there by the entrance under those mangroves overhanging the water. It's in the shadows with the moon behind me. There is no way they will see me if they come into the cove. If they do come, we have them in a crossfire. Now don't get your panties in a wad. This will all work out fine. Unless they have all the right weapons and know how to use them, they don't stand a chance."

Jode was not convinced, "What about us? They'll have us cornered and outnumbered."

Sarge just laughed at him and gave a gentle pat to the M-14, "No worries mate, this IS the right weapon and I damn sure know how to use it. See ya in a few." With that he hopped in the dinghy and idled over to his ambush hideout.

As soon as he got up under the branches of the mangroves, the motorboat got louder and the riverbank started to brighten. Soon the other side of the cove was bathed in light as the go-fast boat moved quickly passed. When it got beyond the cove the darkness returned. Shit! Sarge thought, of course they have a big spotlight on the bow of that thing! He listened as the boat slowed to go under the El Jobean Bridge then accelerated up the river. On the way back the spotlight will be illuminating his side of the cove. Reaching back into the mangroves, he tore off several branches and laid them over the dinghy, making sure they hung well off the stern and drooped into the water. Satisfied that the little boat was totally covered he crawled under the branches and laid in the bottom of the dink. The only thing sticking out was the barrel of the M-14.

About 15 minutes later he heard the boat returning from upriver. They were going slower now, searching for their prey. Soon his side of the cove was bathed in light, not directly in the beam but the peripheral lighting was still bright. Luckily, Old Moe was at the back of the cove and away from the light. The boat continued to motor past and Sarge let out a sigh of relief. His relief was short-lived as he heard the outboards throttle back and then shift into neutral. As they shifted into reverse, he could see the light swinging with the bow back towards the opening to the cove. A moment later Old Moe was lit up like Times Square on New Year's Eve. He hoped Jode had listened and remained out of sight.

As the boat crawled into the cove at an idle, Sarge could see the outline of a short guy at the helm with two big goons standing behind him holding weapons. He waited patiently until the boat was in the cove and directly in front of him. With the spotlight passed, he was once again in the dark. When his night vision returned he rose up and, using the stern to steady his aim he took a shot followed immediately with another. The bright flashes were followed by a defending blast reverberating off the surrounding mangroves and even echoed off the bridge a quarter mile away. Before the noise died down and the shrapnel from two exploding outboards hit the water, the two goons were unleashing a torrent of lead in his direction.

He couldn't help it as a smirk hit his lips. From the sound of the rounds and how fast they were being fired, he knew they were armed with some variant of the MP-5 submachine gun. These compact weapons fire 9 millimeter shells at over ten rounds a second. They are light, hold 30 or 40 rounds and are so well designed they almost aim themselves at close range. They are accurate and deadly at 25 yards, perfect for clearing a room, a house or even a street. It is no wonder they are the preferred weapon of gangsters and drug dealers. In the hands of a trained operator, they can cause mayhem up to 50 yards away. These guys didn't look like trained operators, besides, Sarge was over 150 yards from their boat. At almost three times the effective range the only way they could cause a threat was a round skipping off the water or if they lobed it up in the air and it fell on him. The dozens of splashes more than 50 yards away confirmed it.

All this went through his mind in a fraction of a second. Even though he wasn't in danger, there was no reason to delay the inevitable. He moved the barrel of his weapon a tiny amount and let fly another 3.08 round, this time through the side of the boat about a foot in front of the driver. The dash exploded with sparks and a cloud of fiberglass and metal pieces. The goons stopped firing and took cover, the spotlight went out and the last outboard quit.

When the noise from the blast stopped echoing around the cove it was quiet, except for the screaming of Blue Shorts, the driver. "Ahhhg, I've been shot. I'm bleeding. Help! Help! . . . ." Sarge let him yell himself out before he called out to them. "Ah, shut up ya little baby, you weren't shot. If I wanted to shoot you, you'd already be dead. Now that I have your attention, you've left me with a dilemma. Clearly I can shoot through that chintzy plastic boat of yours so hiding behind the gunnel will do you no good. Soooo, should I shoot you all right through the boat? Or maybe blast some holes at the water line and watch you sink? They don't call this area Alligator Bay for nothing, with numb nuts bleeding; some sharks might want to join the party. But with the cost of ammo being what it is I think I'll go with my favorite, a single round right into your fuel tank. I'm sure that thing drinks gas so the tank must be pretty big and with you guys racing around all night it must be pretty close to empty, one well-placed red hot shell and your all blown to kingdom come!"

Sarge sat up in the boat and waited for their response. He kept the rifle pointed at them but was confident the fight was over. Soon one of the goons called out, "Ok, Ok, we get the message. What do you want?"

"I want you to stand up with your arms stretched out to your sides, with those peashooters of yours in your left hand. Then I want you to Sllooowwly hold them over the side and drop them overboard." He could hear them talking quietly among themselves. "I'm not waiting all night. What's it gonna be, door number one, door number two or door number three or are you going to get up off your ass and do as I say?"

"Ok, Ok, we're getting up, don't shoot!" One of the goons shouted out as they slowly rose up and held out their arms.

"Now drop those guns overboard," Sarge told them. They hesitated and looked at each other. "I said now!" and suddenly there was another flash and explosion as the last outboard was shredded. The two guns were underwater before the echo died and the motor parts hit the water behind the boat.

With it once again calm and quiet, Sarge called over to Jode, "Hey Sailor, hoist that anchor and head behind these guys and pick me up. Be careful to stay as far away as you can. If they make one false move, there will be boat and body parts raining down a hundred yards in every direction." Jode called back an acknowledgment, started the engines and hauled in the anchor. As he cleared the cove Sarge had one more thing to say to the three crooks, "You didn't listen last time and you're lucky to be alive. If I ever see any of you again I'm not shooting at the boat I'm shooting you! Got it?"

They nodded but that wasn't good enough for Sarge. "You know the drill, say it, all three of you." He could hear all three say yes, even Blue Shorts from down on the deck. "Yes what?" "Yes sir," was the response. Sarge let a smile cross his lips as he started the little motor and headed out to meet Old Moe.

After he passed the opening of the cove and was out of sight of the goons in the go-fast boat, Jode shifted into neutral and went to the back of the boat to help Sarge aboard.

Sarge tossed him the line and after it was cleated off, handed up the M-14 to Jode who placed it carefully on the deck and helped him up onto Old Moe. Even with no light except the rising moon it was clear that Jode was shaken. His eyes were wide and his hands damp and clammy. His voice was higher and shaky as he welcomed Sarge back aboard. "Get back up there and get this tub moving. I'll be up in a minute." Sarge said as he turned and went down into the cabin. First he replaced the spent rounds in the clip and made sure the rifle was ready if it was needed again, then grabbed a couple of beers from the fridge and joined Jode at the helm. "Not a good time to tie one on but it looks like you could use a little something to calm your nerves." He said as he handed Jode a can.

"How about you? You need something to calm your nerves? They were shooting at you and what's with all the yes sir crap all of a sudden?"

"Nah, I'm just thirsty and the yes sir crap just felt right. I bet it tasted like shit in their mouths as they said it," He joked. They sat in silence for a few minutes as Jode guided the boat down the harbor towards Boca Grande.

Finally Jode broke the silence. "Damn, when that boat turned into the cove and lit me up like Christmas, I didn't know what to do. Kept thinking you said stay hidden and that seemed like the only thing I could do. Then when those two loud booms rang out I almost shit my pants! Damn, that thing is loud. By the time it stopped echoing I could barely hear those guy's machine guns firing at you."

Sarge let a slight smile cross his lips. "Well those automatics are a lot louder when they are pointed at you, that's for sure. But they were only firing pistol rounds like in Bret over there. Depending on the load one round from the 14 has as much powder in it as 20 or 30 rounds of 9 mil. Those two shots of mine probably equaled all the shells they fired. It just worked out good for us. If they got close, those MP-5s would have torn us up. Luckily at 150 yards, they're nearly harmless."

Jode thought a bit, "Think they'll come after us."

"Not tonight, I think their first priority will be to get that blue-shorted jackass to a doctor to patch up his little cuts and bruises. Could be wrong so we need to keep our eyes open."

"How about the cops?"

This time Sarge took more time to think it over. "There weren't any houses nearby. Those across the bridge probably only heard my four shots. My guess is they would think someone was setting off fireworks. Even if they recognized the sound as rifle fire they would most likely chalk it up to some drunk redneck blasting something out in the woods. No, even if they called the cops there is nothing to see. Don't think those guys will be calling the cops on us either, too much explaining to do. They wouldn't want the cops snooping into their business. Probably on the phone right now to someone to get that center console to tow them in."

"What about later? Think they will be looking for us?"

"Can't say. We sure put a hurting on them tonight. That boat of theirs is trashed and probably cost three or four hundred grand. They'll probably come up with some sort of scam to get the insurance company to pay for it. Maybe tow it offshore some night and sink it. Say it was stolen or some shit. But they are pissed, no doubt about it. That's twice in one day that we cost them a lot of cash and made them look like fools. I'm pretty sure if they run into us it won't be to buy us a beer for old time's sake."

"That's for sure." Jode agreed as he polished off the rest of his beer.

"So where to captain?" Sarge asked.

"Like you said, we can't rule out someone coming after us, so I think we head north in the Intracoastal about ten miles to

Stump Pass. There is a quiet little place to anchor there and when the sun comes up we can see our way out into the Gulf.

"Sounds like a plan." Sarge agreed. "I think we need to keep a lookout for sure. How about I get a little shut-eye while you drive and I'll take watch when we get to wherever we're going."

Jode agreed and Sarge climbed down onto the deck and sat in a deck chair facing back towards the stern. "Remember to check your six, don't want anybody sneaking up behind you. One more thing, if you see something, wake me up. Nothing worse than waking up to the sound of gunfire."

"Will do," Jode confirmed and just that quick, Sarge was asleep with the M-14 across his lap and his finger resting on the trigger guard.

With only the moon to light his way, Jode kept a close eye on the blinking marker in the distance. Every turn in the channel was marked with a lighted marker, but in the harbor they were a long way apart. Soon he fell into a rhythm of following the compass, looking for the markers and checking behind him every few minutes. This gave him plenty of time to think, but what he was thinking about gave him no comfort. Twice in one day he was on the wrong end of a gun. How did things get so screwed up? All we wanted to do was sell some gold. Figured it would be a good deal all the way around. We got some cash and the pawn guy could sell it for two maybe three times as much. Hell, he stood to make 40 or 50 grand. Why come after us? Of course we made up a story. What was I to do? Waltz in there and say, "hey I got some treasure I found in the keys while me and a buddy were out poaching out of season lobsters. It's not stolen or anything, I'll tell ya were I got it. Go check it out, it's all legit!" Everyone was just supposed to make some money and it ended up with attempted armed robbery and some goons shooting machine guns at us.

Maybe the treasure is cursed, he thought, life has sure gone down the crapper since he and Tripper brought it aboard. It feels like years ago he and his lifelong friend were just getting by in the keys, but getting by wasn't that bad. They didn't have much but didn't need much either. Fishing, poaching lobster, hustling a tourist, maybe a few odd jobs around the marina gave them enough money to pay what few bills they had and enough left over for beers on the back deck at sunset and trips to the local dive bars. Not a bad life all in all, but all that changed with the discovery of that gold coin. They had such hopes and dreams but couldn't share them. Then they were run out of town by Big Carlos' thug. No going back to see their old friends or telling lies over beers at the bar now.

Finding the rest of the treasure was hard work but he and Tripper thrived on it. The plans and dreams kept them going. That is, until that one in a million event that left Tripper at the bottom of the Gulf, the worse day of Jode's life. Wrecking Old Moe on the shore of the ten thousand islands could have been the end of Jode just as easily. Spending almost four weeks stranded, hungry and alone was no picnic either. Things just seem to have gone from bad to worse since that fateful day. Showing up at Fort Myers Beach and meeting Sarge was a bit of luck. He was right, Jode looked frightening, "Make women scream and children cry," or something like that, he said. But then things got better and before long, the Beach started to feel like home. Now, with what happened today there's no going back there either. The risk of those goons finding him is too great. He will have to move along. Alone, no friends, starting over in a new place where he doesn't know a soul, trying to get by without getting in trouble all over again. If they had never found that coin, he and Tripper would be just leaving the bar in Key West and staggering back to Old Moe saying goodbye to one more day and getting up the next morning to do it all over again, simple, safe and happy.

Cursed or not his mind was made up. He couldn't stay around here anymore. Tomorrow he would take Sarge back to the Beach, split up the money, he certainly earned his share, top up the fuel tanks, say his goodbyes and head north to who knows where.

He was feeling down but once he got into the ICW, it took all his attention to follow the winding channel in the dark. The moon was up now and giving some light but seeing more than a few boat lengths ahead took all his concentration. Thoughts of curses or far-off destinations would have to wait.

It was just after 2 AM when he pulled back on the throttles and idled into an unmarked channel near Stump Pass. He carefully approached the mangroves as close as he dared, dropped the hook and shut down the engines.

As soon as he had dropped to an idle, Sarge woke up but just sat and watched as Jode made his way to a back corner of the lagoon and got Old Moe settled for the night. "How ya doing? You OK?" He asked.

Jode hesitated, "Ya, I'm Ok one hell of a day. I need to crash. Tomorrow, as soon as the sun is high enough to read the water, we'll head out the pass and I'll get you back to the Beach." With that Jode stumbled down below and flopped onto his bunk.

Sarge couldn't read Jode's thoughts but it was clear something was up. He'd find out soon enough. He climbed up to the bridge, checked the rifle and the pistol and got comfortable, leaning back in the seat facing out towards the ICW and the mainland beyond. The night was still and with no lights on the boat and the nearest buildings a half mile away, he could see millions of stars in the sky. The moon was just setting, as the sky darkened he could even make out the Milky Way. It wasn't as clear and dark as in the desert but it was the closest to it he had seen since. The thought of the desert brought back memories of his squad and being out on patrol in the sandbox. Tonight's firefight was the first shot of adrenalin he had felt since the last time he was being shot at, but back then he had his team. Every man had his six and he had theirs. He knew if it came down to it, each man would lay down his life to protect the others. Back then he never thought he would miss the action, the danger or the hardship of living in a sand pit with enemies trying to kill you, but tonight showed him he did miss it, and not just the guys.

He heard a motorcycle far off in the distance. His watch said 3 AM, probably the bartender heading home after last call and closing up. After that there were no more man-made sounds. Occasionally a fish would pop under the mangroves, a dolphin breathed heavily as it passed, night birds were singing from the trees, it was so peaceful, such a contrast to the gunfire and carnage of just a few hours before.

He had never spent much time on the water. Sleeping on a boat out at anchor with no one else around was so different than the occasional fishing trip out on the lake he recalled from his youth. The peace and quiet almost forced you to think deep thoughts and contemplate where you are and where you're headed. He felt at peace with where he was but had no idea where he was going. After losing his foot and separating from the army he was just moving, no direction, no destination. He felt at home at the Beach but he also knew that he couldn't stay there forever, couldn't live a life of just getting by, not sure where home really was. The VA would come through someday. He would probably need to fit back into society. A job, maybe a career, but doing what? Law enforcement? Military contractor? Go back to college on the G.I. Bill, get his degree and a desk job? None of those options felt right for him right now. He thought of Jode's story about getting stuck on a sandbar. Without thinking, or even knowing it was happening you find yourself stuck so hard aground there is no way to set yourself free. He had run aground at Fort Myers Beach and if he stayed much longer, he might never escape.

The sky in the east started to brighten and the wildlife began to stir as the dawn approached but for Sarge it felt like just another day with no expectations or destination. He was tired and almost dozed off when the smell of coffee brewing in the galley brought him back awake. Soon Jode opened the hatch and made his way to the helm carrying two mugs of the hot elixir. He accepted it with gratitude, and the two men sat in silence, as the caffeine did its work.

Sarge was the first to break the silence. "So, where to next captain?"

"Well, I figure we'll head back to Fort Myers Beach. I'll drop you off there, top off the fuel tanks then head north. I don't feel safe around here anymore. Not much one for the city life so I'll motor past Sarasota, Tampa and St. Pete. Maybe stop in Dunedin or Tarpon Springs. They are kind of like the Keys or the Beach, small towns with a waterfront and enough tourists so being new won't be unusual or get any attention. Maybe try your idea of trading some of that gold for a better boat. After that I don't know. Maybe make my way along the coast to Texas or even Mexico. That's what Tripper and I had planned anyway. For right now we should get going. If you take the controls, I'll get the anchor. Sun is up enough to see our way through the pass."

When Jode returned after hoisting the anchor, he took over the helm and moved slowly towards the pass. Sarge went below deck to pour the last two cups of coffee, stow the coffee pot and anything else that might fall if they got waked and climbed back up to the helm. He handed Jode his cup and sat down beside him. "So, what do you think of me just tagging along with you for a while? Got all my stuff with me and I don't have any real ties to the Beach anyway."

"Thought you had a lot of friends back there?"

Sarge hesitated a long second, "Ya, I do. But I got friends in Tarpon Springs too, just haven't met 'em yet."

That brought a smile to Jode's lips. He'd heard that before. "Well that might be all well and good, but I don't think I need someone 'tagging along.' Me and Tripper were friends forever. Not saying he didn't drive me crazy doing stupid shit now and then but we got along real good. I guess what made it work was, that we were all in, no mine and yours, no me and you. It was ours and us. If one of us was living large we both were. When we were broke, we were both broke and when one of us was in trouble we were both in trouble. He always had my back and me his. Can't tell you how many times I dragged him out of a scrape, probably about as many times as he saved my ass. No, a boat is too small, only way it works is all in, fifty-fifty. No time or space to think about what-if's, you got to do what you got to do when it needs doin. Can't be thinking about yourself all the time."

Sarge let that settle as they reached the pass and turned towards the gulf. After a bit he said, "I get it man. I know how you feel. Sounds like my squad. I was the squad leader but that didn't mean anything when we were out on patrol. Every man had a job to do and if he didn't do it, bad shit happened and those guys always did their job. I had their six and they had mine, never even had to think about it. No looking over your shoulder to check, you knew every man would take a bullet for his buddies and they would do the same for him."

Jode nodded in agreement, "Sounds like that old pirate saying, 'One for all and all for one'."

Sarge laughed, "That's not a pirate saying, that's from the Three Musketeers, but ya, that's the way it was. So, what do you think? I'm all in if you are."

"I admit you were a little help yesterday, but I wouldn't ask Jake Collins for a recommendation on your planning skills, just sayin. I guess if you are all in so am I." Jode agreed as he held out his hand to shake on it.

Raising his coffee cup in a mock toast, Sarge proclaimed, "One for all and all for one! The two Musketeers!" Just then an Osprey swooped down into the wake, snatching a fish. Damn Bird squawked in alarm. "Ok, the Three Musketeers." He laughed.

"But he doesn't get a pirate's share." Jode added, clinking mugs, as they cleared the pass and turned toward the north.

Chapter 16

Having left the pass and turned north the voyage was a relaxing change from yesterday's dangerous adventures. The sun was up and a slight offshore breeze made just enough low rolling waves to remind you, you were on a boat at sea.

Sarge was the first to interrupt the silence, "I think there's some orange juice left in the fridge, if you want me to bring it up?" Jode responded in the affirmative so Sarge climbed down from the bridge and went below. A few minutes later he returned with two cups half full of juice and the last muffin cut in halves. As soon as he put down the muffin, Damn Bird swooped in and took a bite out of Jode's portion.

"Hey you little bastard, that's mine!" he barked.

To that Sarge responded, "Here, you big baby you can have mine," as he swapped out his half muffin for the one shared with the bird. They both gave that a laugh, finished the meager breakfast and leaned back and relaxed.

After yesterday's events and the lack of sleep, it wasn't long before they were dozing off as Old Moe made her way slowly up the coast toward Tarpon Springs. A couple of hours into the voyage they were jolted alert by the screeching of an alarm. Jode glanced down at the gauges, there was plenty of oil pressure, at least for Old Moe's tired old engines. However the port engine showed a temperature of almost 210 degrees. He quickly pulled back the throttles to an idle and shifted the port engine into neutral. He adjusted the steering to compensate for the lost engine and watched the temperature gauge intently. With no load on the engine, the temperature should drop but it continued to move higher. "Well this sucks," he said as he shut down the offending engine.

"What now?" Sarge asked.

"Probably no big deal. Maybe a loose belt, broken hose, or a piece of trash sucked into the sea strainer but I should go below and check it out. Take the wheel and keep us pointed in the same direction." With that Jode climbed down into the cabin as Sarge slipped behind the helm.

The first thing Jode noticed was the telltale smell of old oil and grease cooking off the engine. A whiff of antifreeze confirmed that the temperature gauge was working just fine. Rather than risk opening up a smoking hot engine room, he went to the V-berth and lifted the hatch in the floor that gave access to the forward bilge pump. There was some filthy water sloshing around but no more than usual for Old Moe. Satisfied that whatever went wrong wouldn't sink the boat or catch it on fire, he climbed back up to the bridge.

"So, what's the verdict?" Sarge asked.

"Looks like we won't sink or blow up. Like I said, could be any number of things but it is too hot to deal with now. We'll just run on one engine and if we need to use the port one to dock or maneuver, I'm sure running it for a couple of minutes won't cause any more damage."

"Is it safe to run on just one engine?"

"Ya, no problem, just slower. Tripper and I did it hundreds of times. No way are we gonna make Tampa Bay before dark at 5 knots so I say we pull into Sarasota Bay and figure out what's wrong after everything cools down. On the upside 5 knots on one engine burns like no fuel. Think of it as saving money." With that Jode slid behind the wheel, gave the starboard engine a little more throttle, adjusted course, sat back and relaxed as they headed for Little Sarasota Pass.

Once through the pass and out of the gulf they headed north again. As they approached the city the big mooring field in front of Marina Jacks came into view. "We tying up there?" Sarge asked.

"Kinda, sorta," Jode replied. "Those mooring balls cost money. Besides they require proof of insurance and I.D. things that I don't have or don't want to give them. We'll just anchor a little further out and hopefully be on our way tomorrow morning after fixing the port engine."

About a half hour later they were comfortably at anchor and enjoying a cold PBR on the bridge. "I was thinking," Jode said breaking the silence. "Why don't we take one of those fifties we scored yesterday and head up to the bar for a margarita?"

"Looks pretty pricey to me." Sarge protested.

"Ahh, come on, we've been cooped up on this tub since Sunday. Besides, I bet we saved enough on fuel to cover a round. What ya say?"

Sarge had no response to that so they cleaned up, grabbed some cash, hopped in the dinghy and headed to the marina.

They tied up at the dinghy dock that served the mooring field and walked the short distance to the bar. As they entered,

Sarge headed straight towards the half empty bar. This time it was Jode who reached up and stopped him. Glancing at an old guy at the left end of the bar wearing a gold chain around his neck and one around his wrist, he nodded in that direction and headed that way as he leaned over and whispered, "Just follow my lead."

"Mind if we sit here?" Jode asked.

The guy just waved a hand and said, "Go ahead, it's a free country," without even looking up.

As they pulled out the stools to sit down, Sarge's fake ankle and foot caught the old guy's eye. He turned to look and his eyes moved from the foot to Sarge's cut-off fatigues, passed his tee shirt to this hair, cut high and tight. "Oh, I guess I should be thanking you guys for that freedom, Vets?"

"Yup," Sarge responded without missing a beat. "First Cav, friends call me Sarge. This squid here goes by Sailor."

The old guy stood up and extended a hand, "Names Harvey, thank you for your service and sacrifice," he added, nodding towards the missing limb. "Let me get you a drink," as he waved over the bartender. Sarge gave him their order and Harvey shouted over to the barkeep, "Two margaritas, rocks, salt."

When the drinks arrived they settled into a casual conversation. Harvey observed that he hadn't seen them in the bar before and asked where they were from. Jode, or in this case, Sailor, told him they were from Key West and were delivering a yacht from there to Panama City. He waved his hand pointing vaguely out at the mooring field as if he was referring to one of the million dollar yachts resting in the bay. Harvey shared that he was retired from Wall Street and had an expensive house on the water south of the city on the Intracoastal. It was clear Harvey liked to talk about himself and what he owned. That gave Sailor the opening he needed to change the subject. "That sure is a nice looking chain you have there. I bet there is a story behind it."

That was all it took. "Oh, this?" he dismissed. "Got it up in New York City, the Diamond District. Damnedest place I have ever been, bars on the doors and windows, big burly armed guards, but when you walked in you knew why. Rows and rows of gold and jewelry. You've never seen anything like it!" To that Sarge fought back a smirk. "Well we were looking at this bracelet and the misses says, why don't I buy it? Now I'm not one for jewelry but gold is always a good investment so I said what the hell. Salesman came over, took it out of the case, put it on a little scale, took out his calculator, tapped some keys and proclaimed, that at such and such an ounce it would cost three grand. Imagine that, buying something this nice for just the cost of the gold. Well I had to have it. Probably worth twice that now. Hell of an investment!"

Sailor had hooked what he was fishing for. Now, could he reel it in. "I have a gold bracelet, a little bigger than yours but totally different. It is made from a gold chain from the Atocha." Harvey's eyes widened. "My dad worked running dive boats for Mel Fisher's Salvors Inc. when he hit the Mother Lode. Took some of his cut in treasure. A while back he gave me a little piece of chain and I had it made into a bracelet."

"Why aren't you wearing it?" Harvey asked.

"Well, we go to places not near as nice as this and that could be a problem and on the boat, I'm always afraid I'll drop it overboard, besides a couple of months ago I was working in the engine room and got it caught on one of the engines." Looking over to Sarge he added, "Remember me yelling for you to get the bolt cutters and cut me free?"

Without missing a beat, Sarge said, "How could I ever forget the sight of you stuck to that big diesel?"

"Anyway, I have to get it fixed before I can wear it again and that costs money. I'm thinking about selling it instead, especially now."

Harvey couldn't help himself, "Why especially now?"

Sailor looked back and forth along the bar, making sure no one was close enough to hear, leaned over to Harvey and whispered, "Don't tell anyone but Sarge and I have an opportunity to turn six grand into twelve by sunset Sunday."

"Sounds like something illegal to me."

"No not at all," Sailor protested. "Like I said we're delivering that boat from Key West to Panama City but we hit a broken piling or tree in the Intracoastal south of Venice. Not a big problem now, but we need to get the running gear fixed before heading across the Gulf. Don't want to be two hundred miles offshore with a damaged boat." Harvey nodded in agreement. "So we took it over to the boat yard to get a price and schedule the repairs. Guy there said it would cost twelve grand, give or take, and take a week at least. The owner said go ahead, he'll send us the money. Well, as we were walking back to the boat the guy that actually does the work came up behind us, real quiet like and said if we could bring the boat in at first light Sunday, he'd fix it while it sits in the slings of the travel lift, for six grand, and have us on our way before sunset. Don't know if he was working with or against the guy giving the quote, doesn't matter to me either way. The catch is, we need six large by Sunday and we don't have that kind of scratch."

"Humm, sounds like a classic arbitrage deal, smart." Harvey said with a smile. Both Sarge and Sailor gave him a perplexed look. "Arbitrage, is an investment scheme where you agree to sell something at a higher price before you even buy it. Big banks do it with currency all the time, can't lose, but I never heard of one where you can double your money. Sounds like a good deal but no way would I ever get involved with anything like that!"

"No, no," Sailor protested defensively. "We'd never ask anyone else to get involved. We'd walk away from it first. But since I'm thinking of selling the gold chain anyway, this could work out good for everyone. I know my chain is heavier than that one and you could do a little arbitrage of your own. You get it fixed and it has to be worth more than what I'm asking."

"Well, I do have a jeweler, Masterpiece Jewelry on the circle out on the island," Harvey replied, while stroking his chin. "He took a diamond ring I got for being the top producer at a firm I worked with and turned it into a beautiful pendent for my wife so I'm sure he could fix a bracelet. Might even want to buy it himself."

Sailor shook his head no, "If you wear that chain of mine one time you won't want to sell it. I tell you what, it is a conversation starter. People would ask me about it all the time. Mostly I tell them the truth like I told you but if I had too many margaritas or a pretty lady is asking, I have a hell of a story to tell. Some folks even believed it."

"This I got to hear. Greg, another round for me and my new friends. Now tell me that story of yours." Harvey said as he waved over the bartender.

Sailor took a sip of his new drink and settled in to tell a tale. "When that lady comes up and asks about the gold I say straight away that I found it while spear fishing on a reef in the keys. There I was, 60 feet down, swimming along a coral ridge, spear gun in hand. I see a nice hogfish 10 maybe 15 feet away. I take aim and POW, the spear goes clean through him and he starts shaking as he drifts toward the bottom. All of a sudden, in the blink of an eye, a shark comes out of nowhere and steals my fish. Now it wasn't a big shark only six maybe seven footer and it was a nurse shark so not dangerous but he stole my hogfish. I was pissed. Well, I got my spear back and he went his way and I went mine. No harm no fowl. Next thing I see is a yellowtail, not as good eating as hogfish but plenty tasty. I pop him no problem. Before I can swim over to claim my prize that damn shark swoops in and eats it in one gulp. Now I was really pissed. I tried to scare him away, poking at him with the spear gun, blowing air out of my regulator, anything I could think of, but nothing worked. That damn shark started following me all around that reef. He was like a damn bird dog right by my side, getting all excited every time we spotted a fish.

I was getting low on air and about to head to the surface when we, ok mostly him, spotted a little barracuda about 2 feet long. The bastard could hardly control himself so I gave in and plugged the cuda. The shark raced over and grabbed it. It was too big to swallow in one bite so he shook and shook until he had it torn in half, he sucked down the pieces and swam away. I guess he had his fill. They had stirred up the bottom something fierce. Had to wait for all the sand to drift away before I could see my spear. When I swam over to retrieve it, that's when I saw the gold!"

Harvey started the slow clap while he laughed, "Bravo, good job, that's the biggest pile of crap I've heard in a long time." Sailor gave a small bow. "Maybe I can help you fellas out. I'll give my jeweler a call and ask him what a chain like that might be worth and how much he'd charge to fix it. If he has good news, I'll bring the cash tomorrow and you bring the bracelet. I trust you and all, but we'll meet right here in the bar so there is no hanky panky going on, deal?"

"Sounds good to me," Sailor said as he put out his hand to shake.

"Remember it depends on what the jeweler says and if the chain is what you said it is, but if all checks out, deal," Harvey said as he took Sailor's hand and shook it. With everyone in agreement, Sarge and Sailor said they had to get back to the boat, thanked him for the drinks and headed out the door and back down to the dinghy dock.

Once they were away from the dock and out of sight of the bar and restaurant, Sarge turned to Jode, "Well Sailor that was the biggest pile of bullshit I've ever heard. Makes me wonder if I can believe a single word that comes out of that mouth of yours."

Jode just smiled, "What? I told him the truth! Ok, replace the seven foot shark with a lobster and that's pretty much what happened and hell, every boater knows the cash discount at the back gate of a boat yard can be substantial."

Back on Old Moe, they each grabbed a PBR and headed to the bridge to celebrate. Sarge asked, "You think he'll show up tomorrow with the cash?"

"One hundred percent guaranteed! He'll find out that six grand is a great price and the stories he can tell are worth even more. Next time don't question me when I say I want to go to a bar soldier." They clinked beer cans in toast and laughed as they downed the cold beverage.

The next morning, after having coffee on the bridge, Jode reluctantly went below to inspect the overheated engine. Once the filthy old carpet was out of the way, he hoisted the hatch covering the engines and crawled in. The problem was easy to see. A long streak of rust ran down the side of the hull across from one of the cooling hoses. A closer look revealed a split in the decades old hose. Rather than climbing up and down into the bilge he yelled for Sarge to bring him the duct tape from the drawer in the V-berth. It took him a while to rummage through the collection of useless items but he soon located the tape and brought it to Jode.

"While I tape this up, take a look in the toolbox and see if there are any hose clamps and a screwdriver. Pretty sure the tape will hold but a couple of clamps will add extra strength." He finished the repair in just a few minutes, then had Sarge hand him down glasses of water from the sink until the heat exchanger was full. With the engine rigged up and ready to go, Jode lifted the floorboard near the hull exposing the treasure. They both stood there transfixed. Knowing it was there is one thing, seeing it was an entirely different sensation.

Jose asked for a hammer and after wrapping a piece of the chain around his wrist to estimate the length he used the hammer and screwdriver to cut one of the links. He handed the tools and chain to Sarge, put the broken link in his pocket and covered up the rest of the treasure, before climbing out of the bilge.

As he was admiring his handy work and beginning to close the hatch, Sarge stopped him. "You didn't put the radiator cap on tight."

"Ya, I know, figure it's safer not letting any pressure build up just in case the tape gives way or another hole opens up somewhere else. We'll just use this engine when we need it and putt along on the other one until I can get the parts to fix it right." Sarge just looked at him and wondered when he ever, fixed anything right.

They lazed away the rest of the day aboard the boat until it was time to get cleaned up and meet Harvey. Back on dry land they walked over to the bar. When their eyes adjusted from the bright sun, they spotted Harvey at a table near the back. Jode motioned Sarge to go on over while he headed to the bar, "Guess it's our turn to buy a round." The bartender made the drinks and handed Jode the check. He gave it a quick glance and just left the fifty on the bar. At these prices it was just enough to cover the drinks and an acceptable tip.

Sarge and Harvey were chatting about nothing when he arrived with the drinks. After exchanging pleasantries, they got to the business at hand.

Harvey was the first to bring it up, "Called my guy, he said if it's the real thing and weighs about what you said, then I won't lose too much buying it, even sent me a picture from Fisher's Museum for comparison. Before we go any further I have to know, is this stolen property?"

Both Sarge and Sailor swore it was not stolen and was the real deal as Sailor took it out of his pocket and laid it on the table. Harvey also reached in his pocket and brought out a little digital scale. Sarge and Sailor gave it a look, both thinking the same thing, that scale probably had been used for more than just gold, but neither cared. Harvey inspected the piece of chain, then carefully placed it on the scale. It read just over 7 ounces. Sailor reached in his pocket for the broken link and added to the scale, which now read just shy of 7.5 ounces.

Harvey looked closely at the results, "Well it's a little lighter than I hoped but it looks just like the chains in the picture so I guess it will do. If you gentlemen will excuse me I'll be right back."

Sarge and Sailor exchanged a look. Harvey must have noticed. "Relax guys I have the money in my car. You didn't think I would come waltzing in here with six grand in my pocket did you? I'm an old guy and you're big guys, I could be rolled and in the bay in seconds. Just wait here, I'll order another round and be back in less than five minutes." They both nodded agreement and Harvey headed for the door. Soon the barmaid dropped off the drinks and before they were half gone, Harvey was back at the table. He handed an envelope to Sarge, pocketed the chain, sipped his drink and the conversation about nothing resumed as if no business had ever taken place.

Back aboard Old Moe, they counted the cash, congratulated themselves for the successful endeavor and drank more than a few beers. As the sun began to set, Jode started looking around. "What's up?" Sarge asked.

"Haven't seen Damn Bird since we pulled in. He usually shows up for breakfast and dinner."

Sarge thought about that for a bit, "Well we didn't have any breakfast and haven't brought any food on deck this evening. Come to think of it I do recall seeing a flock of green birds over in the park near the marina. Maybe he found himself a girlfriend or just wants to be with his own kind."

"Could be, either way we will be heading out tomorrow morning. Can't get any parts on this side of town and they will probably run us out for not taking a mooring ball as soon as they notice."

To that, Sarge asked, "Where to next El Capitan?"

"The marinas around here are real expensive if they would even let us in. There's a place up near Palmetto that we can get dockage while we fix the engine and also resupply. We're running low on beer, could use some groceries too." They finished their beers and headed below to crash.

The next morning Jode awoke to the smell of coffee, got up, hit the head, through on his shorts and tee shirt and headed up to the main cabin. Sarge was already on the bridge so he poured himself a cup and climbed up to join him.

"Well, good afternoon, thought you were going to sleep all day," Sarge said sarcastically.

"Everybody's a comedian. How about I get the anchor and we get underway before the sheriff's boat comes by?" With that Jode put his coffee in the cup holder, started the engines and went to the bow to hoist the anchor. He was just securing it in the bow pulpit when he heard a familiar squawking. Looking up he saw a green blob heading towards him in the awkward, clumsy way that parrots fly. He called up to Sarge to head for the channel while he went below and grabbed a couple of crackers for their wayward hitchhiker.

Jode climbed up to the bridge, tossed the crackers on the deck for Damn Bird and slid behind the wheel. He shut down the port engine, adjusted course, gave the starboard one a little more throttle and settled in for a slow but relaxing cruise up to Palmetto.

Chapter 17

At five knots, it took most of the day to make it to Palmetto. As they entered the river, Jode got on the radio and requested overnight dockage. The dock master gave them a slip assignment and apologized that he and the mechanic were busy and couldn't meet them on the dock. Jode assured him that he had help on board and could dock without any assistance.

After they tied up and connected the water and electric, they walked over to the dock master's office to check-in. They introduced themselves and shook hands with Bill, the dock master who also owned the place. Sarge looked over the rates and decided that the weekly rate would be their best option even if they didn't stay that long. Jode, who Sarge introduced as Sailor, gave Bill all the particulars on the boat and inquired about getting the necessary parts to make the repairs.

"No problem, if there is something you need that we don't have in stock Steve can get it the next day from Land and Sea. He might be gone for the day but he'll be here first thing tomorrow." Sarge counted out cash for the dockage fee. With the business completed they walked the short distance back to Old Moe and settled in on the bridge with one of their dwindling supply of cold PBRs.

The first beer went down quickly so they climbed down, grabbed another and decided to walk around the marina and boat yard to get the lay of the land. Jode told Sarge about how he and Tripper had been at this very marina twelve years ago when they picked up Old Moe. It took them almost three weeks to get it fixed up and seaworthy enough to make the trip back to the Keys. It was a lot of work but they enjoyed the time in the marina and since there were no bars nearby, they saved money by drinking on the boat.

They soon found themselves staring up at the biggest boat in the yard. It was only 40 feet or so but looked out of place in the tiny boatyard. It was an aft cabin like Old Moe but was made of fiberglass and had a small cockpit at the stern with a transom door that gave easy access to the dive platform. "That's sweet," Jode said. "Be a whole lot easier to get on and off than Old Moe, especially in bad weather." The boat was far from new and it was obvious by the dirt and neglect that it had been on the hard for a long time. As they were standing there sipping their beers a young guy walked up wearing greasy overalls.

"Hi, names Steve McKenzie the mechanic. Most everyone here calls me Steve Mechanic," he added with a laugh.

Sarge introduced himself and motioned to Jode. "And this is Jode but I call him Sailor cause well, he's a sailor of sorts." Jode just shook his head and handshakes were exchanged all around.

Jode cut right to the chase. "What's the story with this old boat? Looks like it has been grounded here for quite a while. The owner die or something?"

"No," Steve corrected. "Old man Clemens and his wife live out west of town on some acreage. Brought the Irish Lady in here about two years ago. Planned on fixing her up but something came along and it has been sitting here ever since. They come down here every couple of weeks. Stan pulls a ladder out of his pickup and they climb up there on the back deck and have a beer or glass of wine or three. My guess is they are reminiscing about all the adventures they had over the years."

"What's wrong with it?" Jode asked.

"Not much really. Needs new cutlass bearings, shaft seals and bottom paint. That's what they brought it in for. After sitting so long you got to add oil and filter changes, check all the belts and hoses, free up the through hulls, mostly regular maintenance stuff and a whole lot of cleaning, waxing and bright work. If you had to pay for all that it could add up to ten maybe fifteen grand."

"Why doesn't he just sell it? Doesn't make sense to pay storage every month when you don't use it and it just goes downhill every day." It certainly didn't make sense to Jode.

Steve thought about it for a while. "Don't know, but my guess is he doesn't need the money. Can't bring himself to pay to get it back to ship shape and bristle fashion and can't use it or sell it as it is. Plus, having owned it for twenty odd years and gone all the places they've been, it probably has a lot of sentimental value. Seems that way to me when I see them sitting up there drinking wine and sharing stories."

"How much do you think it's worth and you think they might want to sell it as is?" Sarge asked.

"If it were all cleaned up and ready to go I figure it would bring 80 or 90 K. But like I said, that's after a ton of grunt work. As is, sixty maybe less if he likes you. If he is interested in selling and that's a big IF."

Sarge just smiled, "Think he might like us?"

Steve looked them both up and down. "Well I reckon he would take to you just fine." He said looking at Sarge. "Your side kick I'm not so sure." He laughed. Jode just gave him a disgruntled stare. "I have keys to it in the shop. I can give him a call and see if he's open to letting you look it over."

"That would be great. What time do you show up in the morning?" Sarge asked.

Steve got kind of quiet and looked a little nervous before he spoke. "Hate to admit it but I recently lost my apartment and can't find anything I can afford that isn't a long commute. I've been staying in the shop for the past week. Not too bad though, it's got a bathroom, AC and a big couch. Bill doesn't seem to mind. In fact I think he likes someone here to keep an eye on things when he's gone."

"Well if it makes you feel any better, we've all been there a time or three." Sarge said in a consoling tone. Jode nodded in agreement, he certainly had his share of hard times.

Steve said he would give Stan a call and if he agreed he would give them the keys in the morning so they could inspect the interior.

When they got back to the boat the first order of business was to grab another beer from the fridge and some crackers for Damn Bird. Back on the bridge, they sat in silence until Jode got up the nerve to speak his mind. "I know we have more cash than

I've ever had in my life but nowhere near enough to buy that boat. Why are you going through all the hassle for a dream that can't come true?"

"Just let me think on it a while. I have a few ideas that might just work. Not the way you would do it but if we can get our hands on that boat, I'm sure you'll be happy."

Jode gave him a look, "You're not thinking about anything illegal, are you?"

Sarge just smiled again, "Nope just the opposite." Jode accepted that Sarge wasn't going to be anymore forth coming, so they went below to scavenge through what was left of the groceries and fix dinner.

The next morning Sarge and Jode were on the bridge having their coffee and looking out over the marina. When Sarge spotted Bill walking to the dock master's office, he stood up and told Jode to stay put as he headed down the dock towards the office. Jode was curious but did as he was ordered.

Entering the small building, he greeted Bill. "Hey Bill, got a minute? I got something I want to ask you. Might be a total waste of time but you never know." Bill said he did and Sarge got on with his request. "Last night we were looking at the Irish Lady and Steve mentioned that the owner might be open to selling it."

"Folks have asked before and he said no but that was months ago so you never know. What do you have in mind?"

"Me and Sailor really like the looks of that boat and Steve says that mostly what needs doing is stuff we could do ourselves. We would need some help with the mechanical repairs but we could do all the cleaning and painting. I was thinking, if Mr. Clemens wants to sell it, and it was all right with you, Steve could help us with the mechanical stuff, after hours of course and in exchange, we would give him Old Moe. Not the best boat on the water but it would solve his housing problem and you'd get around the clock security."

Bill gave it some thought. "It's a long shot that he would let loose of it but if you make a deal with Stan and Steve, I won't get in the way. What Steve does on his own time is his business and truth be told, having him here would save me the hassle of coming down here from home every time some problem comes up after hours. I think you are tilting at windmills but if they agree it's OK with me."

Sarge thanked him for his time and headed back to the boat. He asked Jode if he wanted another cup of coffee and went below to finish off the pot. As he handed Jode his cup, he was ready for the inevitable questions. "What was that all about?"

"Just needed to ask Bill about the Irish Lady. Want to head over to the shop and see if Stan is open to us looking her over? If he agreed to that we're halfway home."

Jode was getting tired of all the secrecy but he knew Sarge could be an obstinate bastard. "I'm more concerned with the other half, like where do we come up with 50 or 60 grand?"

Sarge just waved him off, climbed over to the dock and started walking to the shop to find Steve. Jode sat another minute, shook his head in frustration and followed along.

Steve was up but his sheets and pillow were still bunched up on the couch. He was kinda embarrassed when Sarge and Jode came through the door. Ignoring the mess, Sarge got right to the point. "Did you call Mr. Clemens?" Steve said he did and dug through the drawer in the desk and handed Sarge the boat keys.

"He said he hadn't decided to sell her but you could take a look and let him know what you think. I've got about twenty minutes before I open up so I can give you a quick tour and then you can stay aboard as long as you like." With that, the three men walked over to the boat, Steve carrying a shop ladder, and climbed aboard.

The teak around the door was a mess and as soon as they walked in Sarge could smell the musty odor but it was nothing compared to Old Moe. The first thing Jode saw was the electronics in the console. Steve gave a brief summary, pointing out the chart plotter, radio and autopilot. "These all work?" Jode asked.

"Did when he brought her in. We can run an extension cord over to hook up the shore power and see if the batteries charge up. If they do, you can try it." Jode was satisfied with Steve's answer and spent another couple of minutes admiring the electronics package. Steve proceeded to open the engine covers exposing the twin engines and a nice generator. Again the engine room was far from pristine but much cleaner and organized than Old Moe had ever been. Steve excused himself to get to work for the marina and left Sarge and Jode to poke around the boat, lifting every hatch and opening every drawer. There were only a few personal items on board but it was well equipped with dock lines, fenders, a selection of boat hooks, spare ground tackle and everything else needed for a long and safe voyage. After locking up, they headed over to the shop to return the keys. While Jode loved the boat he wasn't getting his hopes up. They had less than half the money they needed.

Sarge gave the keys back to Steve and asked him to give Stan a call and inquire if they could talk to him this afternoon. He asked if the marina had something they could drive out there and also stop by the grocery store as they were running low on food and, more importantly beer. Steve said there was an old shop truck they could borrow. Satisfied that everything was lined up, Sarge ushered Jode back to Old Moe before he exploded.

The first words out of Jode's mouth as they climbed aboard were, "I love the boat but how the hell are we going to pay for it? I don't see the Clemens' agreeing to some payment plan bullshit!"

Sarge calmly sat in one of the old deck chairs, motioned Jode to do the same and shared his plan.

"We are going to trade some of the treasure for it."

Jode barely contained himself, "Great plan, that has worked out just terrific so far. I hope he doesn't have a gun!"

Sarge just smiled, "Hear me out. We are going to tell him the truth and he'll believe us and he will trade the boat for gold, I'm sure of it."

"The truth! We're going to tell him about all the treasure we have? Are you nuts?" Jode realized that he had raised his voice and looked around to make sure no one was close enough to hear.

Again, Sarge was calm and spoke softly. "I didn't say we were going to tell him everything but everything we tell him will be the God's honest truth. You've always been dealing with crooks, scoundrels and connivers. You can't believe anything they say and they sure as hell don't believe anything you say, even if it's the truth. These folks are different and I suspect Mr. Clemens is too. These are good folks the type of folks where a man's word is his bond. We are going to tell him the truth about where the gold came from and offer him a deal he can't resist. Like Steve said, he doesn't need the money and probably knows he'll never take another voyage on the Irish Lady. We just need to be the kind of people he wants to see own and take care of her and telling the truth is the only way that will work."

Jode sat quietly for longer than what was comfortable but Sarge just let him stew. "Maybe you're right. If you're not, we'll be gone in a couple of days and I don't think he would be coming after us anyway. What about Old Moe?"

"That's the part of the plan that will make it even easier for Mr. Clemens to say yes. The way Steve talks about him, I bet they are friends or at least like each other. We make a deal with Steve that he helps us with the mechanical repairs and you give him Old Moe. We get work for free and he gets a place to live. I already ran it by Bill, the dock master and it is OK with him. I even think he likes the idea of having Steve live on site. What ya say, you were just going to abandon this old scowl anyway?" Jode was starting to like his chances of getting a new boat. "Now what is the nicest piece of treasure you found? We want to show Stan something he can't take his eyes off of."

"That's easy," Jode replied. "That little gold cross Tripper found on his last dive. It's missing one stone but I think we have one about the right size to make it look even better."

"Great, let's go see if Steve got us an appointment with Mr. Clemens. Then we can dig out that cross and gemstone, get cleaned up and ready to go. You know the drill, we want to be all ship shape and squared away. We play this right he'll be asking us to take that boat."

Not much later they were driving down Stan's long driveway towards a nice house situated on several acres of land. An old couple were sitting on the front porch in matching rocking chairs. Two other chairs were pulled up for what appeared to be this very meeting. Before they were out of the car, Mr. Clemens had walked over to the driveway to greet them. Sarge got out and introduced himself. "Mr. Clemens? I'm Luke but all my friends call me Sarge and this here is Jode but I call him Sailor because, well, he's a sailor at heart."

"Just call me Stan. We've been expecting you. Come on up to the porch and let me introduce you to my wife, Martha." They walked the short distance down the sidewalk and Stan made the introductions.

As they were getting seated Martha asked, "You boys want something to drink?" Both Sarge and Jode were about to say no when she added, "Maybe a beer? I know Stan has been itching to start happy hour a little early." How could you say no to that? After a brief round of laughter, Martha went inside to get the beverages.

By the time she returned the guys were engrossed in a lively conversation about their various exploits both on the water and in Sarge's case in the military. They all tried to keep the conversation light without making any personal inquiries, especially concerning Sarge's missing leg. Martha handed out the beers and sat down with the group. After a few swigs of beer the conversation slowed so Stan got to the point, "Well, as nice as it is sitting here visiting with you fine gentlemen, I suspect that's not why you drove all the way out here this afternoon. So, you want to buy our boat, do you?"

Jode was the first to speak because he couldn't control himself any longer. He asked a few questions then told Stan and Martha how they planned to fix it up and get it back in the water and how much he looked forward to living aboard and traveling. As he slowed to take a breath, Sarge cut in, "Well Sailor, that sure is an interesting way to negotiate the best price. Got any more positive things to add or should we just double our offering price right now?" Jode turned red as everyone else laughed. "All seriousness aside, we talked to Steve at the marina and he thought the boat would fetch eighty thousand or so in good condition but it needs a lot of work to get it back in shape. Now most of that work is just elbow grease and hard labor, something we aren't afraid of. Not something my sidekick here likes but he is not afraid of it." He added in jest.

Jode looked at him and agreed. "That's right I have never been afraid of hard work. I can lay down right beside it and sleep like a baby." That got a chuckle out of Stan and Martha.

Sarge got back on track. "We think sixty would be a fair price but we have something to make it a little more interesting."

"Sixty is a lowball offer so whatever you have in mind better be a lot more interesting," Stan shot back. Martha gave him a look that said, calm down and listen.

"We would like to trade for the boat," Sarge continued.

This time it was Martha who needed to calm down. "We got enough crap around here already. We don't need another boat. Stan has more old cars around here than I can count and don't get me started on farm equipment and all his lawn stuff."

Sarge must have been a Zen master in a past life. He calmly reach down for his rucksack and brought it up to his lap. Without saying a word he reached in and took out a small package wrapped in newspaper, set it on the small table they surrounded and pulled back the paper exposing the cross. Jode reached into his pocket, took out the single gemstone and carefully placed it in the empty indentation, completing the presentation. It was deathly quiet as both Stan and Martha stared at the rare artifact.

Stan broke the awkward silence, "Where did that come from and don't tell me you just found it?"

Sarge nodded to Jode to tell his story, truthfully. "Actually Stan, I did. My buddy and I found that and more on a reef in the keys last May."

"Where a bouts in the keys," Stan challenged.

"West of Key West past Boca Grande Key."

""Dry Tortugas?"

"Not that far out."

"The Marquesas then? Isn't that where Mel Fisher found the Atocha?"

Jode was getting flustered but Sarge had made him promise to tell the truth so he just pushed on. "Ya, near the Marquesas Keys but we weren't claim jumping or anything. We were maybe ten, twelve miles west from where I think they found the Mother Lode, not sure exactly. We were diving a shallow reef about twenty or thirty feet deep looking for lobster."

"Aren't lobster out of season that time of year?"

Jode felt like he was being interrogated by the police. "Yes sir," he responded sheepishly.

Stan had a little smile on his lips. "I guess you're not the first boater to harvest 'summer crabs' and certainly won't be the last." Having gotten Jode to admit to the crime, Stan felt he was probably telling the truth. "Go ahead and tell your tale and we'll decide if it's true or just bullshit."

Jode started again and with few interruptions, soon relaxed enough to tell his story. He talked about that day when he first discovered the single coin and how they used every last breath searching for more. Glossing over their trip to Key West to resupply, he left out all the details of dealing with Big Carlos only admitting to selling the haul to fund their return to the Marquesas. He became much more animated as he recounted their many small discoveries and how he and 'his buddy' celebrated each new find while spending days out on the water. He was careful not to share too much. Stan and Martha didn't need to know how much treasure they discovered. As he was finishing up his tales of recovering the treasure, Stan asked the most important question.

"What's the name of this 'buddy' of yours and what happened to him? It clearly wasn't Sarge," he said as he motioned to Sarge's missing limb.

Jode hesitated and glanced over at Sarge for moral support. All he got was the slightest nod. "His name was Tripper. We'd been friends since we were kids. We had been living on Old Moe for a dozen years. A storm came up and we had to leave. We were headed to Fort Myers Beach when." He stopped mid-sentence. Sarge saw his hand move towards the pocket where he kept his two silver coins. Without saying a word he reached over and grabbed his forearm and held it so it would go no further. Jode's eyes moistened, and in a hushed voice he said what he dreaded most, "The storm hit. There was an accident. It just happened. It was nobody's fault. There was nothing I could do. Tripper never made it to shore." Sarge let go of this arm. Jode's hand reached for the coins and he rubbed them together while they remained in his pocket.

Stan's eyes were watering and Martha was flat out crying. Soon Martha got up wiped her eyes and said she would be back with refills for the now empty beers. The three men sat in silence until she returned. This time, in addition to the beers she had a glass of wine for herself. She passed around the bottles and Stan once again broke the silence. "Well that is one fine looking cross you have there but I don't think it's worth sixty grand. What else you got in that rucksack? It looks kind of heavy."

Sarge snapped out of his funk, opened the ruck and showed Stan the pistol. "No more gold in here just my service revolver. Maybe I'm crazy or sentimental but I've had it with me for years, even before this," he said as he motioned to his artificial foot. "Don't worry. I have a carry permit and I haven't shot anyone with it." He hesitated then added, "As a civilian."

Stan asked if he could see it and Sarge obliged after removing the clip and the round in the chamber. Martha gave Stan a disapproving look. "Don't even think about it. You have too many damn guns around here already. Can't even put away the laundry without knocking one off the shelf."

Jode just shook his head. He knew what was coming next. Mentioning too many guns in front of Sarge was like throwing a rabbit in front of a hunting dog. And they're off!

True to form Sarge immediately had to know how many and what kind. Stan was up for a change of subject. "Well I have the stainless mini-14, call it my boat gun, a blued one with a scope, a cheap old SKS, HK91, a couple of varmint rifles, a few more miscellaneous guns, you know the usual. Haven't shot them in years. Hate to admit it but haven't cleaned them either."

"So you don't shoot them?" Sarge couldn't imagine such a sacrilege. "Isn't there a firing range around here?"

"Ya, about 15 miles out east of here. I just don't feel like going through all the hassle of cleaning them and all that. Mostly had them as boat guns when we went to the Bahamas all the time. Ha, Martha used to say we had enough guns and ammo to hold off Cuba."

"I didn't think it was so dangerous in the Bahamas. I've never heard of any trouble." Jode cut in.

To Stan, a boating story was like guns to Sarge. "Well, I tell you what, it wasn't that way in the 80's. Drug smugglers were thick as well, thieves running pot and then coke from the islands to Miami. Remember that time Martha?" He continued as he looked over to his wife. She gave him a resigned nod, having heard the story many times before. "We were coming back from what was it? Bimini? West End? Or was it Chub? Anyway we were just cruising along maybe Nine or ten knots when all of a sudden one of those cock boats goes screaming past us going at least 60 knots. Next thing we see is a helicopter right on their ass. Those guys in the boat were throwing bales of pot overboard as fast as they could. I was thinking of fishin' for some square grouper when a loud voice comes over the radio, 'Irish Lady, maintain course and speed. Do not approach!' well that ended any ideas of fishing. There were so many bales in the water we hit two. I wasn't about to change course and they wouldn't damage anything anyway. Ya, we always traveled armed and dangerous."

Stan stopped to catch his breath before getting back to the task at hand. "Well we don't need the cash from the boat and gold antiquities will probably appreciate in value so I'm open to your idea but that little cross isn't going to do it for me."

Sarge might not be a salesman but he recognized a buying signal when he saw it. "Oh that. That's just the down payment. We figured we would put together some of our choice items that, in our estimation will be worth at least sixty grand. If we have a deal, we'll bring you the rest."

Stan looked over at Martha and though she didn't even blink, somehow he got the message. "I don't know anything about this kind of stuff but I think I can trust you guys to treat us right. Well, at least you. Still not sure about that one." He said as he waved his hand over at Jode. Everyone chuckled, except Jode that is.

Martha spoke for the first time in a while. "Don't believe that old coot. He knows the price of gold down to the penny and he'll be on the google web looking at Atocha gold before you two get out the drive. I think you'll take good care of our boat and hopefully it will bring you as much happiness as it has us. What are you going to name her?"

Jode was bursting inside. He couldn't believe they were buying the boat, but hadn't given a thought about changing the name. "Haven't thought about a name. Every boat I ever had either didn't have a name or we just left whatever name it had as is. Isn't it bad luck to change the name?"

Martha shook her head like she was talking to an imbecile, then Stan butted in, "You're not Irish and you're damn sure not a lady so you need a new name. By the looks of you two scoundrels, I think Double Trouble pretty much sums it up."

"And if you do a proper rechristening the Gods will not be offended." Martha chimed in.

"Seems like we have a deal," Sarge said holding out his hand to shake on it.

Stan pushed his hand away, "Not so fast there are some more conditions you need to agree to." Jode's face fell. "First we want to be there when you splash her and we will bring the champagne, cheap champagne, to christen her good and proper and once you have her all ship shape and ready to go we want one last ride out the harbor and into the Gulf. I'll bring the beer and pay for the fuel."

"And we will bring the food too," Martha added. With that Stan held out his hand.

"Not so fast," Sarge said. "I have some conditions of my own." Jode was about to burst. "Once we splash the boat, Steve at the marina gets Old Moe. I don't know if you've heard, he lost his apartment and is looking for a place to live so we want to get Irish, or I mean Double Trouble in the water as soon as we can, so he can move aboard. After that's done, you take us out to the shooting range to check out those weapons of yours. Don't worry I'll clean them all afterward before you put them away."

Everyone was more than happy with the contingencies. The Clemens' walked Sarge and Jode back to the old truck and said their goodbyes. After they all shook hands and before they piled into the truck, Martha leaned over and gave Jode a heartfelt hug.

Chapter 18

As they drove back towards town Sarge asked, "How are we going to get all that treasure from Old Moe to Double Trouble without anyone seeing us? Hell, Steve is there 24/7."

Jode just smiled. "We are going to carry it over, right under their noses. We'll just need some more of those tool bags."

They stopped at one of those discount tool stores to load up on tool bags, a couple of off brand buffers, soap, wax and a wide selection of painting supplies. As they headed for the checkout, Jode stopped and picked up a cheap crescent wrench and screw driver. "What're those for?" Sarge asked.

"Well you being such an Altar boy with all that cannot tell a lie crap, I figure if anyone asks what you have in the tool bag, instead of you getting all squirrelly and flustered, you can say in all honesty you have your tools in the bag." Jode joked. Sarge did not think it was funny.

They loaded everything into the bed of the truck and headed to the grocery store. With enough food and beer to last several days, they headed back to the marina. As they drove through the center of town, Sarge spied a library and told Jode to pull in. "You wait here. I'll be right back. I want to check out a couple of books about the Atocha like they had at the Beach. Shouldn't take but a few minutes, if there is a young lady working." He added with a devilish grin. Jode just shook his head and climbed out of the truck to organize the items they just bought.

He was finishing up stuffing the groceries and small tools into the canvas bags when Sarge returned. "That didn't take long. Was she cute?"

"A little old for me but I got the impression I wasn't too young for her." Jode just rolled his eyes, climbed behind the wheel and started to truck. As they left town, Sarge told him to pull into the gas station.

"What now? There's more than a half tank of gas left." Jode protested.

"We'll top it off anyway. We're going to need this truck a lot over the next few weeks and if we bring it back full every time, they'll be asking us if we want to use it." As he headed into the grab and go to prepay.

When they got back to the marina they pulled right up to Irish Lady and began unloading the tools and items they would be using on the job. Before they were done, Steve came walking over. "I'll be damned. It looks like your visit with Stan and Martha went well. What kind of tale did you tell to get them to sell her?"

"Never met a woman that could resist this smile." Sarge said with his white teeth on full display. Jode just slugged him in the arm. "Truth be told, we made him a fair offer and told him we would take good care of his girl. We need to bring the rest of this stuff over to Old Moe. How about you join us for a beer to celebrate after you get off work?" Steve couldn't resist the offer and agreed to meet them after work.

Jode and Sarge were on their third beer when Steve showed up. They welcomed him aboard and offered him a cold PBR. Conversation centered on Irish Lady and all that was needed to get her back on the water. Steve said he wished he could have bought her but would never have that kind of money. You can't finance an old boat.

To that Sarge said, "Well I have an idea." He told Steve about his plan to have him help with the mechanical work on Irish

Lady in exchange for Old Moe. He seemed interested but noncommittal.

"Sounds interesting, mind if I take a look down below before agreeing to anything?" That was fine with Jode so they headed into the cabin, Steve in the lead. "Whoa, this thing has the funk. Is that all mildew or did you sink her?" Jode was beside himself but held his tongue, for the time being! "No AC, how can you sleep on this thing in this heat?"

"We have fans and besides we anchor out most the time so we couldn't run an air conditioner if we had one." Jode spat out.

Steve seemed to ignore his attitude and started rummaging through all the cabinets. He took a small tape measure out of his pocket and started measuring everything in sight. Next came out a note pad and pencil. This went on for more than a few minutes. Jode was losing patience and decided he'd scuttle the damn thing before giving it to Steve!

When the writing stopped Steve turned to Jode and said, "Can we go back on deck? the smell is getting to me."

Back on deck, all Jode could think about was throwing the little bastard overboard but Sarge put his hand on his shoulder to calm him down.

Steve took one more look at his notes and lifted his head to face them. "Are you sure? You're just giving me this boat for helping you out with a little work? I can't believe it?" Jode nodded yes. "This is GREAT!"

Jode almost fell over. "What about the funk, no AC and all that other crap?"

"Oh, sorry man. Whenever I bid a job or make a parts list, I talk to myself. Helps me avoid missing anything. I meant no offense. I love this boat. I'll take out that window, replace it with marine plywood and mount a little window shaker from Walmart. That and a couple of fans and it'll be dried out in less than a week. Wipe everything down with pine sol, clean the bilge and this thing will be fresh as a daisy. You sure you want to give it away?"

Well he didn't see that coming. Jode assured him that the boat would be his as soon as Irish Lady was in the water and he and Sarge could move aboard.

"God I can't believe it, with all the crap I've been through lately this is the best news ever. Can't wait, I'll be able to make the commute to work before my mug of coffee gets cold."

Sarge grabbed three beers out of the cooler and they toasted to everyone getting a new, if old, boat. After downing the beer, Steve said he needed to get going. He wanted to check out Irish

Lady and figure out what needed to be done and what parts and supplies he would need to order. Tomorrow being Sunday and his day off, they all agreed to get to work after morning coffee.

Steve's eyes were misting up as he was shaking hands to leave. When he got to Jode, he leaned in and gave him a man hug. "Thanks man, you don't know how much I appreciate this." With that he hopped down to the dock and gave Old Moe a good looking over, pausing when he saw Jode's improvised patch job. He turned and headed down the dock towards Irish Lady.

"That went well. Was he skipping down the dock and was that whistling I heard?" Sarge joked. "Makes you feel good doesn't it?"

"Yes it does. I totally misjudged him. I thought he hated Old Moe and it turns out he's loving her. Who would 'a thought?"

They grabbed another beer and sat in the deck chairs, this time facing Irish Lady. Neither spoke for nearly a half hour before Sarge turned to Jode and asked, "In a few weeks you will be captaining a fine ship. Where do you intend to take her?"

"I was thinking the same thing. The plans I made with Tripper seem like years ago. Driving from here to Texas or Mexico is out of the question, not sure if I would even want to take Double Trouble all the way over there. Stan talking about the Bahamas got me thinking. With the new boat we could go anywhere we wanted.

Texas, up the east coast or the Bahamas, we could even island hop down to the Caribbean. So many choices."

Sarge thought about all the options. "You're the captain and the choice is yours but if it were me choosing, I'd go back and see if we can find more treasure. Do you think there is any more down there? I know we have more than we can sell but hearing your tall tales and seeing the look in your eye when you tell them, makes me want to see it for myself."

Now Jode was lost in thought. "Hadn't thought of that. Tripper and I were just scraping the bottom with garden tools to uncover the coins and other treasure. If we had a setup like Fisher, I bet we could find a lot more. Of course, if anyone saw that big gizmo on the back of the boat they would certainly know what we were up to, so that won't work. We were still finding treasure by hand until the day we left so we could just do that."

"We would have to go back and forth to Key West for fuel and supplies. After the trouble with Big Carlos and his thugs I'm kind of worried about running into them again."

Sarge laughed out loud as he patted the rucksack that was always at his side. "I was thinking Big Carlos should be worried about us. The last bunch of goons that gave us shit didn't fare so well. Just sayin', if there is gold to be had we might as well be the ones to have it."

"Got a point there. If your game, I guess I am too. If we don't find anything . . . . or find a lot, we can always head over to the islands and live the pirate life there."

With the decision made, Jode went below to grab the box of fried chicken they just bought and brought it up on deck for dinner. As if on que, Damn Bird showed up for his pirate's share.

They awoke early, had their coffee and headed over to Irish Lady to get started. The plan was to help Steve remove the props and shafts then as he did his work they would buff and wax the hull then paint the bottom. With those tasks complete they could splash the boat and concentrate on everything above the rub rail and the interior after they move aboard and Steve had a home on Old Moe.

They organized the tools and supplies while waiting for Steve. Jode was looking at the back of the boat when it hit him. Could a set up like Mel used be mounted below the surface and out of sight and should they risk asking Steve to help get it built and attached? He shared his idea with Sarge.

"Might work. I don't think it would hurt to get Steve involved. We aren't saying we have treasure just that we want to search for treasure. Could explain why we bought the boat in the first place. If it works it's a whole new ball game for uncovering that treasure." Jode agreed and Sarge headed back over to Old Moe to retrieve one of the library books.

When Steve arrived they got to the strenuous task of removing the props and shafts. While resting in the shade Jode brought up the subject of building and mounting the prop wash blower or 'mailbox' to Double Trouble. Steve thought it was a bone headed idea but was intrigued with the project. He took out his tape measure, pad and pencil and crawled under the stern of the boat.

He crawled out and started asking questions, "How fast are you going to spin the props? Do you need to steer while it is attached?" He asked questions they hadn't thought of. Finally he got to the point. "I know a guy that can fabricate damn near anything. Maybe he can put something together. If he can, great, if not, you're on your own."

Jode told him to call his guy and they would be around whenever he showed up. As an afterthought, he mentioned that they needed to change the boat's name. Steve protested that it was bad luck but after being assured that Martha was doing the required christening he said he had a guy that did name decals that could handle the job. That out of the way, they went back to work and got a lot done before calling it a day. Tomorrow Steve had his day job and Sarge and Sailor would be under the boat scraping paint.

It was late afternoon when Jode saw Steve walking towards the boat with a ginormous man. He was as tall as Jode but built like Sarge, big boned and muscular. They all met near the stern of Irish Lady and Steve made the introductions. "Sarge, Sailor, This is Big Jim, the best welder and fabricator in Manatee County."

Big Jim held out his hand to shake, it was covered with scars and callouses and his fingers were as thick as a woman's wrist. Jode hesitated, worried that his hand would be crushed, but Big Jim's hand shake was firm, not painful. A man that big had no need to show off his strength. "Big Jim? I can see how you got that title." Jode commented.

"Oh it's not because of my size. I've been called that since I was a little kid. I was the oldest son and my little brothers called me that. Being a few years older I was big to them. Fact is, now a couple of them are bigger than me."

Sarge shook his hand and added, "Your mom must have had one hell of a grocery bill."

Big Jim just laughed. "She would get the Thursday paper with all the ads and checkout the sales at the three grocery stores in town. Then make a list for each store right down to the department. She would be at it for hours. Don't think it took her that long. I think she just liked that we didn't bother her while she was doing it! We would hit all the stores than stop by the day old bread place on the way out of town. The trunk would be so full you could barely close it. Same with the back seat. Hell, sometimes I would have to ride the twenty miles back home with bags of groceries piled on my lap." They all laughed. "Well enough visiting. What kind of contraption do you want me to build?"

Steve had given him some info over the phone so after Sarge showed him the pictures from the book they got right to work. The tape measures were flying as they hunched over the props and rudders. Steve was calling out measurements as Big Jim drew and labeled a diagram on his notepad. Half an hour later Jim asked, "Where you going to store this thing when you're not using it."

Jode told him under the cockpit that could only be accessed from the inside. Big Jim gave him a skeptical look and said lead on. Big Jim measured the transom door, then the pilot house door and every passageway they crossed to the aft cabin. Jode showed him the hatch leading to under the cockpit and Jim squeezed himself down and let his tape measure fly once again. "Sorry dude, this ain't happening. No way you'll get it in here." He got up and started looking around and landed on the hang up closet. He opened it up and took multiple measurements. "You can store it in here. All this crap will have to go somewhere else." He didn't wait for a response and just headed back out the way he came.

Back on the ground, he did some figuring with a calculator before saying, "Be about a grand to make it out of steel. Good coat of paint and you wash it down every time you use it, it should last a long time. Be pretty heavy mounting it in the water though. My recommendation is aluminum. Materials cost more and the welding is a lot more difficult, cost twice as much but it will make your life a whole lot easier."

Sarge looked to Jode for guidance. With a shrug and a nod the decision was made. "How long will it take?"

Big Jim scratched his chin. "Pretty busy right now. Two, three weeks max."

"That's Ok with us, but Steve here is out of his apartment and looking to move on to our old boat as soon as we splash this one. Anything you can do to speed it up would help him out." Sarge explained.

Big Jim looked to Steve to confirm what he was told. He put his big arm over Steve's shoulder, "Anything to help out my buddy. How about I burn a little midnight oil, mock up and tack weld the funnel that attaches to the rudder. I can bring it by for a test fit. That way you can splash the boat and I'll have the rest done in a couple of weeks?" Seemed like a good solution for everyone. Jim asked for a deposit. Sarge peeled off five C-notes and handed them to him. Steve and Big Jim headed back to the shop.

Jode looked over to Sarge. "I thought we weren't supposed to be tossing C-notes around like chump change?"

Sarge grinned, "That was when you were a grungy boat bum and I was a homeless cripple. Now that we are upstanding Yacht owners, they would expect nothing less. Besides, didn't you tell me that when it came to boats a hundred is like a ten?" They shared a laugh before getting back to work.

As promised, Big Jim showed up three days later with a big aluminum gizmo. It looked like a huge funnel two and a half feet in diameter narrowing down to less than two. He had cut large grooves in it so it could slide on the back of the rudder. There were gussets with mounting holes along the grooves.

Jode held it in place and Big Jim drilled matching holes in the rudder. He took out two long pins and pushed them through to hold everything in place. "These are hitch pins from the Tractor Store. I suggest you get some extras and a bag of cotter pins. When you drop them you won't have to spend hours looking on the bottom for them. Don't cost much for the convenience. I can pick them up if you want." After a brief discussion they decided to drill mounting holes in both rudders just in case. Satisfied with the fit,

Big Jim was packing up to leave when he asked for another five hundred deposit before finishing the job. Sarge handed him another five bills, shook hands and off he went.

They were making good progress and after confirming with Steve that he would be finished by Friday, they scheduled to splash the boat Saturday afternoon. They still didn't have a phone, so Steve would call the Clemens.

Saturday came and everything that needed to be done on the hard was complete. As soon as Stan and Martha arrived, Steve started up the travel lift and positioned it over the renamed Double Trouble. Sarge and Sailor helped with the straps and within minutes it was swinging in the slings. The lift made its way slowly to the haul out slip and the boat was gently lowered into the water. After two years without starting, Steve recommended they wait until he could do one finale check before firing up the engines. Instead they used dock lines and boat hooks to move Double Trouble into her new slip.

With the boat secured, Martha, Stan, Sarge and Sailor walked to the bow as everyone at the marina gathered around to watch. Martha handed Sailor the bottle of champagne and began the christening. She started by thanking Irish Lady for all the great adventures and for protecting Stan and her from danger on their many voyages. She then paid homage to Poseidon and asked that the old name be retired and that in the future the vessel was to be known to Him as Double Trouble. She asked that He grant them fair winds and following seas in the years to come and their voyages be many and productive. Finishing up, she asked Sailor to open the champagne and make an offering to Poseidon christening Double Trouble.

As instructed, Sailor removed the wire from the top of the bottle, loosened the cork and shook it until the cork shot into the air and champagne sprayed all over the four of them and the bow of Double Trouble. When the clapping subsided Sarge and Sailor brought a cooler of beer and sodas to the dock and everyone joined in the celebration.

As the crowd dispersed, Sarge took Stan aside to talk. "We need to get you the balance of the payment and I sure would like to go out shooting with you. Any chance we could go tomorrow afternoon?" Stan was more than agreeable so they planned to meet at his house just after noon the next day.

The dock cleared out and Jode carried the cooler and what was left of beer up to the back deck while Sarge brought out the chairs Stan and Martha had left. They were relaxing and drinking beers proud as can be, when Steve came by. "You guys look good up there. Any chance I can bring some of my stuff over to Old Moe?"

"We already moved everything we want from inside. Figured we would leave the fishing equipment and dive gear over there until we get Double Trouble all cleaned up. Stan and Martha left all their boating equipment, pots and pans and anything else they had on board so we are well equipped. You're welcome to whatever is left on Old Moe and if you want to move in tonight, it's all yours." Jode replied.

Steve thanked them profusely and hustled back to the shop. It wasn't long before he was pushing a dock cart piled high with belongings over to Old Moe. He made several trips loading his stuff aboard then disappeared below deck. Jode and Sarge couldn't wipe the smiles off their faces as they shared more beers and looked out over the marina from the deck of their new home. They noticed Steve climbing up to the helm of Old Moe, beer cooler in tow. He opened a beer and offered a toast over the water to his friends and benefactors. They returned the salute. As the sun set, Damn Bird landed on Old Moe like he had most nights and Steve let him be.

The plan for Sunday was a day of rest and going to the firing range with Stan. As they sipped their morning coffee, Jode asked, "We need to put together the rest of the treasure for Stan and Martha. Not knowing what anything is worth, how are we going to figure out what is a square deal?"

Sarge had an answer ready. "The way I see it, Harvey gave us six grand for the chain and thought that was a good deal and so did we. The coins and chain I sold at the Beach were the same, we were happy and so were the buyers. I recommend we use that as the value for those items and Stan said gold was going for $678 an ounce, use that for the gold bars."

Jode thought that made sense. "Why don't you go below and put that together and I know we planned to take it easy today but I just can't take sitting on this dirty boat anymore. I'll start washing it down." Sarge gave him a surprised look. Jode worried about a little dirt? He agreed and headed below to select just the right items for Stan and Martha.

When they arrived at the Clemens', Stan had the entertainment for the day laid out, four rifles and a pistol along with all the cleaning supplies. Sarge in his element, sat down and got to work.

He picked up a rifle, disassembled it, checked all the workings, cleaned and oiled it and reassembled it before moving on to the next. A few minutes into the process, Martha arrived with a plate of sandwiches and a pitcher of tea. "You didn't even ask the boys how they wanted their sandwich." Stan said.

"I suspect the boys will eat most anything that's in front of them. They're not a picky old coot like you," She protested, smacking him in the arm. She was right, 'the boys' tore into the sandwiches as Stan savored his.

The routine at the firing range was set. Silhouette targets with a bullseye at center mass were set 150 yards down range. Sarge selected the scoped mini-14 first, took a shot adjusted the scope, took another shot, made one more slight adjustment then put six holes dead center in the bullseye. Stan then fired several rounds grouped close to center followed by Jode who struggled to keep the rounds on target. This was followed in kind with the other weapons. With open sights Stan's and Jode's accuracy suffered. Once sited in, Sarge continued to put all his rounds in the bullseye.

With all four rifles sighted in and everyone having several opportunities to shoot, they moved on to the pistol range. Sarge gave detailed instructions and demonstrated the proper way to hold and fire the weapon. At times he reverted to the gruff drill instructor he was, Stan and Jode just laughed and ignored his beratings. Again, Sarge put all his shots dead center but to preserve the target his small grouping was not in the bullseye but tightly grouped between the eyes of the silhouette. Stan followed and as before all his rounds hit within the inner circles of the target.

Sarge spent extra time instructing Jode as he had little experience firing a pistol. He still struggled to hit the target. Sarge was stymied. "How can you spearfish when you can't hit the broadside of a barn door? That little pneumatic spear gun you have doesn't look much different than a long barreled pistol."

"Shit man, I can shoot the eye out of a hogfish at twenty feet like nothin', done it thousands of times."

"Well just pretend the pistol is your spear gun and shoot the eyes out of that target." Jode took his advice, held the gun up in an awkward position and started pulling the trigger. In less than ten seconds the clip was empty and the slide clicked open.

Stan and Sarge just stood there staring, all the rounds hit within the first tree rings of the target. Jode looked over, "What?"

"Oh nothing, go ahead and reload and try again." Sarge then pulled Stan over to the side and had a quiet conversation.

Back at Stan's place Sarge got right to cleaning the guns as Stan dug out beers and passed them around. While Sarge worked, Stan and Jode sat on the front porch drinking beer and telling boat stories. They weren't even done with their second bottle when Sarge joined them. "Everything is clean and squared away. I left them all on the table, wasn't sure where you wanted to keep them." Stan thanked Sarge to which Sarge protested and profusely thanked him for a great time at the range. After saying goodbye to Stan and Martha they headed back to the marina.

Soon, they were relaxing on the much cleaner deck of Double Trouble, beer in hand. Sarge, as happy and relaxed as Jode had ever seen him, reached down for his rucksack and rooted through it. He pulled out a heavy bundle wrapped in an oily old rag, and handed it to Jode. "I got you something for your birthday."

"Not my birthday," Jode said as he took the bundle and unwrapped it. He stared down at the same Glock 19 they were shooting just a couple of hours ago. "What's with this? You didn't steal it from Stan, did you?"

"No, you meat head. I traded for it and some more ammo. We owe Stan two more gold doubloons." Sarge said shaking his head in disbelief.

"Why did you do that we already have plenty of guns?" Jode asked.

"Listen, with what we're up too there is no such thing as plenty of guns. Besides, you're one damn good shot with that thing. Might come in handy someday." He gave Jode a pat on the shoulder and raised his beer in mock salute.

Chapter 19

With the slip paid for another three weeks life slowed to a steady pace of cleaning, polishing and working on Double Trouble in the morning and relaxing during the oppressive heat of the afternoon. Every few days they would drive into Palmetto to pick up supplies and groceries. On occasion they would stop for lunch or frequent one of the local bars but for the most part they spent their time on Double Trouble or wandering around the marina. Damn Bird also had fallen into a routine of sleeping on Old Moe and flying over to Jode and Sarge anytime there was food to be had.

At the two week mark, Steve stopped by and told them that Big Jim would be delivering the 'mailbox' that afternoon. Just after 4pm, Big Jim wheeled his truck up near their slip. They walked down to meet him. After exchanging greetings he led them to the bed of the pickup and uncovered the prop blower he had made. They couldn't decide if it was an engineering masterpiece or a work of art. The aluminum was shiny new and the welds were perfect. The intake at the funnel was over two feet wide, the whole contraption was over four feet tall. As big as it was, Big Jim reached into the truck and easily set it on the ground.

"Here ya go. I added these ears on the elbow so you can attach lines to lower it into the water and on to the rudder. Once you get the length right you'll be able to take it on and off in one breath," he said to Sailor. "Now let me show you how it comes apart so you can stow it below decks. To make it easier taking the funnel off and on, I added extra metal on the inside and threaded the holes so you won't need a wrench on the other side. Don't over tighten 'em or you'll strip the aluminum threads. When you do strip the threads, here is a bag of longer bolts, washers and nylock nuts you can use." He mocked, then got out a cordless drill and removed the funnel then started on the elbow and down pipe that was split in half long ways. "Had to make it this way to get through that narrow door to the aft cabin. If you don't have a cordless drill I recommend you get one. Makes the job a lot faster and easier. Might want to get a box of drill bits too. Handy to have on a boat." Remembering drilling holes with a hammer, wrench and old lag bolt on Lulu Key, Jode could not agree more. In just a few minutes the mailbox was disassembled and Big Jim handed them another bag of bolts, nuts, and washers. Finally he pulled one more package from the bed of the truck and handed it to Sailor. "Here's the hitch pins. I got you four so you can lose two and still be in business and a bag of cotter pins."

They thanked Big Jim and complimented him profusely on how good it looked and how thoughtfully it was designed. Sarge took out the roll of cash and counted out ten C-notes to pay the balance of the bill. Then gave it a thought and handed Big Jim one more. "That is a work of art. Here's a little beer money for your extra effort." They said their goodbyes. Sarge and Sailor carried the pieces over to Double Trouble as Big Jim drove out of the boatyard.

With their departure date approaching, the trips to town were more frequent. At the grocery store they added nonperishables to their purchases. After being shipwrecked for over three weeks, Jode wanted more than enough food and beer on board. A trip to the liquor store yielded several bottles of rum . . . . . for emergency use only, of course.

With three days left they arranged to take Stan and Martha out on the promised boat trip. The entire boat had been cleaned, waxed, polished and where appropriate, painted and varnished. Jode and Sarge were proud of their work and hoped it met with Stan and Martha's approval. Stan drove into the boat yard half an hour before the agreed upon time, towing a small trailer loaded with an inflatable boat. He yelled over to Sailor, "You just going to sit there or are you going to give an old man some assistance?" Not knowing what was going on, Jode hustled over to help. By the time he got there, Martha was standing next to Stan, "This is the dink from Irish Lady. It isn't doing anything but taking up space in my barn. Thought you scallywags might be able to use it. Besides, it'll give me enough room for another car." Martha slapped his arm, "Don't even think about it!"

Sarge had walked over to see the goings on. "This for us? Sailor here has been drooling over these things since the first time I met him. I was afraid he'd end up in the slammer for 'borrowing' one." That got a laugh out of Stan and Martha while Sailor fell all over himself trying to thank them enough.

They disconnected the little trailer, rolled it out of the way and carried the refreshments over to the boat and loaded them aboard. Steve came over to toss the lines as they shoved off. Before putting it in gear Sailor called down to him. "Stan just gave us the dinghy from Irish Lady. That means we have no room for our old one, if you want it you can have it."

"You shitting me?" Sailor assured him he was not. "Man, things just keep getting better and better. I can't wait to take it out fishing. Between snook and reds up in the mangroves and trout out on the grass flats, I'll be eating fresh fish every day!" Be careful what you wish for, Sailor thought to himself as he put the boat in gear and idled away from the dock.

The weather was perfect. They idled out of the creek into Terra Ceia Bay. When they passed Emerson Point, Stan told Sailor to engage the autopilot and they cruised out of Tampa Bay just north of Anna Maria Island and into the Gulf. Stan and Sailor stayed at the helm while Martha and Sarge sat in deck chairs on the bow. When they looked back at the two old salts it was clear they were engaged in a lively conversation. Sarge said to Martha, "I wonder what kind of crazy tale he's telling? He has one heck of an imagination."

To that Martha asked just a little accusingly, "Heck of an imagination huh? Was that story he told us about the treasure just another story?"

"No ma'am, best I know it was the God's honest truth. Now when he has a few beers in him and he is talking to another boater I can't say the same."

"Well in that department he might have met his match with Stan." She laughed.

After clearing the point and entering the Gulf, they headed south along the beach. The white sand was dazzling in the bright sunshine. About three o'clock, they reversed course so they would make it back to the marina before dark.

The goodbyes at the dock were tearful. Sarge wasn't sure whether it was because of how close they had become over the short time since they met or if it was saying so long to Irish Lady but there wasn't a dry eye in the bunch. It seemed especially quiet sitting on the boat that night.

The next day they made one more trip to town stocking up on more groceries and picking up a few odds and ends they would need for their upcoming voyage.

Sarge and Sailor were sitting quietly on deck when Steve came by for one last visit. They invited him aboard and offered him a beer. The discussion focused on how fortunate they were and how nice it was to have a new boat and home. Sailor told more stories of where Old Moe had been and even with all the trials and tribulations she was a good boat and had served him well. Steve said he planned to have the boat pulled and would live aboard on the hard using the bathroom and shower at the shop while he fixed it up. "I've seen you eyeing that patch job I did down in the glades. I bet you'll be glad to get that mess taken care of."

"You got it all wrong. I admire how you took nothing and made a repair under those conditions that not only got her floating but has held up for months now. Not saying it doesn't need a proper repair. I plan to remove the patch, cut out the broken boards and have it fixed good as new. I'm no marine carpenter."

At this, Sarge and Sailor interrupted him in unison, "but you got a guy!" They laughed.

Steve laughed with them. "Just so happens, I did repair said marine carpenter's outboard gratis just a few months back. If you find your way back here six months from now you won't recognize Old Moe. I plan to fix her up, new paint, polish, bottom job, the works. She'll be the classic motor cruiser she was meant to be."

Jode or Sailor as Steve knew him, couldn't be happier. A new life for him and Sarge and one for Old Moe too. After a few more beers Steve took his leave and walked proudly back to Old Moe for the night.

The morning came early. After a cup of coffee in the salon, Sarge prepared two travel mugs and brought them up to the bridge. As they prepared to cast off, Steve and Bill were on the dock as expected. "Didn't think you could sneak out of my marina without a proper sendoff, did you?" Bill hollered up.

"No sir," Sarge responded with a halfhearted salute. He and Sailor climbed down to say so long. Best wishes and promises to see each other again were exchanged. Handshakes were not enough for Steve. He gave them each a man hug. With one last handshake Sarge and Sailor slipped something into each of their offered hands, climbed back aboard Double Trouble and cast off the dock lines.

"Think they will ever find that treasure?" Steve asked.

Bill opened his hand as did Steve, each exposing a shiny gold coin. "I believe they already did."

www.ingramcontent.com/pod-product-compliance
Lightning Source LLC
Chambersburg PA
CBHW040132160726
48006CB00014B/1469